To Shirley
'For auld lang syn'

About the Author

Fredrik Nath is a full-time neurosurgeon based in the northeast of England. In his time, he has run twenty consecutive Great North Run half-marathons, trekked to 6000m in Nepal, and crossed the highest mountain pass in the world.

He began writing, like John Buchan, "because he ran out of penny-novels to read and felt he should write his own." Fred loves a good story, which is why he writes.

Catch Fred online at:

www.frednath.com

Also by Fredrik Nath,

available from Fingerpress:

The Cyclist (A War War II Drama)

Galdir: A Slave's Tale – *Barbarian Warlord Saga, Volume I*

Chapter 1

Be forewarned you old guys,
Be forewarned you heads of families.
The time when you gave your sons to the country,
As one gives bread to pigeons,
That time won't come again.
So resign yourselves to it,
It's over.
– from *Paroles* by Jacque Prevert

1

Spain,
March 10th 1937,

Dear M. Dufy,

I don't know what to write to you. I have terrible news. Jean-Paul was killed yesterday. I was with him and before he died he asked me to write to you. We were retreating through a small village whose name I do not know when a grenade exploded near us. Jean-Paul was badly wounded and I had to carry him a long way. He died in my arms. I do not know what to say to you. A letter

seems so cold. When I return I will be able to tell you all about it. He has been buried in Laneda south of the Basque country I marked the grave myself. You will understand how much I respected him, his bravery and his beliefs.
With great sorrow,
Charles.

The letter informing François Dufy of the death of his only son provoked no reaction—not at first. He stared at the page. He read it again. Although he had been a language teacher since the end of the Great War, the letter could have been written in Hindi, for all the sense he could make of it. There was nothing wrong with the writing, nor was there in the grammar; it was the content his mind refused to recognise.

Minutes passed. The old clock on the mantelpiece struck six. The realisation that the most precious thing in his life was gone seeped into his mind, like water seeping into a crack in a dam. His understanding of the news changed from a trickle to a torrent once it began to percolate through his consciousness.

Slowly and with both hands, he placed the letter on his knee as he sat in the tattered chair beside the fire. He stared straight ahead and a tiny drop of moisture appeared in the corner of each eye. A truck passed by outside and the house trembled, like François' lower lip.

His thoughts went back to the day Jean-Paul left. He recalled how it was a warm summer's morning and they were eating croissants from the baker's shop two doors away. Gentle morning sunshine filtered its yellow rays through the kitchen window.

'You can't go. I forbid it,' François said.

'Thumping the table like that won't make any difference.

Charles and I are going to join the Loyalists. The Fascists will overrun the whole country. Someone has to stand against them.'

'How does that matter to us? It's nonsense.'

'Look Papa, if the Spanish rebels take over, they'll join with the Germans and the Italians. Who knows? They could take over our country too. It's not just because they're unjust and inhumane, it's because we'll be next.'

'I don't care, you're just a boy and wet behind the ears. You can't even shoot straight.'

'Fascist rebels aren't rabbits. They're bigger targets. I believe in the Loyalist cause. You fought in the war with Arnaud and the others; they even decorated you. Now it's my chance to fight for something I believe in. Would you really stand in my way?'

'I was much older than you when I joined the army. You're not going.'

'Charles is coming in two hours' time and I'm going with him. Get used to the idea, will you? I told you I was going weeks ago. You just don't listen.'

'I listen. It's the nonsense I hear that foxes me. This foreigner's brigade of yours is a rag-tag rabble. They don't stand a chance of stopping the rebels. The Fascists have help from the Germans and the Italians. Your brigade is a collection of academics and idealists and they'll be shot to pieces.'

'I won't argue any more. I'm going - with your blessing or without it. Will you really part with me like this? Since mother died, we've needed each other. Can't we be friends?'

'I'll never give way on this. You will stay and finish your studies. If you go now, this door will be shut to you when you come home. I mean it.'

'So damned rigid. Is it your age? If my only son was going

to war, I would at least wish him well.'

'No you wouldn't. Why can't you listen to reason? Spain is not our cause, our country.'

In exasperation, François stood and paced the floor. He waved his hands.

'You're just like your mother. Unreasonable and stubborn.'

'I'm going.'

'At least promise me you'll write.'

'I thought you said you'd disown me?'

François leaned forwards across the table, his hands flat on the scarred surface. His voice softened. 'No. I was angry. You'll write to me?'

Jean-Paul was silent. The two looked at each other, François standing and Jean-Paul sitting at the old oak table. The sound of a pigeon cooing from the eaves came in the open window and a smell of fresh coffee still hung in the air. François felt like a man attempting to push a car uphill: slipping back two steps for every forward pace. He knew his son was determined and he was powerless to stop him. He was not a man who accepted defeat easily, but this time there seemed to be no options open to him.

And now the boy was dead.

Clutching the letter, François got up from the chair and stared out of the window. It was still wintry and a late snowfall painted the rooftops and balconies a dirty white. Occasional cars and motorcycles passed by, churning the St Cyprien cobbles into a mire of brown slush.

Their last conversation took place on the doorstep. He hugged the boy and made him promise to write; unreasonable, as it seemed to him later. Who writes letters in a war?

He did receive one letter at Christmas time and it had been a brief, stained, and crumpled note, passed from hand to hand until, in the end, someone delivered it late on Christmas Eve, while François was at church. Jean-Paul said little, apart from how he was well, but hungry and cold. He mentioned they were passing through the small Basque town of Guernica on their way south. The boy wished him a happy Christmas.

Thinking about that letter caused pain. There would be no more Christmases for François, no reason for church, for laughter or prayer. All gone.

He went down to the tiny cellar and found a case of Bergerac. He recalled how Jean-Paul carried it down and joked how it would last forever if his father were the one who had to fetch the fresh bottles. François took two bottles and carried them upstairs to the poky little kitchen, a place of memories. Arlette, his wife, cooked there. Jean-Paul and he grieved there together. François recalled how he once thought all he had left of her was their son. He opened a bottle and poured a glass. Jean-Paul was everything to him, his only source of hope in a contracting world, filled with politics, anti-Semitism, and pain.

He sniffed the wine and began to drink. It dulled the pain a little by the time he had consumed three glasses. He felt more solitary now than at any time in his life, even compared to the nightmare of the Great War, when men made few friends lest they lose them in death.

And now? He felt it was the commitment and the love causing his pain; a feeling so deep it consumed him. By the end of the bottle, he was unsteady and almost dropped the second in opening it. Life held no attractions for him anymore. He knew some teachers would respond by throwing themselves into their work. Teaching young people could give some reason for carrying on, for such civic bastions. For François, the prospect of teaching dull, resentful children how to speak and write German and English seemed a reason for ending it all rather than something from which he might gain strength.

It was growing as dark in the kitchen as it was in his heart. He fumbled the matches, attempting to light the lamp. Cursing, he got down on all fours to pick up the scattered pine slivers. Jean-Paul was dead. He would never be here again, François would never see his smile, and the tiny kitchen would never again resonate to the sound of his laughter. François stayed like that for minutes, on his hands and knees like some huge canine, then lay down on the cold russet tiles, immobile, silent and uncaring.

Outside it began to rain.

2

If he had been a wealthy man, François would have travelled by car. A schoolteacher in the backwater Dordogne town of St Cyprien had no money for such luxuries however. His motorcycle had seen better days too. He stripped down the ancient Peugeot engine before he left and the head teacher's anger sparked by his sudden absence came to mind as he rode away. It angered him still. 'Yes,' he thought, 'like being stabbed in the back.'

After all he had done for the school over the years, to be told he would be sacked if he failed to return in a month seemed to him typical of the small-mindedness of his superior, but he reminded himself she came from Paris and we all know, he thought, what Parisiennes are like.

He set off on April fool's day and thought it was apt in some ways. What was the use? To visit a grave. To weep and mourn, as if it made any difference to the pain he carried in his heart each day. That pain was there when he awoke, when he went to bed, and throughout each day since the news arrived. Every moment, whether he was occupied or not, contained memories, regrets and a feeling of 'why?'

The border police stopped him. They accepted his explanation and hurried him through the barrier as if he was one among many with the mission of finding a grave, and delaying him might make his grief contagious. The cold wind burned his cheeks as he rode and he began to realise he was seeking to close a chapter of his life, nothing more. He knew he could not settle until he spoke a prayer at his son's graveside. The pragmatist in him insisted it was meaningless, but what man is practical in grief?

Entering Spain, the countryside seemed barren and dull. It was mountainous and steep at first, wide expanses of scrub and empty roads doing nothing for his mood or humour. All he wanted was to arrive, to do his duty and return home to his fire, a bottle of wine and his memories. Small villages lined the roadway and when he stopped, he drank wine, ate bread and cheese, and felt his despair deepen. François spoke to no one unless it was to find a place to sleep or ask directions. He was there; he was doing what was necessary, but he had no wish to interact with anyone even though he spoke their language.

He travelled through Guernica, because Jean-Paul mentioned the place, and in the approaching dusk he found a small hotel where he parked his motorcycle. It was a yellow-rendered building with two balconies, each with a dilapidated flower-box, displaying last year's dead plants. The interior seemed as neglected as the proprietor. Approaching the tiny desk, François took in the woman, who sat sewing. From her appearance, he wondered if she too was a leftover from last year. He stood, and it took a full minute before the woman looked up from her work. She had a weatherworn face, wrinkled beyond her forty-odd years, and her expression seemed tired and disappointed. Yet despite the lacklustre face, her green eyes held something alive but indefinable.

'Yes?'

'A room. I need a room for one night.'

'We have rooms. We have a hotel full of rooms and you'll be the only guest.'

'Suits me.'

She reached behind her to a pigeonhole and passed a key to him across the desk. He signed the register and she directed him upstairs.

'Do I need to take you?'

'No.'

François stood for a moment looking at her. There seemed to be something between them, a common disconsolate feeling, perhaps a mental connection. He said nothing. Since Jean-Paul died, he had felt detached from life, and seldom cared enough to enquire about anyone. This woman was no different.

She looked up. A silent question showed in her eyes as if she too recognised some common ground between them.

'You run this place by yourself?' he said.

'Yes,' she said and paused. 'I do now.'

'Now?'

'My man was killed by the rebels.'

'He was fighting for the Loyalists?'

'No. He was not fighting anyone. He went to the city to buy stores. They stopped him and called him a gypsy. They dragged him out of the truck and shot him.'

'How do you know this?'

'My sister was with him. They only raped her.'

François felt tempted, for the first time, to explain why he was there, but since the letter from Charles he had confided in no one. He was not close enough to anyone to bare his pain. It felt now as if here was someone who might understand. The temptation to open up and burden her with his grief on top of hers was not strong enough however, so all he said was, 'I see. Room twelve?'

'Yes,' she said.

The moment passed for François and he turned, shouldering his canvas bag, and walked towards the stairs. She looked at his signature.

'Señor Dufy?' she called after him.

At the foot of the staircase, François turned.

'Yes?'

'I wondered why you are here. The civil war and all.'

'I am visiting someone. South of here. I am sorry for your loss.'

He climbed the stairs but he sensed she wanted to call him back. He ignored the feeling. What could he say to her? If she wanted a shoulder to cry upon, his were sagging too much; besides, he had his own pain to deal with and it was a full-time occupation.

The room was quiet and comfortable in a Spartan way. The iron bedstead in the corner, the threadbare rug and the chest of drawers, battered and chipped, testified to the woman's situation. It was clean enough, though François would not have cared if it had been filthy. He had not bothered with his own appearance since the news.

He dumped his bag and came back down hoping to find a place where he could eat, and most of all drink. He had a bottle of Calvados in his bag but he wanted oblivion, not sleep, and the combination of the vicious apple brandy and a bottle of wine had served him well in the last month. Passing the woman, he heard her call to him. He thought her conversation unwelcome but he was polite enough to reply.

'Yes?' he said.

'Are you eating here tonight?'

'I didn't think you would be opening the kitchen for just one guest.'

'I have nothing else to do. Just one guest is enough.'

'Well, I wanted wine too.'

'Plenty of local wine in the cellar. There is no one to drink it.'

He shifted from one foot to the other, undecided.

He said, 'When will you serve?'

'Now, if you have a mind. It will take only half an hour to prepare food.'

François' reluctance weakened; he did not want to become drunk in front of this woman, but he had a vague feeling that to turn her down would be rude. It was not like him to worry about what others thought. Jean-Paul had always castigated him over it. François never understood adolescents and when confronted by a teenage son who refused to be seen in town with his father because of the way he dressed, he simply said it was up to others to choose whether he was suitable company, or not.

He felt like a man forced by politeness to eat something he knew would make him ill, but manners demanded he capitulate. On this occasion he noticed he did care but he could not fathom why. The woman was plain. She was grief-stricken and it showed in her face, even her clothing, yet he sensed something between them. Compared to Arlette, she was of no interest in that way, but he wanted to stay more than he wanted to drink, and it was the first time he had found some distraction from his grief in another person. He gave in and went to his room to while away the half-hour while the woman prepared his meal.

François sat on the bed convinced his thoughts were becoming fanciful. He wondered how it would be to talk to this woman about his miserable life. He was now single, but unwilling to challenge himself with a relationship with any woman. It was as if the conflict within him raged between his need for communication and his reluctance to make close contact with another's life.

In recent months, he had felt as alone as he imagined any man could be and his only daily company was a bottle, two bottles perhaps. Yet, despite the truth of it, he recognised now a craving to express his inner thoughts, gloomy as they might be. From his bag he pulled the bottle of Calvados and began to sip it, deep in thought. There was a knock on the door.

'Excuse me,' came the woman's voice, 'your meal is ready.'

'I will be right down.'

Descending the stairs, he began to wonder what he was doing here and he noticed a tension in his neck. He could have nothing to say to this woman. His sympathy was dried up, like his skin, or even hers. He had expended it in his grief and wanted to share it with no one.

3

The pork cutlet with vegetables was the best meal he had eaten in over a month. It was also the only one stimulating his appetite enough to make him eat. He pondered that and realised he had lost a great deal of weight since his son's death.

The wine came from Navarre and although it was lighter than the Bergerac he was accustomed to, he found it pleasant enough. The proprietor served him his meal followed by Manchegan cheese and sliced, homemade bread.

Uninvited, she sat down at his table. He offered her some wine and she fetched a glass.

'So you are French? You've come a long way.'

'Yes, I have.'

'I would like to visit France one day.'

'Perhaps you will. It is a wonderful country, a place of art and peace.'

'But you come here in a civil war?'

'Only passing through,' François said, pouring more wine. He began to get a mild dizziness from it and he wondered if the Spanish wines were stronger than the ones at home.

'But a strange time to visit,' she said.

'I'm sorry. I don't know your name.'

'Alma. It means…'

'I know, it means "soul",' he said.

'Yes. Your Spanish is very good.'

'I am a language teacher. Forgive me, but I need to sleep, I have a long ride in the morning.'

'Yes, of course. I will clear up.'

François stood up. Conversation remained on the tip of his tongue, but something prevented him from saying more. His hesitation prompted her to pause, clearing away his plates.

'Please sit,' she said, 'I will get more wine. We can talk if you like. I see in you there is much to say, but you say nothing.'

'You wish to talk about your husband?'

'No, not really. I have no one to talk to. I'm sorry, I'm being foolish. Please, if you need to sleep…'

'I have plenty of time I suppose,' he said.

He sat down and drained his glass.

'I understand what you must be going through. I lost my wife a few years back and it doesn't get any better. I understand.'

The words disturbed him. He meant them. He sat deep in thought while she fetched more wine.

'You said you understand. No one can understand. I lost all that was precious to me and now I sit here in this dreary hotel. The war has destroyed everything in my life that ever made sense; I can't even earn a decent living. We never had children you see. I don't have anyone apart from my sister, and she is still trying to get over what happened.'

'But you have friends?'

He sipped his wine, then wiped a drop from the corner of his mouth with the back of his hand.

She said, 'No one I can talk to.'

'I do understand. My son died in your war, fighting for the Loyalists.'

'And you are here because…'

'To visit his grave.'

'It is dangerous. The rebels are pushing north; it says so on the radio.'

'I've already been through some of their territory coming here.'

'You were not caught?'

'I saw no one, but I travelled fast. Why stay when there is nothing for you here?'

'I have nowhere else to go. This place is all I have left of my life. We are a small community here in Guernica, mainly women, children and old people. The men have gone to the war. You won't find many rebel sympathisers here.'

'I have no side, though my son had.'

'He was an idealist?'

'Yes. We argued over his coming and I would have prevented it if I could. I fought in the last war. I know war and its face is terrible.'

They were silent then for a few minutes, each lost in their own thoughts. She reached for his hand across the table. He grasped hers in return. It was a contract between them. They had each shed something - given and taken.

He said, 'Until Jean-Paul's death, I had always felt grief was a form of self-indulgence. We miss them and so feel sorry for ourselves. Until now, my son was my life. Existing without him seems meaningless.'

'Yes.'

'Don't misunderstand, I don't find suicide attractive. It is not because I am a Catholic but because I know there can be good things still one day, I just cannot see where or when… I drink.'

'Yes, I understand that. I'm no stranger to suffering either am I? We part in the morning, but my pain will remain you know. It's like a stain, or like something I'll have to step over every time I go there. Look, it's late and I have much to do in the morning. You can take the wine up with you, if you wish.'

There was no embrace, no handshake or other physical contact between them and François took the half-empty bottle to his room. He sipped it, not bothering with a glass, as he stared out at the dark street below. He and Alma had much in common. He understood her grief and felt a softening of his heart. He felt like a man wandering in a mist who, reaching out, found something for which he was searching.

He undressed and lay naked on the bed. It was a tolerable temperature, warmer than at home. His eyes began to close and he dowsed the lamp. A dog barked outside but otherwise, there was silence. He started when his door opened. A faint backlight from the hall lamp framed her. She wore a long pale nightdress. He lay still, watching. She untied the bow at her neck and the nightdress slipped from her shoulders. He felt the beginnings of arousal and it surprised him; he had not been with anyone since Arlette. She approached the bed and sitting, reaching out a tremulous hand, placed it on his chest. He pulled her towards him with gentle, caressing hands. Their lips met, a soft kiss, progressing in fervour and urgency.

As she lay down next to him, he said, 'It has been a long time.'

'Yes, for me too. You will be gentle?'

'I am always that in bed.'

He could sense her smile in the darkness. They made love; he, almost reluctant and feeling unfamiliar with both her body and the act itself. She clung to him afterwards, her head against his shoulder, her hand teasing the hair on his chest.

'Thank you,' she said.

'What?'

'Thank you for giving me this moment. It is the first time I have felt anything but grief. It is almost as if everything happening around me has to be enormous before I even notice it.

My feelings seem to have been so… so blunted.'

'Yes it has to cut to the quick before I feel anything too.'

'Will you stay with me a few days? A few days is all I ask.'

'I cannot. I have a duty to visit my son's grave. I will come back this way if you wish, perhaps stay a while. I have nothing to go home to.'

She took his hand and kissed it, reassurance flowing from the movement. They were silent then and neither of them slept. It seemed to François words were unnecessary and for the first time for months he began to feel human. It was as if this woman, naked and soft next to him, had reclaimed him. He knew he would return and perhaps there would never be a need to return to the Dordogne. He wondered if his thoughts were born of desperation and he would clutch at any straw to escape his feelings in that lonely house in St Cyprien.

Chapter 2

Where are you going, handsome jailer,
With that key that's touched with blood
– from *Paroles* by Jacque Prevert

1

The Peugeot hummed and whined as it hammered the dirt tracks high in the Basque country. The sun shone above and it seemed to François there would be an early spring, the countryside reflecting it with green shrubs and trees, buds and nascent flowers appearing. He felt as if his gloom was lifting. He thought often of Jean-Paul it was true, and the pain seemed undiminished, but he also thought of Alma. When he did, he felt foolish. He had slept with her only once and although they made love more than once, he didn't know her. He knew her grief, knew her body, but the essence of her was still a mystery.

He had only ever loved one woman and she was the one he married. Losing his Arlette to a road accident devastated him at the time, but ten passing years attenuates grief and he wondered if perhaps it was time for him to find a new relationship. The absurdity of his feelings prodded him as he rode, but the memory of the previous night both aroused him and made him question. He wondered if she had been there at a time when he was particularly vulnerable. Was this feeling simply an extension of his grieving heart, or was it more than that?

He passed through a small town on the Basque border and saw no sign of war. He saw no soldiers and no tanks. When he stopped, people were friendly as soon as they heard his French-accented Spanish. The rebels had moved north months before and now had retreated after the Loyalists had counterattacked. It didn't look good for the Loyalists however, and local people referred to them with an air of pessimism.

With directions for Laneda, he headed south after drinking wine and eating local bread and cheeses. He thought he might turn into a cheese if his diet did not change.

The tiny village of Laneda consisted of a single street, or at least it once had. There were three burned out buildings, craters in the road and no church. A café displayed ancient wicker chairs and rickety tables, but when he stopped there, he found no one in attendance. François walked around the building, down a narrow alleyway, seeking some living soul to guide him to where Jean-Paul's grave might be. He entered a yard, a scruffy affair, with a grimy water-barrel and a cobbled, enclosed area. A shed with an open door stood at the far end. He approached.

A plump man of François' age appeared, holding a shotgun. He wore a beret like François and sported a thick beard. He pointed the gun at him.

'What do you want? We're closed.'

'I came only to ask directions,' François said.

'You're French?'

'Yes, I'm visiting my son's grave.'

'Well it isn't in my yard or my café is it?'

'I just want to know where he's buried. I don't want any trouble.'

The man looked at him as if trouble was inevitable. After a moment his demeanour softened and he said, 'I seem to recall a French boy who died here. Another lad tried to take care of him but it was hopeless. You're his father?'

'Yes.'

'You sent your son to fight in this stupid war? It's a river of blood with no end and you sent your boy?'

'I wanted him to stay, he wouldn't listen. He died because he believed in a cause. He thought it would help people like you.'

The man looked down at the ground and said, 'I'm sorry. We don't get many people visiting us. The last ones brought war and death. You saw those burned out houses?'

'Yes.'

'The people who lived there were taken out and shot. The rebels burned their homes. That's what you get for being Loyalist sympathisers. I had known those people since I was a child.'

'Where did they bury my son?'

'Same place as my friends. I'll take you.'

He pushed past François and led him up the street to a small enclosed area framed by a low white wooden fence and containing rough wooden crosses hammered into the ground.

'I can't tell you which one is your son's. Probably the only one with no name, unless his friend had time to carve it. I suspect he didn't. They weren't here long. They were retreating from the Fascists.'

François began looking at each cross and walked between the three rows bending to each in turn, oblivious of the café owner.

'I wish you luck, though there seems little of it for anyone these days,' the man said as he walked away, his shotgun broken now, under his arm.

All the crosses had Spanish names except two. One of those looked ancient and François ignored it. The other was fresher but with no name; he felt uncertain whether it was Jean-Paul who lay there or not. He concluded it had to be him if Charles had been right in his letter. He pulled up the cross. He felt determined no son of his would have an unmarked grave. He sat in the dust by the graveside and, unfolding his Laguiole knife, began carving. He heard birds singing in the afternoon sunshine and a smell of juniper hung in the air, though he was not interested enough to look up to find its source.

When he finished, the horizontal piece of the cross read "Jean-Paul Dufy, N.1918 M.1937."

Replacing it at the head of the grave, he knocked it in with a stone; then he knelt, remembering the boy he would never see again; the son whose smile and laugh were denied him forever. He tried to pray but no words came.

'Our Father who…' he began.

It tailed off into silent tears. If there was a God in heaven then why take my son? If there was a God in heaven then why let him die in some strange country fighting for strangers who did not care enough to put his name on a rough wooden cross?

He found he could not pray. In the end. It seemed meaningless. It seemed a travesty to utter any kind of religious cant. If this was God's will, there could be no God, no Superior Being. He denied God then, he shunned him for the pain and the injustice visited upon him. He was not Job and he knew it. Fascist scum had taken Jean-Paul away and neither God nor the church had raised a finger to prevent that injustice. It could only mean there was no God, he reasoned. If there was a

God... No, it was all shit.

François stood up, a feeling of hopelessness enveloping him. He had done nothing to save his son from this. He looked down at the dark earth and cried bitter tears.

He said, 'I don't know how this could be, my son. All I came to say was I love you. I miss you.'

He turned away, and as dusk descended, he mounted his motorcycle and rode back towards the border.

2

Darkness overtook him on the road, and for the first time he lay down by his motorcycle, in the lee of a small hill, and slept a few hours until dawn. He had taken a few pulls on his half-empty bottle of Spanish brandy, purchased from the café owner in Laneda, and when he awoke he noticed the bottle was empty. He could hear the sounds of myriad far-off explosions. He stood up but saw nothing from the brow of the small rise next to him. It sounded like shellfire, but north of him. It was the first hint of the war he had experienced since leaving France.

He shrugged and started the motorcycle. He headed north wondering what would await him in Guernica. Perhaps he would see Alma in a different light, perhaps she would feel differently about having a grieving Frenchman hanging around the house. He clung to the memory of the night they were together as if it was a last chance, not of happiness, but of solace. He realised also this was the first morning in months he had not awoken from dreams of his dead son.

He was a mile from the town when he heard it. Aeroplanes, bombers in the sky. They were too far away for him to see but he realised they were not fighter planes. Mounting a hill, he stopped astride his ride and looked out on the valley where Guernica nestled. He saw a bomb drop. It was huge. The explosion vibrated beneath his feet, even at this distance. There was smoke and then more explosions, massive ones. He had never seen a place razed by bombers before and his mouth gaped as he witnessed the destruction. All of the bombers dropped their loads over the little town.

It made no sense. All he had seen there, days before, were old people, women and children. It was not even a place of strategic importance to anyone. It was an ordinary rural town, no soldiers and no military presence of which he was aware. He stood there for an hour until the planes spent their deadly payloads. A low flying bomber passed overhead and he noticed the black cross of the German air force. He realised Jean-Paul was right: Germany was extending aid to the fascist rebels. Uppermost in his mind was Alma. He wondered if anyone could have survived the carnage he knew would have engulfed the town.

François realised he had remained static on the hill watching, and wondered whether he should have gone down to the town. He knew also that to have done so would have been suicidal. There was such heavy destruction below in that cloud of dust and smoke, little could have survived of the town.

It was quiet now. No birds sang, nothing moved. Half a mile away he could smell the smoke.

Craters from stray or badly aimed bombs pockmarked the road and at times he had to dismount and walk his motorcycle to make progress. He entered the main thoroughfare.

There was an acrid smell of burning and he seemed to be in a fog of steam and fumes. Flames crackled around him as he walked and he saw no living soul; heard no one calling or even crying. He started when a wall collapsed to his right and he coughed in the pungent smog surrounding him. Not one building escaped unscathed. A butcher's shop sagged and caved in, the roof absent as if blown away by some gust of malevolent wind. Overturned cars and trucks littered the destruction and he had to pick his way between burning vehicles and craters in the road. He left his motorcycle propped against a hairdresser's and looked up at the balcony. A woman sat there silent, oblivious. He called out to her but she rocked backwards and forwards, forwards and back in a repetitive cycle. She clutched a bundle, baby shaped and sized, to her bloodstained chest.

He stood with his back to the street, facing where the hotel once stood. Motionless, he understood what lay before him. Where the hotel had been, with its peeling render, balconies and flowers, now lay a crater. Delved out of the ground, all it revealed in the dust and smoke and haze were the remains of the foundations and a pile of smoke-obscured rubble; not one brick stood upon another. Alma had gone if she was in that building. He recalled how he first saw her behind the lobby desk. The likelihood of her being elsewhere was small and so he assumed the worst because he felt nothing in his life was happening for the best. Alma had gone, and with her his reclamation and his hope of re-joining humanity.

Perhaps she had gone out. If she had not been in the hotel, maybe she had hidden. But where? In this blazing, smoking place, could anyone hide from the destructive German rain falling from those spring skies? He thought he could wait. If she had escaped, she might come back. He knew it was fanciful, but all the same there seemed no other option. He sat down in the dust, legs dangling over the edge of the hole occupying the space where once the entrance to the hotel stood.

Two doors away, he heard groans from a baker's shop. He got up and entered, thinking he might help. A woman lay on her side. She was the source of the sound, her blackened face distorted and burned. He turned her over and realised it was pointless. A table-leg projected from her chest and he knew she could not survive. He knelt and held her to him. She opened her eyes and for one brief moment they connected with a silent communication, until François realised she was beyond pain. Getting up, he left her there and emerged from the ruins, begrimed with dust and soot, soaked in blood.

He stumbled, tripping on a dog's corpse lying twisted in the roadway, and realised there were several, even the body of a horse further up the road.

François felt as if he stood at the gateway to Hell. Fire, dust, death and destruction all around, and still that choking acrid smoke, wavering when the breeze took it but returning when it lulled.

He felt robbed. He was pinning so many hopes on Alma and now she was gone. It was the same nightmare as losing Jean-Paul, but attenuated because he knew much of what he felt had no basis apart from his own expectations. There was so much left unsaid on the one night he had spent with her. He had saved it for his return, but now she wasn't here. Had she been killed? He had no idea what to do. He could stay here in the dust and reek, or move on, putting Alma down to a missed opportunity. But in the end, he had to know. He was desperate to find out if she had indeed met her death in the bombing.

Why had he waited to tell her how he felt about his life and the importance of that tender moment she gave him? He cursed himself for waiting. Waiting for what? To carve a name on a cross in some far-off place? It made no sense to him and as the town returned to life around him he sat, legs swinging into the void where once had been his hope of relief. Hope of a return to feelings and normality.

It was as if he was left with nothing, his own life already at an end. He knew he didn't love the widow, but seeing her grave he realised his anticipation of reciprocated feelings for another human being had died with her. The events in Guernica stole his soul and left him empty of caring, empty of love. Sitting there, he began to think about the perpetrators of this theft. It was none of Germany's business what happened in Spain. Yes they shared a common aim, the rebels and the German Nazis, but to send bombers to destroy women and children? It made no sense. He felt the beginning of a festering hate both for Germany and for the Fascists in general.

A woman leading a child by the hand walked past him as if he was invisible. Tempted to speak to her, he stood up, but she had moved on. He looked around. Death was in the street but signs of life were appearing. The shells of brick and rubble disclosed those nascent islands of survival. People began wandering about, confused, deafened and bloody. He saw tears and heard lamentations, most of them female, as if this was a town of women; women violated by their unseen attackers in the sky. It was a sky that for them had always been bright, friendly and benign, but he could understand if none of those survivors would ever look up at the azure canopy with those feelings again. This place confirmed his view there could be no God in heaven. How could there be, if He allowed hell to thrive in such a place?

Still he waited, thinking and wishing. Would she come? Had she escaped? What else could he do? He felt strange about his presence here. He was not Spanish, he did not belong, and Alma had been only a single night of love to him.

Love? Had he thought of that word? It was impossible. He wondered if he had become some foolish adolescent, at the age of forty-seven, to feel love in exchange for a single night of lovemaking. He shook his head and jumped into the crater, looking for some sign. Not signs of life, for he had not become a fool in his newfound infatuation. No, he sought some sign of death; unwilling yet determined, and when he found it, he wished he had never looked.

It was an approximation, but he guessed where the lobby desk must have stood. There was rubble there though the structure of the building had gone. Some charred wooden remnants remained. He kicked them away and realised with horror what lay beneath. The body was incomplete, almost unrecognisable as a once-human form. He knew the truth of it despite its mutilation. It was more the shape than any visible landmark, making him realise this was the remains of a person. A person he had held in his arms and to whom he had whispered endearments. He turned away; he had no desire to touch the carcass, smouldering in death.

It was Alma, but he knew he had no right to bury her, no right to mourn. Yet that was what he did. He searched the nearby ruins and eventually found a pickaxe and a spade. Dragging the still warm remains to the edge of the crater, he hauled it up to the edge, wondering how a limbless corpse could weigh so much. At the back of the place where once the hotel stood, he began digging. It was hard work and took an hour of continuous labour. He pulled the remnant of her body into the three-foot deep grave and filled it in. He had no words to say. He stood for a few moments and then made his way back to his motorcycle, passing distraught people, charred human remains, and the carcasses of animals and cars.

He started up and rode north. He didn't look back. His

mind was absorbed in hatred.

3

François arrived home to an empty house and an empty life. He didn't go to the school the following week. He drank. He drank wine, he guzzled Calvados until his days merged with his nights, and yet no solace came. In his waking moments, sober and thick-headed, he only felt pain. He banished the pain with a morning eye-opener of wine. He lunched on wine, and his evenings became a blur of alcoholic reminiscences and regrets.

If only he had prevented Jean-Paul from leaving. He could have forced him somehow. Why had he allowed it? Tumbling into bed at night, he thought of Alma. She became larger than life. She became beautiful and a potential salvation denied him by the filthy Fascists. He raved, he swore, he broke things in his home in his violent rages.

After two weeks of this, the head teacher Madame Lusard appeared on his doorstep. She was scrawny, her lips puckered in a permanent expression of intolerance. She was strict with the children and stricter with her staff and François disliked her with an intensity accentuated now by his alcoholic haze.

It took him minutes to answer the door. When he finally roused himself from his near comatose state, he stumbled through the hallway and fumbled the latch. Opening it, he confronted his superior. He made no attempt to step aside and ask her in: he needed his grip on the door-handle to remain upright.

'Yesh?' He squinted at her, unsteady, swaying.

'You're drunk Monsieur Dufy. It is eleven in the morning.'

'Yesh.'

'I am afraid we cannot have this kind of behaviour at the school.'

'I'm not at the school.'

'But you have not returned, which is why I am here.'

'Come in. Have a drink you old trout.'

'I beg your pardon?'

'Oh, why be so po-faced? Always so humourless. If you had seen what I have seen you would want a drink too.'

'You don't make sense. I am here because you failed to turn up at the school and we are going to have to let you go. We cannot have… have… this behaviour in front of our children. I will have to dismiss you, and the school board will back my decision.'

François remained jovial. 'Give us a kiss you old tart.'

'I hope you remember this conversation, but I doubt that very much. I will send a letter in due course. You are entitled to one month's salary. You should be ashamed of yourself.'

It was the word "ashamed" which rankled. François felt he had nothing of which to be ashamed. The word sparked anger and in his alcoholic haze, he experienced no reluctance in expressing it.

'You stupid stuck-up Parisian bitch. You think you can come here and preach at me about shame? Shame is the monster all of France should express for not fighting the Fascists in Spain, in Germany and all over the world where intolerance and prejudice raise their ugly heads. Yesh! Even in schools where stupid snobbish women are in charge. You can take your stupid job and stick it in your vagina! It would be the only thing to visit that stink-hole in half a century.'

She stood there a moment. She looked at him. His diatribe seemed to François to cause no reaction at all. The head teacher turned away, but her gait was less determined and he began to regret his words. He realised he had gone too far. He was an educated man and he had never been rude to a woman in that way before. He slammed the door shut in disgust. It was anger with himself, more than with Mme Lusard. He sat in the living room and picked up his glass. He sipped, and then in another fit of pique he threw the glass, half-filled with red wine, against the wall.

François took his head in his hands and tears came. They were tears of anger and frustration and he knew it. He hated himself then and wished everything would end. He fetched another bottle from the cellar. He fell down the stairs descending and slipped on the top step when he emerged. He looked down at the cellar and shook his fist, muttering curses.

'Bloody bitch of a house. Bloody bitch of a woman.'

He sat in his chair drinking from the bottle, unable to find a glass.

'Moving on,' he said. 'Bloody moving on, get away from them all. Sell the house, that's what I'll do. Go to Bergerac or maybe Bordeaux. New start. Do a bit of fishing, hunting, get a dog.'

Despite the time of day, he leaned back cradling his bottle, and his eyes closed in an alcoholic nap.

Chapter 3

It's war, it's summer,
Already summer, still war,
And the desolate, isolated city
Smiles, still smiles...
  – from *Paroles* by Jacque Prevert

1

François listened. He heard a finch calling, off to his right. With a slow, almost imperceptible movement he raised his rifle to his shoulder where the stock fitted snug and firm, comfortable in his experienced grip as he slid his finger to the trigger. A gust of autumn wind rippled the long yellow grass of the meadow while the hare stood on its hind legs, looking around and sniffing the breeze in the approaching dusk. François stood downwind. He was careful where he hid because he understood the ways of the creatures he hunted. He squeezed the trigger. It was a slow gentle movement and despite the slight tremor in his hands, he knew the hare would die.

The creature startled as the gun went off. The bullet was faster than any reaction in its brain. The impact lifted the hare into the air and its legs kicked for a fraction of a second in its descent. It lay still, a yard from where the bullet took it.

François picked his prey up by the ears and examined it. Urine ran, dripping from its hind legs. His .22 bullet had passed clean through the chest but it came as no surprise to him: he had hunted game in that way since he was a child. He knew he was different from most. Whether he was drunk or sober, he could shoot as straight as a Roman viaduct.

He stuffed the limp creature into his satchel. He had taken half a dozen this evening and intended to sell four in the market. It would pay for a few bottles of wine. Crossing the forest along tiny paths and tracks, he whistled to himself. Drinking was the only thing he had to look forward to these days. His one-storey house, purchased from the proceeds of sale of the house in St Cyprien two years before, left him with enough to live on for a few years. The new home was isolated and close to his beloved forest where he hunted, fished and sometimes slept rough.

Hearing the sound of men talking ahead of him he slowed his pace. He knew he should not have been hunting in this forest as it was private land, so he removed his satchel and hid it in the undergrowth. He marked the spot with an upright twig. The voices came closer.

'Dufy. What are you up to you disreputable fellow?'

The voice came from a short, stocky man with close-cropped hair and an air of authority. His face was serious, but behind the eyes there was laughter. The other was tall and broad, with long brown hair and a large hooked nose. He too seemed on the verge of laughter.

'Nothing, Inspector Ran, just out for a walk.'

'With a rifle?'

'I often take it with me. There's a war on isn't there?'

The big man said, 'This is not a good place for hunting. It is a private area and the owners are part of the Dubois family.

They might treat you as a trespasser.'

'I don't know you,' François said.

'I'm Pierre Dreyfus. The Inspector and I are old friends. As to the war, the Germans are halted at the Maginot line, hadn't you heard?'

'No. I keep myself to myself.'

Inspector Ran said, 'Look Dufy, I would not arrest you for poaching, but make it a little less obvious will you?'

'Naturally,' François said, 'good day to you gentlemen.'

François walked on. When he was certain Ran and his friend had gone, he doubled back and found his satchel. He opened it. There were only two hares inside. For a moment, he stood staring in disbelief.

'Fucking thieving police bastard,' he said to himself, shouldering his bag.

2

The annexation of Austria, the invasion of Poland and the defeat of the French army all passed by François. He began to realise he was not in touch with the world and he did not care. All he wanted was for people to leave him alone with his dog Cognac, his guns, and with his grief. There were long nights when sleep became elusive, long nights when he drank copiously. Those nights he often spent slumped on the tattered sofa, in the small sitting area of his simple house on the outskirts of the town.

Nothing disturbed his peace. He began to think this was all he wanted for the remainder of his life, and although he didn't become morose, he isolated himself in the certain knowledge that no one could break into the world to which he had banished himself. All around him food became scarce, people complained, and German soldiers began to appear in places where François would never have expected to see an occupying force. He was not a stupid man, but in his narrow cycle of fishing, hunting, reading and drinking he had given up on normal everyday life. He was happy too, in a perverse way. There was a kind of peace in his existence. He had no need of cleanliness, no need of social interaction, and on those days when ordinary people went to church he watched, never tempted to join them but gaining a strange reassurance from the fact of their worship.

How nice for them, he often mused. How nice to have the anchor which religion provided. He knew inside he didn't need that anchorage himself; it was cessation he sought. An end to what had become a miserable existence. He denied to himself he was suicidal but that germ of a thought often grew in his consciousness.

Sometimes François gave in to feelings of uselessness, as if he had wasted his life in his monogamous relationship with Arlette, going nowhere. She died and then Jean-Paul too, and he was left with nothing and no reason to continue living. An intestate man in his forties. He wondered what use he was to society, the world even.

It was a Thursday when his life changed. He would re-member it for the rest of his days. Thursdays were hunting days. Rifle on his shoulder, beret firmly settled on his balding head and his canvas bag across his shoulder, he set out ready to earn enough money at market on Saturday to finance his drinking and pay for the meagre diet to which he was now accustomed.

The forest was quiet; no birdsong impinged upon his sens-es and the sun filtered through the tall pines above, lighting his way as he walked. Had the burden of his grief not weighted him down so much, he might have enjoyed the environment, the sunny world he moved in.

Close to the road, as he entered the Dubois forest, he heard a new sound. It was human, and it struck him hard. He thought a child cried out in pain. The noise seemed to François to be a travesty, a violation; it brought with it pain and misery to an extent he had never experienced since his days in St Cyprien. He stopped in his tracks and listened.

'Filthy little Jewish whore,' he heard.

It was a German-accented voice.

With a hunter's caution, he approached the road, listening and looking. At first he saw nothing. As he emerged from the tree line and came closer, he saw the source of the miserable whimpering. A military car crouched at the verge of the road. Beside it stood two German soldiers in green uniforms and between them a child of perhaps ten or twelve years, hunched and curled up in the dry summer dust.

François saw one of the men draw back his foot and dispense a vicious kick at the child's head. The black boot glanced off her dark locks as the second soldier landed another boot-blow on her back. The child screamed, her hands about her head, her knees drawn up as if they could protect her. François knew they would not. The soldiers wore black boots, heavy boots, shiny and clean, vicious and clean. It was as if the clean black boots spoke to him. The clean black boots so soon to become smeared with blood.

At first he only felt anger, then the beginning of release of the hatred buried so long ago in Spain, in Guernica, in Laneda. At last he realised he could retaliate. He felt like a child bullied in the playground who in one moment understands he can fight back, standing up against the aggressor.

François raised his rifle. He worked fast. He drew the bolt and nestled the butt of the rifle where his shoulder met his chest. He was twenty yards away. There was no doubt in his mind. It was simple. Easier than a rabbit. Jean-Paul had been right: they were bigger targets.

The first bullet struck home through the eye-socket. The report was soft, it was a .22 rifle after all. The second shot took the remaining German in the front of his throat. Another entered the chest to the left of the sternum. Both men were down. But François knew they might not be dead. A .22 in the skull ricochets inside and cannot exit like a heavy bullet. Within moments he realised the first man lived. The German was crawling, sightless, towards the vehicle.

François took out his skinning knife. No hesitation, no remorse. He did this for Jean-Paul. He did this for Alma and he did it for the girl who still lay curled up, silent now. Most of all, he did it for himself.

He stood straddling the man. He leaned forward and drew the bare head back by the hair. The blade sliced from left to right in a second. Blood spurted onto the ground, pumping, as if it had a life of its own but weakening with each spurt. François watched with a strange fascination. He had killed many in the First War, but never close up like this. He had shot men, but never despatched a man with a knife. He realised he could smell the blood but it barely made inroads into the anger and hatred consuming him in this instant. He stood for a few moments, straddled across the corpse, and he then felt he had spent his hatred.

François turned to the child. She lay still, her whimpers quieter, head still covered.

'My little one? Can you stand? We must clear up and get out of here.'

The girl looked up at him through bruised and blood-shot eyes. She was older than he had thought. In a moment she spoke.

'I'm Jewish.'

'Yes and I am nothing. Don't fear me. Come.'

He proffered a hand and she stood with slow painful movements. With one eye closed by swelling and with a limp, she made her way, supported by her rescuer. He lifted her into the front seat of the open vehicle. Next he dragged the two bodies into the back. It was hard, heavy work, but nothing to a man with strong arms, trained now for years in lifting carcasses. This act seemed no different to Francois than the end of a good day's hunting; the stag, limp and lifeless in his hands, needing a hard pull and heavy lift. He brushed the path with a branch and hoped the blood would not be too obvious to a passer-by.

Getting into the car, he pressed the ignition and drove into the forest. The evidence had to go where no one would find it, and he knew where. The whole event occurred as if he had planned it, as if he had followed some path to revenge after a long absence. To his surprise, François felt more alive now than at any time since Guernica.

He thought of Jean-Paul and he ruminated on Alma as he bounced on the forest track. He had miles to go but he was sure of his destination.

The edge of the forest hovered over a bend in the Dordogne. The undercut bank created a ledge with a sheer drop into the muddy waters. François knew the water was deep here; had he not fished this river and its tributaries now for years? However deep the pool, he knew he also had to secure the bodies to prevent them floating into the current, once nature caused the abdomens to bloat.

He dropped the girl off at the tree line and told her to wait. She would not allow him to leave.

'This will not be a pretty sight. I don't want you to see.'

'I don't care,' she said, grabbing his sleeve.

'You will. I have to slit their stomachs open or they will fill with gas and float.'

'I won't look, but please, please don't leave me.'

François positioned her facing away from the car. He used his knife, efficient and fast. When he finished, he strapped each body into place with the crude lap belts.

They stood hand in hand and watched as the vehicle struck the brown swirling waters of the river. It did not sink at once. The vehicle seemed to hover in the water for moments before the front dived. The bodies jerked when the bonnet submerged, as if the dead men braced themselves in readiness for their watery grave ahead.

'Well, my child, what do we do now? Find your parents?'

With her only open eye, moist and compelling, she looked up at him.

'They took them away this morning. The soldiers grew angry when I tried to run away.'

'Well,' he said, 'looks like we're stuck with each other for a while. What's your name?'

'Rachelle.'

'The water carrier?'

'What?' she said, as he took her hand and led her to the path.

'Don't they teach anything in school these days? In the Bible she was a beautiful young woman who carried water from the well. Married Jacob, I think.'

'Papa said it was a name that came to him in a dream.'

'Oh.'

Looking up, she turned her puffy eyes towards him and said, 'Will you kill more Germans?'

François looked at the swollen lips, the bruised cheeks and he smiled. 'Are you scared?'

'Not now. I want to see my Maman and Papa. Where have they taken them?'

'Who can say? Perhaps we can find out. I will keep you safe until that day.'

She tried to smile but her contused lips moved only a fraction. It was enough for François. He understood.

Chapter 4

Oh
Lost gardens
forgotten fountains
prairies in the sun.
Oh suffering,
splendour and mystery of adversity,
blood and flickered light
stricken beauty.
Fraternity.
– from *Paroles* by Jacque Prevert

1

'Your face looks a bit better,' François said.

'My lip is still swollen and my back is still sore.'

A week after the killings they stood in a meadow half a mile from his house. A warm summer sunset cast red beams of light behind the forest and the rosiness of the closure of the day illuminated the girl with a radiance reminiscent of a statue of the Virgin Mary François had once seen in the cathedral in Sarlat. He shook his head to free it of his strange and foolish thoughts, and turned to walk through the thigh-length yellow grass.

Rachelle caught him up.

'Uncle, where were the Germans taking me when you killed them?'

'I don't know, my little friend. I heard about a camp near Bordeaux. I don't know.'

'What if they find me?'

'Rachelle, I am an old man next to you. When I was fifteen the world was very different. I have seen many changes and they made me withdraw. No one comes here. It is safe.'

'You drink.'

'Yes, that too. I live alone. I speak only to people who buy game and fish from me. No one will see you and they will not find you.'

'Why did you...'

'Shhh. See that movement? It's a rabbit.'

'Poor little thing.'

'You will never make a hunter.'

'Can I try to shoot the gun?'

'No, but I can teach you when we have hunted. When I was your age,' François whispered, 'I could kill a rabbit at a hundred paces.'

'I don't want to kill rabbits.'

'Oh?'

'I want to kill Germans.'

François regarded her with surprise. He almost dropped the rifle.

'You are a young girl, but full of hate. It is wrong to kill for revenge. If we have to kill to make them leave then it is all right. Not for revenge.'

'They touched me.'

'What? Oh look, the rabbit escaped.'

'They touched me down below. Both of them. It was why I tried to run. Then they beat me.'

'They are dead. Gone. Don't think about these things.'

'I can't help it.'

'We can talk later. Tonight we hunt.'

'Yes Uncle.'

'And stop calling me Uncle. We're not relatives. Friends yes, not relatives.'

'Yes Uncle.'

François smiled. He looked at the girl and their eyes met in the dusk light. He saw strength there, anger, and determination too.

He pulled her to him, patting her back with a gentle but clumsy hand. It felt strange. He had not had physical contact with another since Guernica.

'You smell bad, Uncle. I'll wash your clothes tomorrow.'

'I smell this way because I hunt and sleep rough. It is an honourable way to smell. It is the odour of hard work.'

'And drink.'

'Oh, you.' He turned in irritation and stomped off through the field. Rachelle followed, head bowed, thoughtful.

2

The rays of early morning sunshine sneaked past the tattered hangings draped across the windows of the small house. Cognac, François' Border-collie bitch, whimpered and scratched to come in, hunger-driven. François awoke with a start and looked at his watch. It was well past dawn and he was still on the couch. He lay unmoving at first, then scratched a midge-bite on his buttock. Turning onto his back he stared at the ceiling where a patch of damp had appeared. He noticed with irritation a fungus in its early stages seeming almost to grin at him.

He rubbed his chin and sat on the edge of the dilapidated couch. He wondered why he slept so well in a war-torn world. He was naked and for once he covered himself up as a reflex, one that was new, since Rachelle's arrival.

He wondered what she would change in his life today. Already she had washed his clothes, changed the bed linen and cleaned the house. It irritated him because he couldn't find anything. Every time he looked for shotgun shells, for a spanner, or even his clothes, the reply was the same.

'I found them on the floor and now they are in the cupboard.'

He had not experienced this feeling of someone looking after him since Arlette died, and he began to wonder after three weeks with Rachelle how he ever coped. It was not resentment at losing his privacy, nor even the inconvenience of needing to think about someone else; it was the feeling, sneaking up on him, that he enjoyed someone else in his life. True, her company was often harrowing. She would cry, and though he tried in his clumsy way to console her, her bitterness and nostalgia made her difficult company at those times. But she often smiled, she laughed and she badgered him. When she petted Cognac he tried to scold her, pointing out she was a working dog, but it made no difference.

Bare to the waist, he emerged into the sunshine and began to wash. He lathered his face to shave and the words of an English song came to mind,

When I was in love with you,
I was clean and brave,

And miles around the wonder grew
How well did I behave.

Putting down the razor he changed his mind. If he became clean and brave, people would notice the change and he wanted no one to become suspicious.

And now the fancy passes by,
And nothing shall remain.
And miles around they'll say that I
Am quite myself again.

He sang in English and smiled to himself. He must resist the urge to clean up too much; he must now play a part, like an actor. No one could know.

Was that what was happening to him? Was he becoming clean and brave? He recognised he had no sexual feelings, only an intense sense of guardianship for the girl. It went deeper than that. He thought perhaps she represented something to him; something which had been elusive before. He knew what it was: a form of resistance, a way of getting back at the Fascists who had invaded France, just as Jean-Paul predicted they would, on the day he left for war. He hated them and so it was natural he should love Rachelle as a friend and, in his dreams, as a daughter.

A sound behind him roused him from his thoughts. He continued to wash.

'Uncle,' Rachelle said, her voice sleepy and soft.

'Eh?'

'I have not been to school since the Germans came.'

'School. No. You can't; they will arrest you.'

'No more school?'

'You sound sad. Most children would be delighted not to have to attend school.'

'I miss my friends and my mother wanted me to go to

school and later University in Paris.'

'Paris? Lousy place, full of snobs. You're better off without Paris. I can teach you here if you want. I have plenty of books. I can teach you French, German, and Rosbif, even Spanish.'

'You speak all those languages?'

'Yes, I was a teacher in St Cyprien for many years.'

'If you are a teacher, what are you doing here?'

'You ask too many questions. Now wash and we will have breakfast. By the way don't wash any more clothes.'

'But they smell like a mixture of old ponds and sweat.'

'All the same. If people round here see I'm clean all of a sudden, they will suspect something. Leave half the clothes dirty, you hear?'

'I need something else. When you go to market…'

'What?'

'Each month… I didn't mean to embarrass you.'

'I was a married man once, as well as a teacher. I understand these things. We can begin your lessons tomorrow.'

'I need to learn how to shoot a gun. You promised.'

'First I will teach you how it works, then how to strip it down and oil it, then about sighting. Only when you understand a gun and can look after it will you learn to shoot one. Understood?'

Rachelle looked at him with an expression of pleasure and she nodded. It was as if, having said all she needed to, he was rewarding her. She turned and walked back into the house. He dried himself and heard the clatter of pans in the kitchen. The sun was shining and a dove cooed in the eaves of his house. The beauty of the moment made no impression on François. He knew he could not trust the good times anymore; they ended in grief too often for him to smile now. He felt as if every time a chance of happiness came, events he

44

could not control took the opportunity away, so now he was determined never to commit himself again. Perhaps the Germans would come, perhaps the girl would become ill. Perhaps the sky would fall in upon him. Whatever happened, he would be ready.

3

François hated market days. Usually it was on Saturday, but on feast days the townspeople demoted it to Friday. He found contact with the locals difficult and it was his reason for drinking in the morning on the way there. On most Saturdays, he downed a bottle of wine by the time he arrived at six in the morning.

Not so today. Rachelle had hidden his bottles of wine the night before. He remonstrated with her, he shouted, he swore. She refused to budge however, and in the end he left, his foul temper expressed in expletives as he walked. The barrow stuck in mud at the side of the road by the bridge and he almost toppled and fell down the bank to the wide brown swirling waters of the river.

He cursed again but desisted when a plump woman stopped on her bicycle. She was well groomed and she wore a hat with a lace veil, white and clean.

'M. Dufy. What are you doing here?'

'A little trouble with my wheel, Mme Arnaud. Stuck in the mud.'

'Can I help you?'

'No. I can manage.'

'Have you rabbits?'

'Yes, one hare and ten doe rabbits. I have some venison too

but it's hanging and won't be ready for a week.'

'I'll take two rabbits from you. Fish?'

'Just the usual trout, Mme. Arnaud.'

'Two of those will be nice. They are fresh?'

'Naturally, I caught them yesterday.'

'You will deliver them?' she said seeming unsteady propped on her right leg on the bank.

'When would you like them? I will finish at the market by two in the afternoon. Would this afternoon be all right?'

'My husband will be there then. He even works on Saturday mornings nowadays.'

'Nowadays?' he said.

'Yes these filthy Germans cause so much trouble, arresting and bullying.'

'The Germans don't have powers of arrest; our police do it all.'

'The SD does what it wants. It has all changed since the Germans moved their men into Vichy,' she said.

'I don't bother with such things you know. Keep myself to myself these days.'

'But you fought alongside my husband against the Germans in the Great War. Don't you care?'

'Well, yes, I care but what can I do?'

'Resistance. That's what.'

'Resistance?'

'Yes, Sergeant Dufy, have you forgotten? It is the duty of all Frenchmen to resist. Some do it in small ways: they paint slogans on walls, they sabotage machinery, they cause inefficiencies in the postal system, they re-route trains to the wrong place. It is all resistance, is it not so? Even an old woman like me can do her bit. France has fallen but she will rise again. I know it.'

'Yes Mme. Arnaud. I will do my best.'

'I remember when you received your decoration, my husband was so proud of you.'

'Yes. It was a long time ago though, Madame Arnaud.'

'My husband will tell you. We are French and you must begin to resist now.'

'Yes Madame.'

François, taken aback by her vehemence, raised his hand to salute then realised it was inappropriate and pretended to scratch his head.

'Now don't forget, as soon as you finish today, deliver two rabbits, and two of the larger trout. You will keep the best for me, do you hear?'

She mounted her bicycle and rode towards the market, no doubt to lecture someone else about the value of fighting unassailable enemies, he thought. Resistance indeed. There was no organised resistance to the German occupation. Everyone had become poor overnight. Filthy scum had overrun the land and there was no one who would help. Not even the Rosbifs could do anything. François doubted they could hold out until the spring; a little country against a huge aggressor—hopeless.

He pulled the barrow loose with a strength fostered by his ill temper. He did not like anyone to lecture him and he disliked the insinuation that he was not doing what he could for his country. He believed in France and he knew, although his country was on its knees, it would, as Mme Arnaud said, rise up once more, with him or without him. Anyway he was doing his bit. Had he not killed two of the filthy sauerkraut-eating bastards? Had he not taken in Rachelle?

He realised he was pushing his barrow too hard for he had become breathless with the exertion, so he paused in the cobbled roadway. It was then he heard the beeping behind him. His barrow was not blocking the road but there was insufficient space for the black Mercedes following behind. He waved his hand behind him. They would have to wait. There was no room for them both.

The beeping became more insistent and more frequent. François slowed down. If they were so rude, they could learn to be patient. Damned Germans.

He felt the impact before he was aware of them closing the gap. The front bumper hit his calves and he fell forward, striking his chin on the barrow. The world became a swirling starscape of coloured lights and blurred movements. Dizzy, he realised he lay in the road. Struggling to get up he felt strong hands lifting him by the arms and dragging him to the narrow pavement. They dumped him without ceremony against the wall of a building. Unable to stand, he saw two men clad in green uniforms, grabbing his barrow and tipping it up. It lay disconsolate to his eyes, broken against the same wall holding him up.

The soldiers dusted off their gloved hands and one of them spat as he passed. The glob of spittle landed on François' arm and the second man laughed. They got into the black car and drove away. The last François saw of them was a pale face staring at him from the back of the vehicle. The man was young and thin, blond and scowling. François never forgot a face. In this case, despite his dizziness, he knew he would remember. He got to his knees and then to his feet, holding onto the wall with an outstretched arm, lest he fall. Moments later he tried to tip his now one-handled barrow onto its wheels but it was heavy and old-fashioned and he strained hard in his efforts.

'Here, let me help you.'

It was the big man from the woods, that day when Inspector Ran stole his rabbits.

'Leave me. I'm all right.'

'It is heavy, my friend. Let me help you.'

'No. I can manage.'

'You don't want the help of a Jew, is that it?'

François noticed the man had a yellow star sewn onto his right arm. 'I remember you from the forest. You stole my hares.'

'Yes, I did. Happier days those. Here let's get this upright.'

'Dreyfus is it?' François said, less certain in his vehemence.

'Pierre, yes.'

'Thank you for the help. Jewish eh? Lucky the Inspector is your friend. Bad things happening to your countrymen these days.'

'I am French. You are all my countrymen.'

'I meant your, er... religion. Good to have contacts, eh?'

'Him? He was my friend once. Now? Well, he interns my friends and sends them away to be killed. No friend of mine now. Tell you what, can I buy a rabbit? I have a child at home and we are very hungry. They won't let us work, won't let us buy.'

'Child?'

'Yes, my daughter Monique.'

'You helped me. Here, take one, no, two, you look like you need a good feed. I can always get more. Where do you live?'

'Couple of miles out of town east of the bridge, south-bank.'

'I know it; near the quarry. Is it the big posh house facing the river? Sell it and get out my friend. This place stinks of death.'

'I can't leave without papers. I can't even pay you for both rabbits.'

'Take them I said.'

'I am not allowed to sell the property or goods over a certain value either. I am registered at that address so I have to stay there. That's why I can't leave.'

'You have a gun?'

'Not allowed.'

'Fishing rod, then.

'Yes.'

'Meet me tomorrow evening Rue de Matisse, far end of the road, low building. We can talk and fish. I know all the spots.'

'There is a curfew. If I'm caught, they will send me to Germany and take my daughter away.'

'So I'll come to you. It may be late though.'

'You're fishing?'

'Well I use nets too. Illegal, but a man has to live.'

'And drink.'

'My reputation goes before me.'

'Auguste—you know, Inspector Ran—always said you were the town drunk.'

'We'll see won't we?'

'I don't understand.'

'Do you know who the man in the car was?'

'I think it was a man called Meyer. Works with Brunner, the SD Major at the Mairie.'

'Big man? Important?'

'I don't know; the rank in the SD is lower than the equivalent in the army. He's maybe like an SS major.'

'Meyer, eh? Well good day to you M. Dreyfus. I will see you soon.' François turned. Wiping the German's spittle from his sleeve with distaste, he pushed his barrow towards the market. The face in the car felt imprinted in his memory and he would not forget. Nazi bastards, they would pay.

Chapter 5

It's terrible
The faint sound
Of a hard-boiled egg cracked on a tin counter.
It's terrible that sound
When it stirs in the memory of a man who is hungry
– from *Paroles* by Jacque Prevert

1

The Arnaud house stood out from most houses in Bergerac. Locals called it the 'English' or the 'Rosbif' house because it was constructed entirely of red brick and roof-slates with no balcony or shutters. It was an old place, built fifty years before by an English sea captain who settled in the small town after long sea travels. He left his mark. The English appearance of the house and the big, rusty anchors adorning the garden showed who lived there all those years before.

François rang the doorbell, shifting from foot to foot. He had no wish to meet his old commander from those terrible wartime days of mud and trenches, mud and death. Despite the warm sunshine, he shivered as recollections of those times entered his mind. He had only moments to wait before a maid opened the door.

'Deliveries round the back,' she said. She was young and

seemed flushed. She straightened her hat and smoothed her skirt as if she had just dressed. She had beauty he had to admit, but she was just a child in his eyes. What would she know of the bond between soldiers? François knew all she could see, was a dishevelled smelly old man with parcels.

'The Colonel knows me. He may wish to know I'm here.'

'Doubt it. Go round the back then and wait. I'll tell him you are here.'

François made his way to the side gate.

She called him back, 'Hey. You.'

'What?'

'You have a name or should I just describe you?'

Her expression indicated to François how much she would have enjoyed the task of describing him.

'Sergeant Dufy, he knows me. We were in the war together.'

The girl lifted her little retroussé nose and with a haughtiness François felt was unnecessary, shut the door. He walked with one of his two packages under each arm to the back of the house, and waited.

Colonel André Arnaud was older than François. He was balding and he wore a small grey moustache. When he came to the back door, François was surprised to see him in a dressing gown and slippers. It was mid-afternoon and he wondered what his old commander might have been doing to have his clothes off at this time of day. He recalled the girl at the door straightening her clothes and he felt a stab of admiration for his old superior.

'Sergeant Dufy. At any other time, I would have been pleased to see you. I am very busy just now. Can you come back?'

'Your wife, Colonel...'

'What? She is coming?'

'I... don't know, she asked me to deliver these. Fresh game. She wanted the best.'

'Deliver? What is it?'

'Fresh game sir.'

'Ah yes, she did say something... Why are you delivering it?'

'I catch and sell it sir.'

'I thought you were a school teacher? Haven't you found a job or something?'

'No sir. I hunt and sell nowadays.'

'Bit rum for an educated man isn't it? Never mind, I suppose you had better come in.'

The Colonel stepped back indicating for his old sergeant to enter. François tripped on the threshold, nervous.

'Steady on my old man. Are you drunk or something?'

'No sir. I tripped on the rug.'

'Ah, well sit down. What have you brought?'

'Two rabbits and two trout. I picked the biggest ones specially.'

'Good man. Always reliable. We go a long way back don't we Dufy?'

'Yes, sir.'

'Château Labégorce Zédé will do.'

The Colonel shut the door to the hallway and, returning, reached towards a wine rack on the kitchen table. The screw-pull, ancient and rusted, hung on the wall and he extracted the cork in silence. Two glasses poured, Arnaud sat opposite his old sergeant.

'So. You shoot creatures and go fishing?'

'Yes, sir.'

'You are on holiday.'

'Holiday?'

'Yes, you do the things others do for leisure and you say this is your living. Is it not so?'

'I have had a hard time, sir.'

The Colonel's face changed to a subtle shade of madder.

'Look Dufy. We are as much at war as we were in 1914 and you go fishing. What has happened to you?'

It was all on the tip of François' tongue to tell the Colonel why he was where he was, but something stopped him. Later he put it down to foolish pride but in that moment, he had nothing to say. It was as if the Colonel spoke the truth. He had been on holiday. Not a joyful break from a stressful job, but a holiday from life; a holiday from life's responsibilities and his sense of duty to his country.

'I'm not well up with the war business, sir. I live out of town and live alone.'

'No excuse my boy.'

The term 'my boy' brought back a scene in François' head. He stood before his Colonel. Rain lashed the tent and the sound of the Colonel's voice attenuated by the downpour reverberated in his ears.

'Dufy, you are the best shot in the unit. We need you. I need you to do something for your country.'

Today, it felt the same. It was the same message. To do something for his country. But what could he do? He could kill the enemy, but for what reason? It made no sense. This time they had lost the war. It was a waiting game, not one in which he could do anything. The voice of Mme Arnaud came into his head. He could hear and see her in that moment.

'Resistance,' that was what she said. He looked at her husband and he was saying the same thing. François wondered if it was some kind of infection. Perhaps they both hoped to infect him, inoculate him with their passion. He wanted the aspirin of peace.

'Well?'

'Colonel, what do you want me to do?'

'We must find a way to communicate with each other. Ways for everyone who stands against this tyranny to join hands against it. I may need you to take messages for me.'

'But messages to whom?'

'We have men in the forest. From time to time, I may need you to help me. I have a radio left from the first war. I use it to communicate with the Rosbifs. They have a new network of agents who will come to us if we can keep them safe. I will need your help.'

François pictured Rachelle in his house. He pictured her with an agent of the British in his house. He despaired for a moment.

'Well?' Colonel Arnaud said.

'Colonel, I will do as you ask. I will serve you and my country as I did once before. My son died fighting the Fascists in Spain. He tried to tell me they would come here but I refused to listen. I owe it to his memory to fight back now. What do you want of me?'

'I will tell you in time. Be ready. Be prepared. It is all I ask. More wine?'

The two men, one impassioned with a fervour to fight and the other wishing he had never come, drank wine and talked about old times. They were times of blood, times of carnage, but the Colonel reminded François they were times of courage.

2

When François arrived at his house, it was late. He had not eaten, and the three bottles of wine he and the Colonel consumed in the afternoon had taken their toll, for he noticed he bumped into things as he tried to find the oil-lamp. The place was silent and dark, even Cognac failed to bark. He wondered whether Rachelle slept and he tried to be as quiet as he could.

Lighting the lamp, he peered around the corner of the doorjamb, proffering the light. Rachelle was not there and he puzzled for a moment where she could be hiding. Realisation came to him like a summer dawn. Of course, she must be in the shed behind the house. He remembered telling her if anyone came, she should hide there. It had a hatch in the back wall where she could escape into the forest if need be.

François knew sobriety comes fast to a man in danger and faster still when someone close to him is in danger. It was so for him then. He heard a shot. It came from the forest. He almost dropped the lamp but managed to put it down. He searched for his rifle. Unable to find it, he grabbed his hunting knife and burst through the backdoor. Cognac was not there. He saw nothing but the looming darkness of the tree line, despite the bright moon above. The close-grown pines seemed impenetrable yet he knew the paths and he headed for the shed across the yard.

No one was there and he experienced a feeling of dread, multiplied tenfold when the next shot rang out. He judged it came from a hundred yards away and he darted into the darkness with greater speed than a drunken man might be entitled to.

He cleared the hundred yards or so in a short time and breathless and dizzy he looked around, obscured by a pine tree. There was a clearing ahead and he heard another shot. Then he saw her. It was Rachelle. She stood leaning against a tree holding his rifle to her shoulder. He realised the barrel did not waver. There was no trembling, no uncertainty. Another shot and he peered into the moonlight to see what she fired at. There was nothing there. Then he saw it. A rabbit lay at the far end of the clearing. Its legs quivered in the little dance of death with which François was so familiar.

He stayed behind the cover of the pine tree and called to her. He had no wish to startle her, lest she fire at him.

'Rachelle. Rachelle, you hear me?'

She was silent for a moment and then replied.

'Uncle?'

He came out from his shelter.

'What in all of Christendom are you doing?'

'I am hunting. You did not come home and I was hungry. I cleaned the gun. I made sure it was in order and I and Cognac went into the forest.'

'Damned fool. Suppose someone else heard you? Suppose the Germans came here thinking you are a partisan or something?'

'There are no Germans here in the night. What was I supposed to do? I had no idea when you would return. I was starving and wanted food.'

'You're a fool. Give me my gun.'

She surrendered her weapon. He was about to chastise her further but she turned her back on him and ran to pick up the rabbit. She held it aloft and François realised it still wriggled. He approached her and took the struggling creature from her.

'It is cruel not to kill with one bullet. One shot has to be enough. Look how this animal suffers.'

He held it aloft and it began to whimper. Her face was set. No anger, no feelings.

François used the side of his hand to chop at the rabbit's neck. It hung limp; forlorn, he thought. He had no pity for it though. He was being pragmatic. One shot. Save bullets. One shot to finish it. He turned and walked back, saying nothing.

When he reached his house, he left the backdoor open and began skinning the rabbit over an old newspaper in the light of the smoky oil lamp. They could spit roast it. He wanted to sleep but he recognised his hunger.

François felt a hand on his shoulder. He half-turned and looked up.

'What?'

'I'm sorry. I was impatient.'

He felt his heart soften. That rankled.

'Don't worry,' he said, 'you did well. I just didn't know where you were. I worried.'

'Thank you.'

'What for?'

'For caring, Uncle. I have no one else now.'

He shrugged her hand away.

'Damned silly thing, hunting in the dark. Next time tell me or ask me, else don't do it. Hear me child?'

'Yes, Uncle.'

'Go light a fire outside. I'll show you how to spit-roast a rabbit. And get some of those carrots, we can roast them. Oh and potatoes too. I'm hungry.'

He listened to the sound of her footsteps as she made her way outside. He turned, but the words on his lips froze. It felt as if it was all happening to him again. First Arlette and Jean-

Paul, then Alma, and now he recognised he was scared, scared of loving, scared of caring. It was all so painful. He cut himself on the back of his hand and realised he was still drunk. Damn this life. Damn his feelings. How could he focus on Arnaud's resistance when all his mind wanted was to turn to silly feelings about a young girl? He felt moisture forming in his eyes. He shook his head and wiped his eyes on his sleeve.

They ate the rabbit and long after Rachelle was sleeping in the only bed in the house, François sat up by the embers of the fire, cradling a bottle of Calvados, oblivious to the tears running down his cheeks. Cognac nuzzled him, prodding at his face, but he did not notice. All he felt was sorrow.

Chapter 6

Whenever you drew straws
It was always the ship's boy you dined upon.
But the time of joyous sinkings is past.
– from *Paroles* by Jacque Prevert

1

François was drunk this time. Rachelle had failed in her attempts to hide the wine and he had drunk one and a half bottles by the time he arrived at the market. He set up his barrow opposite the Prefecture and he kept his eyes open as best he could, considering the amount of alcohol circulating in his veins. He had briefed Rachelle on what to do, and made certain he left her with food and drink before he left. He felt confident she would be all right. He left her his gun too. He loaded it himself and he knew now she could shoot. Her target practice revealed a steady hand and a steel nerve and he was proud of her. He knew he had no right to that pride. She was not his, yet he had become reconciled to his growing affection for the girl.

Rachelle was not moody like the girls he once taught in St Cyprien. She got on with the business of life, day to day, and never complained. Yes, at certain times of the month when she was sad, she needed a shoulder to cry upon but she was very stable and good company most of the time. For the first time since Jean-Paul died, François felt on the verge of feeling happy. It was a strange feeling for him. He had shrugged off the cloak most men wore to ward off the rain-clouds of emotion. It was a cloak, always protecting him before, but now it was in tatters and he struggled to hold the deluge of his feelings at bay. He loved Rachelle as if she were one of his own.

When he caught himself feeling this way it was always easy to shake his head and bury those feelings, but since the night she shot the rabbit he realised he cared, and it became less frightening to him. His greatest fear was something happening to burst the bubble in which he seemed to exist.

He wanted people to leave him alone in that bubble. He wanted to see no one. He came to market to sell his game, but he desired no conversation, no jolly drinking company when the market day closed. People said he was always drunk. They stayed away from him and it suited him. At market he wore his dirty clothes, the ones he forbade Rachelle to wash. It often amused him how he wanted to preserve his image as much as the middle-aged ladies did theirs, with their hats and their flowery dresses, trying to impress the world with who they were. He wanted to be the drunk. The dirty, dishevelled, alcoholic remnant of a man with whom the town had become familiar.

No one could know about Rachelle - the Jewish girl who loved him, cleaned for him, and cared for him. It sometimes made him smile as if he was a man with buried treasure for which he was the only one with a map. François felt it gave him an edge. It put him above others he met. He had a different world to come home to and he did not care what the townsfolk thought of him.

A black uniform interrupted his thoughts. He looked up

from his barrow and realised who the man was. It was Meyer. Flanked by two SS soldiers, the man was watching François. Meyer was tall, blond-haired, and young. François thought he might have been in his thirties. The SD officer stood still, gazing with a look of disgust at the barrow.

'What is this?' the German said, indicating a haunch of red meat.

'Venison sir,' François said.

'It looks like it's off.'

'Off?'

'Rotten. Like its seller.'

'It is well hung. In France we like game to be hung.'

Meyer took out his Luger. He prodded the meat with the barrel-tip, pushed it onto the cobbles and stamped on it. François watched but did not move. He knew the German wanted to provoke him.

'It is illegal to sell food that is rotten. It will make people ill. I have a good mind to offer you the accommodation of the Mairie, but the stink of you would contaminate the building.'

François said nothing.

Meyer grabbed at the corner of the barrow and began to tip it up. François watched as the trout slithered, as if still alive, onto the cobbles. It amused him because he could almost see them wriggling as they had when he caught them.

'You think this is funny?' Meyer said. The look on his face was one of fury.

'No sir.'

'But you smile? Are you drunk or just stupid?'

'I had a little wine.'

Meyer swung his Luger at François' forehead. By reflex, François leaned back and the blow went astray. The German raised his arm again.

'Is there a problem Scharfürer?'

The voice, deep and calm, came from behind and the SD officer turned to see who spoke.

'Inspector Ran. This man is selling rotten food. I am protecting the public.'

'With a gun?' Ran said.

'Whatever. The man is drunk and his food is unhygienic; he should be locked up.'

'It is a civil matter, not one of state security. It is for me to decide who is arrested not you. If you do not leave now, I will report your actions to Major Brunner. Understood?'

Meyer's face reddened but he said nothing. He turned and walked away towards a parked black Mercedes, and his men followed.

Ran said, 'You should not provoke these people. It can land you in a lot of trouble. Stay away from that one in particular, he has taken a dislike to you.'

'Yes, Inspector. Want some fish?'

Auguste Ran smiled. He stood close, looking straight into François' eyes.

'You are a strange man Dufy. He wanted to provoke you and all you do is stand there and take it. I know your war record and so your behaviour puzzles me. I sometimes wonder if there is more to you than meets the eye.'

François burped. It was a belch laced with wine and garlic and the Inspector turned his head away in disgust. He walked back into the Prefecture but on the top step he turned, staring back at François who was engaged in picking up and salvaging those of his goods that could still be sold.

François knew what he wanted to do. The .22 was not powerful enough for what he planned and he decided to get a bigger gun, maybe a .303 like the English used, or similar. He thought deeply about it until he sold his remaining goods, and on his way home he had an opportunity for which his run-in with Meyer had prepared him.

2

A low sun cast long shadows in the dusty roadway as François wheeled his barrow across the Dordogne Bridge. He glanced down at the shallow brown waters swirling twenty feet below. He spat and watched as his spittle disappeared into the cool, café-au-lait shades of his beloved waterway. He looked down-river and saw movement. There were two men swimming a quarter-of-a-mile downstream. He could see their clothes, de-posited on the bank. Better still, he saw they were green uni-forms, and two rifles stood propped against a tree, two or three yards from the bank. He knew what he was going to do and felt his heart leap at the thought. There was no one around and the bridge was empty of traffic. He pushed his barrow towards a sparse wood on the far bank and hid it in bushes on the south side of the bridge. He felt an unfamiliar exhilaration, as if this new situation lit a fire within him. It was a flame of enjoyment as powerful as any hunting.

François knew the ways of animals. He had to in order to hunt them; he also knew how to move without any sound betraying his presence. Ten yards from the river, he lay down and belly-crawled towards the swimming Germans. He kept the tree on which the rifles leaned between him and the swimmers. It took minutes, but he was a patient man and he knew what he was doing.

He reached around the bole of the tree. His hand lighted upon one of the rifles and he laid it down beside him. He took the other and examined it. It was a beauty, a Mauser K98K; a little short for François' liking, but he knew the weapon from description, and he understood the internal magazine held five bullets. He placed the stock against his shoulder and used the metal sight, absent from the first weapon. Lying flat, invisible from the river or road, he sighted his targets and took careful aim. One of the soldiers stood up in the shallows, laughing and splashing his companion. He seemed not to have a care in the world.

François knew he did not need to kill them and he recognised a risk if anyone heard the shots, but he wanted their ammunition belts and their clothing lay too close to the river for him to search without the two soldiers seeing him.

His finger found the trigger. He began to squeeze. An easy headshot.

Then he stopped. Neither of the two men seemed much older than Jean-Paul would have been. The sound of their laughter reminded him of his son too. The thought they might have parents and family lanced him to the bone. He lifted his head. He sighted the other soldier; the lad was swimming away but still an easy shot. Torn, he paused again. The delay increased the risk of discovery but he remained undecided.

No, he couldn't do it. They were boys. If they had been older, if they had been men, he would have killed them with no more compunction than killing a rabbit or a deer. It was the similarity in laughter and movement to Jean-Paul which stayed his hand, and he crawled back towards the barrow with his prizes. It took only a moment to hide the rifles in some sacking and tie them underneath the vehicle, and he continued on his way, wondering where he might obtain more German ammunition. It had to be 7.92mm and they didn't manufacture it in France. It wasn't as if he could, with confidence, walk into the gunsmiths and ask for German military rounds. No, there had to be a better way. He pondered the conundrum as he pushed the heavy barrow.

Then he thought about Meyer. The German had offended him, tried to strike him and Meyer was not a man who resembled his son. He was not a boy, naked, playing in a river and facing a courtmartial for losing his weapon. No, the first war had killed enough children. He cast his mind back to the trenches in which he once found himself, where Arnaud was the one man he trusted. What had the Colonel said to him?

'We need a sniper. It has to be a man whose cool aim is reliable and Dufy, you are that man. We need you and your country needs you. There is a man who has to be erased to further the aims of your country, this war.'

It had been a night mission. A silent mission and one in which death would come to one or other of the antagonists. To kill a General and live through it seemed impossible, yet they trusted him to do it. It filled him with pride still. It was a time when he felt he truly belonged somewhere. He never felt that elation again. The praise and the adulation from his success remained elusive for the rest of the war but Arnaud saw to it he received his decoration anyway. It was one of the reasons he held his old commander in such high esteem: Arnaud had not forgotten what François did, and it still mattered to François.

The sun sank pink on the horizon and François smiled as he pushed his barrow. He had another mission, self-appointed, but no less real and no less dangerous.

3

François was becoming used to surprises on his return home from market. If Rachelle was not out hunting or practising with his rifle, she was preparing some kind of culinary surprise or she had cleaned or tidied something in the house. He had begun to look forward to returning home whenever he was away, even for a day.

This time she greeted him in English and forbade him to speak any other language. They ate and spoke in Rosbif, with 'please' and 'thank you' at every turn. They laughed and they enjoyed the joke.

'You may have to speak English soon enough,' he said.

'Are we going away?'

'No but an English spy may be coming. If I have to baby-sit, I cannot keep your presence secret. It doesn't matter because if there is an Englishman here he will be as keen to avoid the Sauerkrauts as you are.'

'Is something happening?'

'I don't know. Colonel Arnaud told me to be ready and he would contact me. I think there are many young men who wish to escape being sent to Germany to the work camps and they are running away to form partisan groups. There is nothing organised yet, but I may have to help in some way.'

'Is it dangerous?'

'I don't know.'

'I can look after myself as long as I have a gun.'

'And what will you do with a gun? Will you kill all the Germans? Will you lie in a trench and shoot them? No. You must hide. I don't know where this war will end but I do know that France will never cooperate with these Fascist pigs.'

'You hate them too don't you?'

'You know why.'

'Yes.'

There was silence then, each of them lost in their own thoughts.

Presently, Rachelle said, 'I will be sixteen in two days' time.'

'Sixteen? Why, you will soon be an old lady. If we were free we would celebrate.'

'I don't want to celebrate without my Papa. I miss him.'

'Yes.'

'I miss my Maman too but my father was special to me.'

Another silence succeeded in making François think about his own son. Jean-Paul had often said he loved his father but François had never made much of it. He was not a man to wear his heart on his sleeve and he always avoided emotional conversations. He regretted it now and wondered if supporting this young woman would be enough to substitute for all the things left unsaid to Jean-Paul.

'I have a present for you for your birthday,' François said, animated all of a sudden.

'A present? Have you been shopping? You were careful?'

'Not that sort of present. Here.'

François stood and went to the door. He found his barrow outside and brought back the sacking parcel. Unwrapping it, he showed the girl the contents. Wondering what she would make of his "present", he looked up towards her from the floor where he sat next to the guns.

'Uncle. There could be no better present. They are beautiful.'

'You like them?'

'Oh yes. I will kill Germans with these.'

'Hey, who said anything about you killing Germans? You are just a child. I will show you how to use these guns but it is only for self-defence.'

'What sort of rifles are they?'

'They are made by the Mauser factories. The German troops used Mausers in the last war and they've designed these in a similar way. Here, feel how light it is.'

He opened the bolt from old habit, and passed her the gun without the sight.

She checked the spout with her little finger to make sure it was empty and pressed on the bullet in the magazine as he had always drilled into her. She closed the bolt, then opened and closed it again, engaging the first of the five bullets into the chamber. François reached for the gun.

'You've loaded it. Get that bullet out of the chamber. It will go off. Some of these guns have hair triggers.'

Rachelle laughed and made for the door. François followed and he watched as she put the stock to her shoulder. She fired the rifle.

François knelt and reached out a hand to his now recumbent charge.

'I hadn't realised it had a kick like that.'

'Powerful enough to put you on your back. Next time try asking first. We have only nine rounds left now, until I can get more.'

'But how can you get German ammunition?'

'I don't know. I will make a plan. Let me sleep on it.'

'This rifle is so powerful compared to yours.'

'It is yours. It is late, we should sleep.'

'Uncle?'

'Yes, my friend.'

'If we run, will you stay with me?'

'How do you mean?'

'If I have to run away, will you be there?'

He looked down. 'I don't know. Arnaud may send me away for long periods. You must stay here but run if the Germans or anyone else comes. You understand? Run as far as you need to, in order to get away and don't look back.'

'But when they have gone I can come back?'

'You will have to judge that yourself. My advice would be to make contact with some partisans and stay with them. I will find out where they are and we will make an emergency plan.'

Rachelle was silent and he could see her eyes moisten.

She said, 'If I lose you too Uncle, I don't know what I would do.'

'If I am in the hands of the SD you can be sure I will talk. I will make sure I keep silent for as long as I can hold out after they take me. It will give you time to leave.'

'How would I know if they take you unless I go with you?'

'Go to bed now Rachelle. I will puzzle it all out and we will talk in the morning. There is something I must do and it is possible I will be caught. They could arrest me anyway, even for a minor offence, and you must be vigilant. I could be locked up a long time and you might have to fend for yourself. Cognac will warn you if anyone comes. We will make a plan, but now, I am tired.'

They both stood. She reached for him and his arms, more natural than before, encircled her. He patted her back and he kissed her hair.

'Uncle. I love you,' she said.

'Love? Love is dangerous. We are good friends, but love? Love hurts. It brings only pain and either of us could be captured or killed anytime. I know what you mean. Try less love and more thinking will you?'

She pulled away and looked up at him.

'You still smell.'

She smiled in the lamplight and disappeared around the corner to the bedroom; her room, her solace. It had ceased to be part of his world as soon as she came into his life and he had no regrets. He sat down on the couch. He knew danger lurked all around but he wanted Meyer's blood so much he could taste it.

Chapter 7

A horse collapses in the middle of an alley,
Leaves fall on him,
Our love trembles,
And the sun too.
– from *Paroles* by Jacque Prevert

1

François set up his barrow in a side street where he could see the doorway to the Mairie. He knew it was dangerous but he threw caution to the wind to-day. The SD took over the place as soon as the Vichy Government decided to capitulate and collaborate with the Nazis. It was once a beautiful building, a place of French municipal authority, although the informality of the administrative workers there had made it a pleasure to deal with these local bureaucrats. Bergerac was after all, a small community and everyone knew everyone else. They knew everyone's business, and gossip too. The Germans converted the five-storey building into a fortress, with cells in the basement where prisoners suffered and often never came out.

Everyone in Bergerac knew how if one became imprisoned there life would end, or if they survived they would emerge as broken men or women.

He had something he needed to do and he would do it

whatever the place's reputation. A sloping drizzle began to fall, and he watched as the two rabbits and three partridges on the barrow in front of him, began to soak up the moisture. He could smell them since he had hung them for four days and they were ready for the table. The proprietor of the shoe-shop came out under an umbrella. She was a plump middle-aged woman with ginger hair and a slight limp. She frowned.

'Why are you here? It is illegal to sell food outside market days.'

'Who made that rule?'

'It is a new one. I can sell shoes but you cannot sell food, now go.'

'My God, woman. Can't you let an old man earn a living?'

'Look, if they come out of that place,' she pointed to the Mairie, 'you will wish they hadn't. They might think you are spying on them.'

'Me? Spying? Do you want to buy some rabbits?'

'What?'

'Rabbits. I shot them myself a few days ago. Well hung. Good in a stew. Add some wine and it tenderises them. '

'Well maybe, but you need to move away from the doorway.'

'I could refuse.'

'You could, but why would you? You want to cause trouble? I could telephone the police.'

'You'll buy the rabbits?'

'Very well, as long as you go away.'

'But it's raining. You would send an old soldier out in this weather? I might catch pneumonia or influenza.'

François sniffed as if he had a cold. She looked at him and smiled. They shared the little joke.

'Coffee?'

'Real coffee?'

'Yes, my nephew brought some back from Africa. I can spare a cup.'

'Madame, you are very kind. Do you own the whole building?'

'Yes. All the way up, four floors.'

'The view must be grand.'

'No. All I can see is the building across the street and the Mairie, ruined as it is.'

They entered the shop. It was empty. He looked at the empty shelves, the naked stands and the ownerless counter. To François there was something sad about the shoe-shop, which he could understand. It was like a café with no wine or a prefecture without policemen. Shoes were a necessity and the emptiness demonstrated the economic climate, which bit into everyone.

'You do good business?'

'Not now. The war makes it impossible to import shoes, so prices are high. We used to get them from Italy and Spain. Italian shoes are too expensive, Spanish ones are impossible to get now, after the civil war. They have reduced the franc to such small value too, the Germans.'

'Yes, no one has money these days.'

'Before the Germans came we were happy. We all earned a living. And now?'

'And your husband?'

'He is in England.'

'England?'

'Yes, he was in our army and escaped to England. I told him it was a stupid war but he went to fight anyway.'

'He is with De Gaulle?'

'Who?'

'Charles De Gaulle. He is the leader of the Free French army.'

'How can a man have a name like that? "From France"? It's ridiculous. There is no such person.'

'I don't know about that. Colonel Arnaud tells me they will come back and drive the Germans away. Maybe not so easy, but I hope.'

They sat in the back of the shop, in a small room, bare floorboards, no window. François sat on a chair which had seen better days, with his back to a door.

'This is the stairs?'

'Yes, all the way up.'

'May I see?'

'But why?'

'Oh, just curious about the view. I can't see how it can be as limited as you say. If it is really good, then I may rent one of the rooms.'

'Who are you?'

'Me?'

'Yes, you sound educated, but you smell like a tramp. You ask questions and answer none. Now you want to see my view of the Mairie. Am I stupid? You think I am?'

'Madame, I would never think that. I simply ask if I can rent a room, no questions asked,' his gaze pierced hers. He was seeking truth.

'What is going on? Maybe you should finish your coffee and move along.'

'Madame, you are a patriot? Do you believe in France?'

'What sort of question is that?' She sat forward and glared at François.

'I ask because I want to be free of this "yoke" imposed by evil people. The Fascists and Nazis who want to destroy our country and our way of life. Even the Rosbifs in the eleventh century did not treat us like this.'

'Who are you?'

'No one… maybe everyone. I want to do something. Something which may bring danger but I cannot tell you what it is. I only ask that you trust me. I need access to the top floor and I will do what must be done for resistance, for France.'

'You're going to kill someone.'

'I can't tell you that but clearly I trust you. Is it not enough? Your man is in England. He would say yes immediately. He would understand.'

'He would do anything for France, but if you do something illegal on my property they will hold me responsible.'

'I will give you a good story to tell. I could, if you wish, tie you up before I do my business, but I must act. I have to do something, for hate maybe, for my dead son, for a wish to create a semblance of resistance, visible to all. I want it to rouse the people, the partisans, the workers on the land and all good Frenchmen. We have to fight back or all of our world will crumble and disappear.'

She sat in silence trying to make sense of this mad, illogical man who confronted her. After a few minutes, during which they both stared at each other across the empty space and the coffee-cups, she stood and began pacing the floor. She waved her hands. She spoke. The woman sweated as she conversed. François could see how emotional she had become and he felt a strange satisfaction at that. Had he not felt the same, talking to Arnaud? Had he not sworn his commitment to the cause? He knew she would capitulate as he had done, months before, but he waited for her to finish.

'All right. I am a member of a group of people who wish to resist. I know someone who communicates with England. Yes,

England. The place where your husband is waiting. He is waiting for the day when we will drive the cruel Huns away to their own country, away from France, and we will have our lives back. We have allies, friends across the sea, who will fight with us, and your husband is part of that. To refuse me is like betraying him.'

'Betray...'

'Yes, naturally. There is a German SD officer called Meyer. I wish to kill him. I have a rifle and ammunition but I need to see where and when he goes out. I can kill him on the Mairie steps, however I need to have an escape route. Your building is my only platform. If you say no now, I will go away and never bother you again. I beg you not to say no.'

She looked uncertain. He knew she needed more collateral, but what had he to offer her? If the SD took it into their heads to arrest her, she would talk within hours. She could describe him and they would come for him. It was simple deduction on their part. He possessed the reputation of being the town drunk but it would never protect him. He wondered if in the end, he would have to kill this woman, this patriot. It would silence her and reduce his risks. The thought made him take stock. It was a sudden revelation to him; he felt like a man who decides on a course of action and realises it has changed him into a monster.

He began to wonder what he was doing. Why did he want to kill Meyer anyway? Had his pride grown such that a simple insult in the market place marked the man out for death? No. It was not his own pride, he reasoned. If this man could treat the town drunk like that in the Market Square, what else would he be capable of behind the closed doors of the Mairie? Would he not kill and torture others more vulnerable than François? He became certain he was right.

'Here I am drinking your coffee and I do not even know your name.'

'I am Madame Breton, You may call me Lucille.'

'Enchanted, Lucille. I am François Dufy. I should tell you I am sometimes clean.'

He smiled as he spoke and she understood the joke. They laughed together. It was a brief fracture in the tension between them.

'I can trust you?' he said.

'Do you not know that?'

'I worry.' He smiled as he spoke, but there was ice in his heart.

'No, Monsieur Dufy, I can see you don't. You will not need to do anything to protect yourself. I am, as you put it, a patriot. I care about France and would never collaborate with the invaders. If I had the skills, I would do what you plan to do myself, but I am only a seller of shoes. I will pray for your soul for it seems to me it is in jeopardy.'

'No, Lucille. If there were a God, would he really allow these pigs to do what they are doing to our people and the Jews? No there is no God, no Supreme Being, only us.'

'You are a Communist?'

'No.'

'I really will pray for you then, but we have a common cause. If you do what you say you will, you must make sure they do not suspect me.'

'That I promise. You must be far away when it is done.'

'Then let me show you the upstairs rooms.'

She gestured towards the door. François began to think it had all been too easy and it made him even more cautious. He climbed the stairs behind her ample backside and began to wonder whether he should talk to Arnaud about his intentions. He was acting alone and he knew it. Arnaud was not a loner and would surely condemn him for this, but François' hatred for the Germans seemed to have taken control. He wanted them all dead, and Meyer was a good beginning.

2

Rachelle wrenched the door open before François could get his hand to it. He saw a look there he had not witnessed before. She was close to panic. She frowned.

'Why do you leave me alone like this?'

'What?'

'A man was here.'

'A man?'

'Yes, he tried the door and I hid in the shed. If Cognac had not barked I would have been caught.'

'But what did he look like, this man?'

'I looked through the spy-hole like you told me. He was old, bald. He had a light coloured suit and a grey moustache. I was frightened.'

'Ah, nothing to worry about. If it was SD they would have arrived in military vehicles and they wear green uniforms. You know this. "Race Verte" and all that.'

'But he scared me.'

'No need to worry, he is one of us.'

'Jewish?'

'No. Resistance. He is my old commander from the war.'

'You were in the war?'

'Not this one, the First World War.'

'You killed Germans?'

'Never mind. What happened? Did he see you?'

'No.'

'Then why all the panic?'

'I was scared.'

He looked at her face. There were care lines there, a vertical crease, drawn over the middle of her forehead, deep like a trench. He felt his heart soften; he knew about trenches.

'Here,' he said.

He reached for her and took her in his arms. He patted her back, gentle slow movements intended to reassure. He remained uncertain whether it was the way for him to behave. He felt awkward, out of his depth. His experience of girls and women was limited to Arlette. Yes, he had related to Alma but the brevity of that confluence robbed it of meaning for him at this moment. He felt as if he was losing his grip on the situation. It was as if he wanted to support his newfound friend but he felt ill- equipped to do so.

'Uncle, How dangerous is it?

'You mean strangers at the door?'

'Yes,' she said.

'Well, you can rely on Cognac. She knows a bad 'un from a good 'un and she will tell you.'

'You think I'm a child, don't you?'

'Well...'

'You don't understand what I've been through. It makes you grow up: to lose your home, your parents and have to hide in case Germans will come and take you away to God knows where.'

'You will be safe with me.'

'But you aren't here all the time. I was so frightened. You told me no one came here.'

'My dear girl, I cannot be here all the time. If I were, people would soon be asking where the town drunk had gone.

They would come and search for me, for no other reason than they want their pheasants and fish. I have to pretend to be someone else. I have to be the drunk but we both know there is more to the story than that.'

'What am I to do Uncle? Should I not leave and go somewhere where the Germans are far away?'

'There is nowhere accessible. Africa is not good, it is a long journey by sea, and there will be patrol boats. Switzerland is a long way away. I could do it but not with a young pup in tow. No. We stay here. We fight. In the end, I believe France can win. Perhaps we need the help of the Rosbifs, but we can win.'

'But what does winning mean?'

'It means the Germans are defeated and they go back to their own country. Do you know, even in the Roman times, the Germanic tribes used to try to take our country? In the end, the Franks who ruled all of it had German origins.'

'So it's all right for them to come here now?'

'No, I only meant that...'

'What?'

'I don't know what I meant. Let's not argue about it. I understand you had a fright. We have to work on that to ensure it does not happen again. Maybe you always sleep in the shed when I'm away and if Cognac barks you run into the forest. Come, let's eat. There is venison hanging in the shed and we have vegetables too.

She looked at his face. He was smiling but he knew he was not fooling her. He understood how she felt and knew his bravado was meaningless to her. In food and wine, he hoped to distract her, to make her relax into the world in which he moved. She could shoot a gun. She might even be able to protect herself in some circumstances, but he knew also how vulnerable she was. If he was away a long time, he feared what might happen; he knew also the only way to combat his fear was to train her to be sharp, to be cautious, and above all to be sceptical of anyone who came. Whom did she have but him? He was afraid of that. He knew her life depended upon him and he was terrified at the consequences of that. He had a job to do now, or so he thought. Reconciling the assassination of Meyer with protecting Rachelle seemed an impossible task.

3

François spent three weeks in a small box-room on the top floor. He was watching the steps of the Mairie for Meyer's movements. He kept a chart of when the man entered and left. He watched who accompanied him and whether he had transport. He watched to see how many men went with him, and he tried to estimate their response times, if he could get in a shot. At the end of two weeks, he felt he could predict when the man would be accessible. It would be a long shot, but he had done similar things in the Great War. He was confident, but certainly not blasé.

He climbed the ladder to the loft and then out through the doorway to a flat roof. There was enough space there, he felt, to launch himself to the next building and then the one beyond. Descending was a worry, but he had an idea. It would mean a little preparation though.

Lucille brought him coffee and bread with cheese during the day, but he refused her invitation to fill the bathtub.

'It would be no trouble François. I can heat the water easily.'

'No thank you Lucille. If I come in here looking like an old drinker and emerge a well-scrubbed gentleman the whole town will suspect.'

'You are not even tempted?'

He patted her cheek.

'Lucille you would tempt any man, but I must keep my mind on my work. Now, leave me to do it.'

By the end of the third week, he knew Meyer would be leaving the Mairie at midday. François assumed it was to have lunch somewhere, but he did not care why, as long as he was there. He practised the shot several times without using any rounds in the magazine and he thought it should be possible to kill Meyer if he managed a headshot. It was one hundred yards, but he was not worried. The escape route caused him more concern than the act itself.

It was a Monday. He sent Lucille away to stay with her nephew in Saint-Julian. Almost no one braved the soaking weather. The autumn rain descended in sheets and as midday approached François looked out of the tiny window at the top of the shoe-shop building, allowing only the tip of his rifle to project beyond the sill. The shiny wet cobbles reflected a silver light and the grey canopy of cloud darkened the Mairie but not enough to obscure François' view of the steps. He took in the scene with a clarity aided by his sharp and hawk-like vision.

He looked down to the steps then adjusted the metal sight with practised ease, his deft fingers moving fast. He looked at his watch. Five minutes to twelve. Any time now. A covered military truck pulled up in front of the steps. He cursed. If Meyer came out now, he might lose his shot and have to wait until tomorrow. He bit his lip and noticed he was sweating. His mouth was dry and he wished he had time to drink something. With his heart beating a crescendo against his ribs, he saw his target.

Meyer, prompt as usual, walked around the truck and peered inside. François wondered what he was looking at. The German stepped back. A brown-uniformed soldier emerged and he turned, gesturing to someone inside the truck. A woman appeared, ejected from the vehicle, alighting on unsteady feet before Meyer. The man struck her face with the back of his black-gloved hand. He was shouting. François took careful aim.

The brown-uniformed man moved and obscured Meyer for a moment. François realised his finger trembled on the trigger but he steadied himself with the thought he would get his man if he was patient.

Then it happened. The soldier stepped aside. As if guided by some second sense, Meyer looked up, straight toward François. There was only an instant in which to react. François took it.

He heard the report, felt the hard thump of the stock on his shoulder. He did not wait to see more than the German falling.

François shouldered his weapon and grabbed his rope. In seconds, he was up the ladder, drawing it up behind him. Emerging onto the roof, he took a running jump onto the adjacent building then another and he was two roofs away. His rope had a grappling hook and for the first time he felt a strange anxiety that the rope might be too short. It could leave him dangling in mid-air if that were the case.

He threaded the rope through the climbing harness and attached the hook to the edge of the flat roof. He abseiled down. It took moments only and he felt exquisite relief as he realised the rope was long enough. He left it where it was, swinging in the autumn rain and gained his bicycle. Glancing over his shoulder, he confirmed there was no one about, no doubt because of the rain, and he cycled towards the market square and the Prefecture. Dismounting, he placed the rifle under his barrow, hidden in a long narrow conduit, constructed the night before. He took off the harness behind some bushes and pulled out two rabbits from his canvas bag. Standing at his barrow, he held them up. In the distance, he heard a siren. The sound approached fast. The rain turned to drizzle and he stood, alone, swaying as if drunk and shouting. The doors to the Prefecture opened and an angular face peered out.

'Here, buy my rabbits. Fat as Göring. Lovely fat rabbits, fat as Göring!'

A tall, thin, gangling man approached, wearing the uniform of a senior police officer.

'What are you doing Dufy?'

'Just selling my rabbits.'

'If the Germans hear you they will arrest you and probably send you away.'

'Inspector Desour, would you like a drink?'

François reached into the inner pocket of his coat and produced a half-empty bottle of Bergerac, which he raised to his lips.

'It is not a market day, you old reprobate. I'm taking you in. Disturbing the peace.'

'But I'm just selling my rabbits.'

'All the same,' Desour said, grabbing François by the elbow. 'Come on. You stink, you know that?'

They mounted the steps of the Prefecture.

In the back of François' mind, he wondered how long they would keep him and whether anyone would search the barrow before he came out. Mounting the steps, he thanked God for the rain. The streets were empty and no one saw him, or so he thought.

Chapter 8

Real and surreal
Terrifying and funny,
Nocturnal and diurnal
Usual and unusual
Handsome as hell.
– from *Paroles* by Jacque Prevert

1

François drank in his freedom as he stepped down the stone staircase outside the Prefecture with the same pleasure he would have downed a good wine. Three days was a long time to him, he thought. His main concern as he ate the prison food and tried to chat to the police guard, was Rachelle. When the lights went out and silence reigned, he thought about her. He knew he was putting her at risk. If the police even suspected a connection between him and Meyer's death, they would have kept him in custody and he knew it. When Desour questioned him about it, he denied any knowledge of the death. Desour was full of the massive manhunt sweeping the town and François for his part, betrayed only innocent ignorance. He hoped no one would examine his barrow. If they did and they uncovered his rifle, he knew he would never return to his house, his dog or to Rachelle. They told him he was too un-important to occupy the cell for longer and the officer who saw him to the door told him to keep an eye out for terrorists and report anyone suspicious.

François smiled and said, 'I don't see a lot of people except on market days.'

'Huh,' came the reply, 'the amount you drink, old man, I guess you don't see much even then.'

François descended the steps and reclaimed his barrow. He wheeled it home feeling pleased with himself, though his concern for the Jewish adolescent whom he hoped would be waiting for him marred his pleasure. His relief when he found her irritated him. He began to feel guilt over leaving her alone. He knew also, the more he felt chained to her the less freedom he would have to move around or do Arnaud's bidding.

Arnaud returned two days later. This time Rachelle remained hidden and François opened the door to the Colonel. It was a fresh morning and as autumn began to close the curtain on the summer months, the world around was full of gold and bronze, leaf-fall and drizzle. Cognac barked a warning outside but became quiet at a word from François.

The old man stood on the doorstep dressed in his Gendarme's uniform, the peaked cap in his hand, his pate glistening in the rain which streaked his epaulettes. François ushered him in with apologies for the mess.

'There is no one here?'

'Of course, unless you count Cognac who informed me of your coming.' François smiled as he spoke.

'This is a serious matter, more so than you realise.'

'It is dangerous for you to be here is it not? What if someone sees you?'

'No one saw me, Sergeant. I am a little old for this clandestine way of life, but I have not lost my intellect.'

'Some wine?'

'No. I have had a message from London. I need you to do something for me.'

'Of course.'

'They are sending an agent. Parachute drop at Cazenac. I need you to take a message to a group of patriots who stay in the forest around there. They need to meet the agent and transfer him here to Bergerac. He will know how to sabotage railroads and transport. They are dropping radios, explosives and weapons too.'

'When will this happen?'

'Tomorrow night. I need you to go today. Here,' he said, taking a map out of his pocket, 'this is the drop area. The plane will pass over the hill at midnight.'

'It is not safe to carry such things, even for you. I know that area well so I will burn the map.'

François for the first time thought the Colonel was an amateur. He had always respected his old commander, but who would carry such an incriminating thing with him?

'You must never come here again. If you need to pass a message, send your wife on her bicycle, she can return with some game or fish and it will look natural.'

'But how can I involve Marquite in this? It is too dangerous.'

'She feels no different than you do sir. She told me we all have to fight. She need not know any details either.'

'Perhaps you are right. I must go.'

'You haven't told me where the partisans are.'

'Oh, yes. They are in the forest near Fontaud. Head for the farmhouse at Nord Fontaud and they will be there at six o'clock in the evening. The farmer is a sympathiser. It will have to be tonight because they won't come again for a week.'

'But it will take me two hours to get there, even if I walk very fast.'

'You must cycle and then walk.'

François still felt he was dealing with an amateur. Arnaud had not left him enough time to give a comfortable margin of error and as he looked his Colonel in the eye, he realised this had dawned upon Arnaud too.

François said, 'Well, I will do what I can. I must hurry then. Until we meet again.'

Arnaud left in his jeep. François walked through the house and called Rachelle.

'I have to go out. I will not be back until tomorrow. Be very careful. Cognac stays with you and don't pet her, she's a working dog not a pet.'

'Uncle?'

'What?'

'If you don't come back...'

'Why should I not return? I am in no danger. I will come back and we will have venison and wine.'

He patted her cheek and turned to gather his canvas bag. He could feel her eyes boring through his back. He turned.

'I will have to take my rifle. You have the other two and the shotgun. Don't try to fight anyone. Run. Always run and hide. Cognac will be your signal, your warning. Trust her.'

'What did the old man want?'

'He wants me to meet some people and deliver a message. Nothing dangerous.'

'Can I come too?'

'But of course not. If we were seen, there would be trouble. Besides I have to cycle, time is short and we only have one bicycle.'

'Uncle, I will be alone again. It is hard.'

'Yes, life is hard. There are no lucky breaks for any of us. No one said life was fair either.'

'I miss my Maman and Papa.'

'I know. I can't help you there. I can be your friend but cannot change what has happened or make things better for you.'

He hugged her and said, 'It will be all right. You'll see.'

Her tears as he left seemed to sting him more than he expected. He realised how fond he was becoming of the girl and he was sorry he had ever met her. He cycled through the rain thinking of her, waiting alone and scared, and he wished he could have been there to help. He also resented the fact he felt this way. He thought when he first came to Bergerac he could escape all his grief and his sentimentality but nothing had been predictable, nothing was easy. He felt like Job, oppressed and picked on by God. He put that thought out of his head; he had shrugged off the trappings of his religion when Jean-Paul died and now was determined not to weaken or slip into a religious lifestyle. No, let God look after his flock, François Dufy was no sheep.

2

The strap from his rifle chaffed his shoulder as he cycled. It was fifteen miles by road and he had almost two hours in which to reach Fontaud. He rode first on the main road heading east towards St Cyprien and then turned south on small tracks after five miles or so. The roads were empty, though one tractor passed in the opposite direction. He thought it would be a farmer heading home at the end of his day. He envied such a man. To own land and to work it, to have a family to come home to and a hearth at which he could sit. And what did he have? He had a small house, a drink habit, and a Jewish girl who wept whenever he left the house. No, that was unfair. He was fond of her. She had changed his life for the better, not in material ways, but she had brought out in him a wish to care about someone else; something, which had died in him in the years since Jean-Paul's death.

A mournful sun peeped out from behind grey slats of cloud as he approached his destination. Long shadows stretched across the yard, magnifying everything, as if this was a place of giant dimensions, a place where ogres lurked. The thought made him smile. He did not enter the farm by the gate, he was cautious. Leaning his bicycle against a tree in a small copse, he walked through a field to better survey the scene. The farmhouse stood next to the road and there were two barns, a hen house, and a shed for the pigs. He could smell them but he was not a man to be put off by any odour.

Standing in the shade of a tall pine, he waited. He took out his tobacco pouch, rubbed the tobacco and filled his pipe. Lighting it, he kept his eyes fixed on the farmhouse. The nicotine made him a little dizzy which was unexpected. He had smoked a pipe since he was sixteen, but he now realised he had been too busy to keep up his nicotine levels. He remained uncertain what he waited for, but he needed to see something that might lead him to believe it was safe. The sound of a fractured twig behind him made him turn. The faint snap came from his right. He drew the bolt of his rifle, priming the gun with a bullet. Safety off. He waited but did not move.

'You there.'

Still he did not move.

'You with the rifle. I can see you clearly. There are three

guns aimed at you. Who are you?'

François opened the bolt of his gun and with his thumb prevented the bullet ejecting. He pushed it back down into the magazine and shot the bolt again. He held up his rifle.

'Who are you?'

'I am Jules Janisson. Who are you?'

'François Dufy. Colonel Arnaud sent me with a message.'

'Are you stupid? For all you know we could be Germans.'

'Germans don't speak French with a Breton accent.'

Out of the shadows emerged two men and a woman. François took in her appearance first. She wore a long brown coat, loose and baggy. Her small silver earrings reflected the waning sun and she had dark brown hair, cut short under a small beret. In her hand, she held a rifle, a .22 such as François carried. Her companions were young men. One wore a beret, the other a peaked cap above a bearded face, and a dark jacket. Each of them carried a rifle. It was the one in the dark jacket who had spoken.

'How do we know you come from Arnaud?'

'Listen Sonny, do you think the Germans know who he is? If he didn't send me then all your plots will be in the German's hands anyway because it would mean he's been captured. Have some common-sense.'

'Well, I suppose you're right. We trust no one.'

'I am Josephine Laval,' the girl said. She proffered her hand and François took it. He noticed it was dry and the handshake firm.

'Enchanted to meet you,' François said.

'Enough of this,' Jules said, 'what is the message?'

'Arnaud has had word there will be a drop tomorrow night at midnight.'

'Where?'

'Cazenac.'

'Tomorrow night?'

'Yes, there will be a Rosbif too.'

'An agent?'

'Yes and supplies. Now, if you don't need me, I'll be on my way back.'

'No,' Jules said, 'you stay.'

'I need to go.'

Jules pointed his rifle at François.

'You stay,' he said, 'it will make me more comfortable with your message.'

'Jules always suspects a trap. If you stay until the drop we will know you are not working with the Germans.'

François had no option but to comply. He wondered how Rachelle would fare without him. He had prepared her for one night on her own. If these children did not release him, he might be away two nights.

'Look, I can stay one night. No longer.'

'You stay until we know you can be trusted.'

The group made their way to the forest and although François was reluctant, he did not feel out of place. It was like one of his hunting trips. Their camp was deep in a forest and there were three tents set out around where, it was clear to François, they used an open fire. He wondered how they had managed to avoid capture. If he were a German, he would have looked for smoke as the first sign of partisans. The feeling he was involved with amateurs, young people, full of life and humour pricked him; their inexperience would bring their deaths. It was the same feeling as when he spoke to Arnaud, but his lack of professionalism was born of a lack of familiarity with clandestine matters. These children were simply too young to be involved in warfare.

As he went to sleep in one of the tents, guarded by Jules and his companions, it occurred to him he too had been young in the last war, yet he survived. Not only had he survived, they had labelled him a hero for killing at Arnaud's request. He knew in those days he was no different from these young people, and the thought reassured him as his eyes closed and he drifted into a dreamless sleep.

3

'Monsieur Dufy?'

The voice came through the thin canvas of the tent, accompanied by sharp rays of sunlight projecting through small holes in the canopy above his head, and François realised he must have slept later than his usual time. It was Josephine.

'Yes, yes I'm awake. I will come out in a moment.'

He lay still trying to gather himself for a long day. His thoughts were still fixed on Rachelle and he wondered what she might be doing.

The tent flap opened and Josephine entered with a cup of chicory, the only substitute for coffee available since the Germans ruined everyone's life. He took the tin cup and swung his legs over the edge of the straw pallet on which he had spent the night.

'I wish it were coffee,' he said, and he meant it.

'Yes, I have not had coffee for almost a year. We cannot get any. The farmers are kind. They supply us with what they can and we eat well.'

'What are we doing today? Sitting still and waiting to be

discovered?'

She smiled. It was as if she understood his concerns.

'We may be young but we are not stupid. We abandon the camp in the day and move north. We kill Germans when we come across them.'

'Which Germans? Any of them? You need to eliminate their Generals and their commanders.'

'And you know about such things?

'Yes, as it happens I do. I was in the last war. We walk to Cazenac?'

'Cycle, but not until this afternoon.'

'Why are you here? You are young and you have a beautiful face. What makes a girl like you want to live rough and kill people?'

'I believe in my country and in my man.'

'Your man?'

'Yes, Jules and I have been together since the beginning of the war. When the Germans are gone, we will marry. His brother is one of us too but he disappeared yesterday; we are waiting for him to contact us again. He lives in Bergerac and delivers groceries.'

'You may be old and grey by the time this war ends, particularly if you don't organise and join all the groups together. Your intelligence seems rudimentary. For Arnaud to be the one with the radio seems foolish. He has no skills in this kind of thing. Don't get me wrong, I admire him, we fought together, but he is no secret agent.'

'I understand that. It is why we requested an Englishman. We need guidance on which targets to strike and how to cripple the Germans.'

'Perhaps the Englishman will help you organise. He may know about bombs too. You need radios.'

'Yes they are dropping radios with machine guns and ammunition. I think that is why Jules wanted you to come too. We can't carry everything away from the drop zone by ourselves.'

'Don't make me laugh. I'm not a young man like your Jules. I can't carry as much as you even.'

'All the same, we will need you to come too.'

'What about the Englishman? He will stay with you in the forest? '

'Yes, naturally.'

'This gets worse. He will need to be nearer Bergerac and he will need intelligence if he is to know what should be destroyed. He will also need to know about troop movements. Do you have such contacts?'

'No not yet.'

'Well I wish you luck, it sounds as if you'll need it.'

He downed the hot bitter liquid and grimaced.

'I'm going back to sleep. Call me when we move.'

François lay down again, not to sleep, but to work out how a small group of children could be of value in a clandestine war, against terrible odds. He closed his eyes and a feeling of hopelessness overtook him. Jean-Paul invaded his thoughts. Any of these partisans could be his son or daughter. He needed to help, not for Arnaud, not for De Gaulle but for Jean-Paul. He would point them in the right direction. He made up his mind he needed to meet this new British spy arriving like a bird of prey, swooping from the sky to solve all their problems.

A likely story.

Chapter 9

1

The four of them cycled the muddy paths towards the St Cyprien road. They joined it east of the town and turned towards Beynac, heading north before the small conurbation. The ancient ruined chateau loomed above, grim and desolate. François glanced up at the familiar grey stone shell and wondered if in some way it was responsible for the gloom pervading his thoughts. He had an uncomfortable feeling things would go wrong.

It was mid-afternoon and a few farmers passed in the opposite direction, but they saw no Germans, no soldiers. François knew the area well. Beynac was only ten kilometres from where he used to teach. The sight of the road brought back memories of times when he and Jean-Paul had spent days out after Arlette died. He pictured them fishing in the Dordogne tributaries and shooting game in the woods around the area.

He pictured how he showed his son to skewer the worm

on the hook and let the unweighted lure float downstream on the fine line. He recalled how delighted Jean-Paul was when a fish sucked in the bait and he landed his first trout. It was only seven inches in length and not a fish François would have taken home, but the boy would not let him put it back. Camping by the stream, they cooked their fish, frying it in butter and swilling the pan out with dry Spanish sherry. His mouth watered at the thought and he wished, as always, he could have prevented his son from going to Spain.

He could not shake off an uncomfortable foreboding this time however. He entertained no trust in these young people's ability. They seemed hell-bent on sabotage but seemed to have no knowledge about how to do it. Considering their lack of experience, François found himself in fear of his life if it all went wrong. But what could go wrong, unless someone talked? He felt concerned about the idea of one of their number disappearing and no news of him for two days. He reassured himself however, that these people could not have survived this far into the war if they were inept.

The road snaked upwards and they stopped for a break halfway up the track leading to the tiny church at Cazenac. To their right, the fields, surrounded by pine forest, were planted with hay, but François realised it was a hopeless fight. How could farmers maintain their finances in this economic climate? The invading Germans devalued the franc so they could pillage the country. There were now twenty francs to the deutschmark and he knew it was like robbery. If Germans paid, they paid a tenth of the true worth of anything they bought. Often the invader paid nothing; they only took. It all fuelled his hatred. Meyer was a personal kill. The next ones would be strategic, even if it did not fit in with Arnaud's plans. François decided he would concentrate on high-ranking military officers and collaborators. He wanted to kill them all but he would settle for key figures if it helped assuage his hatred.

They cycled on for a mile and came to the church, where they turned left up a small hill to a collection of buildings owned by three farmers. Josephine said they were all sympathisers and it was one of the few safe places in the Dordogne valley.

Fifty yards short of the little crossroad in the centre of Cazenac, was a farmhouse. Here they stopped. The farmer's wife came out, all flowery dress and plump friendliness and François warmed to her immediately. An Alsatian dog barked at them when they dismounted. François stood and called the dog to him. There was no response from the dog at first, so he greeted it with a long and tuneless whistle. The effect was extraordinary. He pointed to the ground in front of him. The dog came with tail down, whining softly. It rolled on its back and François stooped, tickling the canine's chin.

The farmer's wife, whose name he learned later was Camille, said, 'How did you do that? He has never done that before. We rely on him to protect our farmhouse.'

She seemed offended but he said, 'Dogs know who to trust. They are more sensitive than we are. They know a friend better than any partisan can.'

She smiled at that and they went inside. It was a typical French farmhouse with a large kitchen. Strings of garlic hung from a rack swinging from the ceiling, and a black range stood against the far wall. They sat at the old oak table, scored and dented from long use. François gained reassurance from its wear and tear as if it was an indication of the durability of the French way of life in such troubled times. He thought of Rachelle, alone and frightened back in Bergerac, and hoped the partisans would let him get away soon, whether they needed his guidance or not.

They dined on rustic cheeses, pâtés, and wine. The farmer arrived by six o'clock and they drank more wine while he ate. They laughed and joked until François began to feel relaxed and although he had trouble admitting it to himself, he felt happy.

They drank the evening away until the farmer brought out some rough bread and foie-gras. When they finished, François said, 'We need to prepare for the drop.

'How do you mean?'

'You mean there is no signal? Do you not light beacons for the aircraft to aim at?'

Jules said, 'We need to do this? You never told us that.'

'I assumed you knew it. How is the pilot supposed to know where you are?'

'This is the first drop we have received. I didn't know.'

'For the love of Christ,' François said, 'are you all complete amateurs? Don't you know anything?'

'We have not been in touch with anyone foreign before. Colonel Arnaud has been our only contact. We have tried to shoot soldiers and damage the railroads but we have only been active for a few months,' Jules said.

'There is more to this than drinking wine and eating paté. You have to plan meticulously. Every step you take from now on must be carefully considered. So this drop tonight, the first one?'

'Yes,' Josephine said.

'You'll need more people, you know. You need to communicate, and above all you have to be very careful. Understand?'

'And what do you know about it old man?' Jules said.

'Seemingly more than you. I was killing Germans before you were born.'

'You are not our leader.'

'Nor would I wish to be. I can help you though. No Jules, you are the leader here and it means the others depend upon you to take advice as well as lead the group. Yes?'

Jules looked at François and his expression softened.

'Naturally, you are right. We will light some beacons.' Turning to the farmer, he said, 'We need some oil and rags and tin cans, if you have them.'

In the dark, they scrambled about on a field half a mile from the farmhouse, placing the cans of oil. François was relieved there was no sign of rain. The preparations made, they returned to the farmhouse to wait until midnight, the time Arnaud indicated the flight would pass overhead. They spoke little as they waited. Tension mounted.

2

The sky was clearing by the time they lit the beacons. They chose a field where there was enough space for the parachutes to land without entanglement in the trees. François looked up at the sky with trepidation. If an informer spotted the plane, there would be little time in which to collect the materials from the drop, let alone to hide the contents. It would be impossible to transport everything on bicycles so they had agreed to hide anything they could not carry and return for the rest.

They waited. Standing at the edge of the tree line, Josephine shivered visibly and François placed a reassuring arm around her. The odour of him made her withdraw and he smiled to himself in the darkness questioning whether he could blame her for her reaction. It was fifteen minutes past midnight when they heard the low drone of the aeroplane high above. It swooped low the first time. Then, having seen the beacons, the plane ascended for a second pass, to drop its load at a thousand feet. In the dark and outlined against the inky sky, François thought the parachutes looked like winged creatures swooping to attack.

The partisans split up to find the fallen gear. There were three packing cases, but François could see no parachutist descending. He looked around as the others scrambled to find their flying prizes. François glanced over his shoulder. A movement in his peripheral vision grabbing his attention. He saw the fourth parachute suspended in a tall pine tree two or three yards into the tree line. He was tempted to call to the others but, for no reason he could have explained, thought better of it. He jogged towards it.

The parachutist hung suspended from the tree, five feet from the ground, the parachute having snagged in the branches. He reached up and supported the British spy and the sudden weight as the parachute came free toppled him and its occupant to the lush turf.

François was on his feet first. He reached a hand towards the parachutist who sat on the ground, removing a leather flight helmet.

'Here, let me help you,' he said in perfect English as far as he knew.

'Thanks, I can manage.'

François stepped back in surprise. The voice was unexpected. It was a woman.

'I thought you would be a man.'

White teeth grinned up at him reflecting the faint light remaining from the beacons. 'Don't worry, I'm fully trained.'

'No, not that. I had assumed they would not send a woman for this kind of work.'

'We hoped the Germans would think the same,' she said, still grinning.

She stood facing François. Her overall smelled of fuel oil and her hair, lank and greasy, hung in straggles about her shoulders now that she had discarded the helmet.

They shook hands. 'François Dufy, at your service.' He bowed his head, feeling formal and polite. The darkness obscured her face but he felt she seemed attractive.

A shot rang out in the night.

'What the...' François said and he threw himself to the ground, pulling the girl with him.

More shots came and the flames of the firing rifles seemed to fill the field.

'Damned amateurs,' he said.

'What's happening?'

'I don't know. We need to get out of here. Come with me.'

François began to crawl towards the forest. The girl followed, belly-crawling low, invisible.

Twenty yards in, they stopped and sat up.

'What's happening?' the girl said.

'Treachery,' François said, 'someone must have talked. We need to go all the way through this forest and out the other end. A steep climb uphill and we can reach some ruins where we can hide for the night.'

'What about your friends?'

'They will have to fend for themselves. They have little experience but may escape. The radios and the weapons may be lost, I'm afraid.'

'That's a disaster. All my explosives were amongst those boxes.'

'Too late to worry about that now. Come.'

'I don't even have a fucking radio now, old chap.'

He said nothing and led the way through thick bushes of gorse and hazelnut under the dense screen of trees. They struggled on for three hundred yards and the girl said, 'I'm Shirley Doone.'

'Ah,' he said, 'like Lorna, in the book.'

'Well, something like that, but maybe not so tragic I hope.'

He smiled and searched for her hand. He shook it again and said, 'Is it Madame or Mademoiselle?'

'I'm not married if that's what you mean.'

'Mademoiselle Doone then. Enchanted. You are not hurt?'

'No, a few scratches that's all. The tree you know.'

'Of course. We cannot stop. We must surmount the hill opposite. Is that the right word?'

'Surmount? Well sort of. Where did you learn your English?'

'I am a language teacher, well, I was. Come, it's only a few miles.'

They cut through the forest and emerged onto a small road, which they crossed. Making their way across fields, ever upwards, they came to a crossroads. There they turned right and found a steep path leading to the old Chateau Beynac, ruined for centuries and deserted apart from birds and foxes. The keep still stood, upright and proud, in daylight looking down at the whole Dordogne valley as far as Castel Naud in the far hills.

They found a space under the ruined archway of the keep and sat facing each other, backs against the ancient stonework, sheltered and François thought, perhaps secure.

'What now?' she said.

'We rest. In the morning, we find our way to Bergerac and

I will need to know what to do with you, Lorna Doone.'

She smiled and he noticed for the first time she was beautiful. She had high cheekbones and a small mouth and her eyes glittered like diamonds in the faint moonlight. He could not make out her features with clarity but he thought she must have been young. He reflected on what he would do now. He had lost his young partisan group and now had a young British spy to look after. He felt like a man rolling downhill in the snow, he was acquiring more and more layers of baggage in his life, and he wondered what Rachelle would say. He knew he could not abandon his charge in the woods and there was now no option but to bring her to his house. As sleep took him, he sighed. It was all hopeless.

Chapter 10

The scavenger's coming to carry you away,
It's over, the Three Musketeers,
Now's the sewer man's time.
– from *Paroles* by Jacque Prevert

1

A hailstorm battered the ground around them in the morning. The sloping ice balls sought the space between François' collar and his neck and he shuddered as the young woman and he made their way down the steep hill upon which the ruined castle stood. They hit the main road before dawn showed its yellow prongs of light and they turned up towards where he had left his bicycle the night before. He wondered if it was foolish and whether the attackers would be watching to see if anyone retrieved their transport. If the Germans thought they had killed all the partisans they would not be watching, François guessed. Half a mile before the place where the bicycles stood, they took to the woods. Neither of them spoke. There was not much to say and the tension and risk of their predicament seemed to make conversation difficult.

The bicycles were still where they had left them the night before, and he scouted around the area before venturing to the edge of the forest to regain his ride. He wondered if the attackers missed them in the dark, but he wondered also, who the attackers might have been and how they could have known with such precision where the drop would take place. Trees surrounded the field on three sides and there was no chance of anyone seeing the beacons from any distance.

Two of the bicycles were gone but two men's cycles remained and he apologised to Shirley about that. She smiled and shrugged off the inconvenience of having to ride a bicycle with a bar. Despite her long Mackintosh, she seemed at home cycling with François and he passed no comment. Still not conversing, they rode downhill to the main Sarlat road and despite the rifle slung across his back François risked the main road. He could have been out hunting for all anyone knew. He was not a Jew after all.

It took an hour to get to St Cyprien and before entering the town, he tied his rifle to the cycle bar between his legs to hide it. It would be sufficient for a passer-by but not close inspection. From there Bergerac required another hour. They stopped at a roadside café and bought chicory and croissants, and sat on the grass verge as the sunlight began to warm them.

'This road connects Sarlat and Bergerac,' he said.

'I know.'

'You have been here before?'

'Many times, as a child. My father was French but I grew up in England.'

'So you speak French?'

'Naturally,' she said, in French with a perfect accent.

François looked at her. He realised his English had been unnecessary and he smiled at his stupidity. Assumptions had been made. A shot in the dark, and he felt as if he was leaving all common sense behind. Why would the British send a spy who spoke no French?

'Funny?'

'Yes. For some reason, I thought I should speak Rosbif to you.'

'Very good. I don't mind. My mission obviously requires I speak French fluently. Your English is very good. Where are we going?'

'To my place. There is something I must tell you. It may increase the risk but I have no control over that.'

'Risk?'

'I have a Jewish girl living with me.'

'So?'

'I am hiding her. Her parents were interned and she stays with me. If the Germans find out she will be killed.'

'If the Germans find out I am here, we will all be killed.'

'Yes, but Rachelle must be protected.'

'And I don't need protection?'

'You understood the risks when you jumped from the plane. She has never volunteered for the risks she faces. She is a civilian.'

'Of course. How old is she?'

'Sixteen.'

'You and she...?'

'What do you take me for? A beast? I am an old man. I have no interest in a child.' He stood up, restless, agitated.

She said, 'You don't look so old to me. Look, I'm sorry; I didn't mean to offend you. It is important I know about everyone. Strengths and weaknesses, you understand? It is my life on the line here too.'

François regarded her with a look of understanding. 'Yes, I know. I do not understand how a beautiful young woman would be sent here to teach the children I was with, to lay bombs and kill Germans.'

'Children?'

'Yes, younger than you and you are a youngster to me.'

'I'm old enough at twenty-seven. Besides I have my own reasons.'

'Reasons?'

'I don't want to talk about it.'

'It's all right.'

'I heard there were reprisals last year for the killing of an SD officer.'

'Yes?'

'A sniper shot him and they shot seventeen Frenchmen in a village north of Bergerac in return. London Office is still puzzled why anyone would have done it without their knowing.'

'Perhaps the sniper was a Communist. I don't know about such things. I keep myself to myself mostly.'

'Oh. So you are not one of us?'

'Colonel Arnaud was my Commander in the last war, he asked me to help carry messages—I'm an old man after all. That's what I do. I wouldn't hurt a fly.'

Her look was disparaging. She seemed to know whom she was dealing with and François decided to say no more about himself. He had a distinct feeling this girl could see through him, and he didn't want her to know him. He wanted no one to know him. When he analysed it, even Rachelle's questions about his past or his feelings were unwelcome. He felt prickly about it; like a hedgehog whose private burrow was disturbed by children poking it on and on with their sticks.

They cycled and François tried to distract the young woman with stories of the countryside around them. He talked about Richard the Lion-heart, and how the crusader died at Chateau Beynac, but she seemed always to ask more penetrating questions: about the layout of the land, the strength of garrisons, the number of people who could be counted upon as sympathisers.

He gave up in the end. She was too sharp for him and he knew it. It began to dawn upon him how the British did not select fools to wage their clandestine conflict in France. His main feeling about that was relief. He began to trust this 'Lorna Doone' and a sense of relief came to him. He had met the first participant in this secret war whom he felt could trust.

2

It was dusk when Rachelle ran from the house. She threw her arms around François' neck. He held her there.

'Ma petite. I am so sorry to be away so long. The partisans kept me because they did not trust me.'

'You've seen partisans?'

'Yes, I told you.'

'So there really are fighters in the forest?'

'Yes.'

Cognac greeted him, her tail down and her back arched sideways. She showed her teeth in the emulation of a grin. He leaned forward and cuffed her with gentle calloused hands, 'Silly old dog.' Her tail wagged even more. 'Damned dog. Useless.' He turned and with his right arm still around Rachelle, said, 'Can I introduce you to our guest?'

Shirley appeared around the corner of the building. She smiled and François thought she looked as beautiful as he had thought her in the ruins of Chateau Beynac.

Rachelle's reaction surprised François. Her face contorted

into a grimace of anger. She tensed and pushed him away.

'Who...Who is this? It is my life you are gambling with, you stupid old man.' She ran into the house.

Shirley said, 'I'm sorry, maybe I should have waited longer.'

'No. Not your fault. I have spent months telling her to stay away from anyone who comes and you are the first person I have brought here without warning her to hide. Months. I had better go and talk to her.'

'No, let me.'

She pushed past him and Cognac sniffed at her legs as she passed. François wondered why the dog did not bark and he recalled his own words about dogs knowing whom to trust. He almost believed it himself.

François entered the house. He heard the two "girls" talking. Their voices were hushed but he eavesdropped.

'No,' Shirley said, 'I am with a British Government department called SOE. We are here to help the partisans set up a network and to show them how to use explosives.'

'How can we trust you?'

'I was dropped from a British aeroplane last night. Ask François if you like. If they caught you, it would risk my life as much as the Germans catching me would risk yours. I am on your side.'

'Hah.'

'Really.'

'I don't trust you.'

'That is a perfect beginning. I need to stay here for a while then I have to get a job. The railroad maybe or even the post. I will move to town. Do you think I would tell you if I didn't trust you?'

'So?'

'If I trust you, maybe you will come to trust me. We both want the same thing, don't we?'

'I want my parents back; you don't care about them do you?'

'Maybe I do. Isn't their plight what the war is all about?'

'Doesn't mean you care about my family does it?'

'No, perhaps it doesn't seem that way to you, but we both want the Sauerkrauts out of France, don't we?'

François, standing at the doorjamb, cleared his throat.

'Now girls...' he began.

'Uncle, what have you done? She knows about me. When she is captured, they will come for me.'

'Perhaps; so it makes sense for us both to make sure she isn't caught then.'

'I'm going to leave. You can't stop me.'

'Where would you go, you silly girl? The place is full of police informers, SD, and soldiers.'

'I'll go and join the partisans. I can shoot a gun. I will be alright.'

François said, 'Rachelle, talk sense. You are very young. The Rosbifs sent Shirley to help the partisans. I promised Arnaud I would also help. I need you to trust me.'

'I trust you. I won't trust her,' Rachelle said pointing a finger at Shirley.

Shirley said, 'Give it some time Rachelle. You will learn to trust me. I can teach you a lot of things, useful to us both, for surviving and fighting this war. I like the Germans even less than you, if the truth were known.'

Rachelle said, 'What do you mean?'

'I can teach you to blow up a train for example.'

'You would do that?'

François stepped into the bedroom and said, 'You will not

involve Rachelle in your operations. She is not a sympathiser, she is a victim. I won't have it.'

'It's up to her isn't it? It's her parents who have been taken away to God knows where and her family torn apart. Maybe you should let her do her part to defend her country and people?'

'No. She is just a child. If she died or was captured, I don't know what I would do.'

'Uncle,' Rachelle said, 'do you mean that?'

'Of course I mean it. You think I risk my life if I don't care?'

Rachelle ran to him; she threw her arms about his neck and he could feel the raw emotion in her embrace. It seemed to François the presence of a third person pressurised them both to express these feelings, hidden before, on his part at least. It was as if a stranger's mere presence was enough to bring them to a point where it all needed to be said—laid bare and exposed; understood and then forgotten like a few drops of rain in the whirlpool of daily life.

He smoothed her hair and said, 'Rachelle, my poor little one. Didn't you know?'

'What?'

'Stop it.'

'Know what?'

He pushed her away. 'Damn all this sentimentality and emotion. It will never win the war. We must be more practical.'

Rachelle looked at him. When he returned her gaze, she smiled and he knew that perhaps he should be more open, but Shirley's presence seemed somehow to interfere.

'No,' he said, 'we need to arrange a bed for our guest and get some food cooked. I'm starving.'

Shirley and Rachelle looked at one another. It was as if his very intransigence and wish to hide his feelings created a bond between them, for they both understood what François was unable to express. Through it, Shirley became in moments part of them, part of François' world—unbidden and without his consent, it was true, but she was joining them.

In his mind, he rejected such thoughts. He had known Shirley for only twenty-four hours or less and yet she had his complete trust. It was not his nature to trust anyone, and it irritated him. He walked out of the back door and set up the grille over the stones they used for a fire when they spit-roasted.

'Bloody women. What sins have I ever committed to be punished in this way? A secret life with two women, both of them young enough to be my daughters.'

And then, he thought of Jean-Paul and that special catch in his throat came. The faint choking feeling, so familiar, yet so unwelcome. It was a kind of pain, mental and physical and it was with him still. If only life had been fair.

He began stacking the sticks for the fire and as he worked, he recalled a time when his son had lamented the unfairness of life, as young boys do. He remembered saying how no one promised life would be fair, and to expect fairness would lead only to disappointment. He hated himself then for that. It was as if he had denied his son something of himself, pushing negative thoughts into Jean-Paul's head. Small wonder the boy had gone to war against what he thought was unfair; his father had always extolled the virtues of unfairness and Jean-Paul rebelled. He was so like his father in that and François recognised it. The thoughts brought the pain back and he shrugged it off, stoking the nascent blaze.

'I'm just hungry,' he said to himself.

3

Christmas was a strange time for François. He was used to spending it alone, thinking of his dead family. If he could have had his wish this year, he would have been alone again. It seemed to him as if the presence of the two women disturbed his reminiscences, his hate, and his pain. They took something away from him by their presence - something indefinable, something firing the devil within him, who faded to become only grey embers of the disgust he felt with the world.

He sat outside in the shed. The roof consisted of wooden slats sealed with pitch. Each night he lay on the hay-stuffed mattress and pondered what the two women in his life meant to him. He considered how Rachelle came into his life. How could he have left her to be beaten or raped by the Germans? Disposing of them was as natural to him as shooting a deer or a rabbit. At least he did not have to hold them up by the ears to stop them pissing on him after they were dead. He smiled at the thought.

Shirley was a different matter. Arnaud said the radio had broken and he needed to get word to other resistance groups to inform London, but he seemed to have stalled in his efforts. François reminded him each time he saw him, but nothing happened and time drifted on. It was now six weeks since the drop and Shirley seemed worried. She nagged, she cajoled, but what could François do? He had no contacts, no secret army with which to prosecute the war Shirley talked about with such passion. And that was another thing. He had no passion for the war. He hated the Germans, the Nazis, but he did not see his role as that of a resistance fighter. True, he wanted revenge. François wanted to repay them for Guernica, for Alma and for Jean-Paul, but he baulked at the inexperience of the fighters he had met. He could not imagine they would succeed. What François wanted was to fight in his own way; to cause damage to the Germans, to expend his revulsion of them by killing when it suited him, not when some wet-behind-the-ears youth told him to. And London? Who were they to direct things? He would have taken orders from De Gaulle or any of the men who were exiled in Britain, but Englishmen? What could they know of life in Aquitaine?

Arnaud, with his broken radio received no news of the partisans and he suspected, or so he told François, they either all died on the night of the drop or else they no longer trusted him. François, on one occasion searched the forest around Fontaud, but saw no sign of Jules and Josephine. They were at an impasse and Shirley seemed more frustrated with each passing day. She had come with the intention of training partisan groups and achieved, in her own words, nothing.

And time? It passed. François' home became a place of bickering and irritation. When he returned after shooting geese at the quarry, he heard them. Back and forth, they argued. Rachelle wanting Shirley to leave. Shirley saying she would love to, but it was too dangerous and the war would suffer if the Germans caught her. It was true, they shut up as soon as he entered through the back door, they both enthused over Cognac and she in turn seemed to love them both, but François struggled with their presence more with each week that went by. The three of them could not co-exist for long.

Maudlin, Shirley called him. There were times when he found it hard to choke back the tears of genuine sorrow but they were sometimes tears of hatred too and when the women interrupted him, they gave little sympathy. It would have felt like an insult if they did offer it in any case. He had no capacity to receive such words from another and he knew it.

On Christmas morning, a light snowfall brightened the yard as François arose. He stretched and yawned. Swinging his legs out of the sleeping bag, he sat on the edge of the striped mattress and rubbed his stubbly face. Finding his boots, he shivered as the icy leather gripped his feet and he realised his age was making him sensitive to the cold. As a young man, he never felt the freezing temperatures of winter. He recalled how one morning his father scolded him for going out without a vest and he had laughed at him, saying, 'Don't worry Father, I'm fired with enthusiasm, it keeps me warm.'

Almost slipping over on the ice in the yard, he greeted Cognac and wondered whether the girls were awake. He cracked the ice on the rainwater barrel and threw some water on his face, disdaining a strip-wash in the sub-zero temperature. He knocked on the door. The house was silent but he decided to risk disturbing Shirley to get out of the cold. The gaps in the drawn curtains shed a glimmering light on the room. Shirley was not there. He shut the door and crossed the room towards the kitchen.

Entering the kitchen, the place had changed. It had become for that one day a place of merriment. Paper streamers made from old newspapers hung from the ceiling, four candles burned at the table and there was a sense of celebration. It failed to puncture his shell of indifference but he recognised it meant something to both Rachelle and Shirley. A celebration, fresh bread baked from François' little oven, cold meat and warmed, spiced wine greeted him. There were no frills. There was no banquet with which to celebrate in style, only this meagre spread adorning his kitchen table, but he realised that what they did have was a companionship and a camaraderie hidden before in the mists of their bickering and his moodiness.

'But Jews don't celebrate Christmas,' he said.

'Do you celebrate pass-over? Yom-Kippur? You don't have to be religious to feel like celebrating,' Shirley said.

François looked from face to face. 'No, I suppose not. Are you religious?'

'C. of E. but not a church-goer.'

Rachelle said, 'What is that?'

François said, 'it is the substitute for Christianity the Rosbifs practice because one of their Kings wanted a divorce. The Pope forbade it and they formed a new version of Christianity.'

'I have lost mine,' Rachelle said.

'What?' Shirley said.

'My religion. I can't pray because I've forgotten the words and I have no holy book. My papa always led the prayers at home. Without him it seems to lack…I don't know.'

'You can celebrate anyway,' François said. 'This is the best Christmas morning I have had for a long time. Tonight we eat roast goose and drink the best wine of the house.'

'Which one is that?' Shirley said.

'The same as the one I drank last night, and the night before. It is the only one we can afford.'

They laughed and the memory of that laughter stayed with François for a long time. It was almost as if it was illicit, forbidden. He felt he had no right to laugh. Who can laugh when all his family is dead, and his country overrun by Germans? Christmas nineteen forty-two was a moment when time stood still. It was a single day when hostilities ceased between Rachelle and Shirley, and François smiled from his heart.

Chapter 11

And I stand rooted there,
With the sad whip of reality,
And I have nothing to say,
Your smile is just as true,
As my home truths.
– from *Paroles* by Jacque Prevert

1

It was early, even by the time they finished breakfast. The sun had yet to peep through the clouds and a mist hung in the Dordogne valley, sending its minions into the neighbouring forest behind the one-story house François had now lived in for five years.

'You were up very early?' Rachelle said.

'Yes, maybe five o'clock,' François said.

'And you cycled all the way to the baker's for the bread?'

'When my son, Jean-Paul was a little boy, we used to go hand in hand before the dawn, to a baker's close to the house in which he grew up. It was so early in the morning, before his Maman was awake, and we would buy fresh bread and croissants and sometimes as a special treat, Danish pastries. Today, all they had was these plain loaves. I was lucky to get them: that judge's wife, Mme. Dubois was trying to push into the queue.'

'You pushed her out?' Rachelle said.

'Not quite. I put my arm around her and she withdrew.'

He laughed then. It was a strange boyish laugh from a man of his age and he caught himself short, stifled it, realising he was no longer a young man and no longer a father. The thought made him morose. He looked at their faces and stood.

'I must feed poor Cognac.'

'No, Uncle, not yet. What did he look like? Jean-Paul?'

'I don't want to talk about it. Leave me alone.'

'Uncle?'

'What?'

'I'm sorry. I was clumsy.'

François stood there. He looked at the girl's face.

'No. it's not you. Not your question even. I had happy times with my boy. To remember them is painful. Not your fault.'

'François,' Shirley said, appearing from the back doorway.

'Yes?'

'I have to meet with Colonel Arnaud. I've been kicking my heels here for far too long. I need him to find a way for me to communicate with London and to get me radios. I also need to meet the partisans, if any of them survived. François, you must arrange it.'

'This clamp-down since you came has made it difficult for even me to visit him. Besides, I'm no partisan really. I just take the odd message.'

'You're in deeper than you think my friend.'

'How so?'

'I'm stuck here. Stuck with you. If you have any sympathy for the cause, you will help me.'

'I'm just not used to taking orders any more that's all.'

'You need to now.'

'Perhaps. I will go to the Arnaud's house and take your message. Meeting Arnaud will be very dangerous for you both.'

'And not for you?'

'No. I am the town drunk. I smell and I smoke a pipe. I have yellow teeth. If they arrested me, the SD I mean, they would not want to torture me in case my bouquet drove them mad.'

'He won't let me wash all of his clothes,' Rachelle, said.

'It is to our advantage I guess,' Shirley said, 'not easy to live with though.'

François grinned and left. He went into the yard behind the house and fed his dog with goose-breasts. For once, he stroked her head as he put down the cooked meat in her bowl.

'I saw that.' Rachelle said.

He started and said, 'She's a good dog. We depend on her for our security. She has never let me down.'

'Don't be defensive Uncle. I stroke her all the time when you are not here. She sleeps on my bed if you are away.'

'What?'

'On my bed. She guards me.'

'You'll make her soft.'

'Is that so bad?'

'Yes. She is a working dog. She needs to focus on her work.'

'Like you? You aren't soft are you?'

'I... I...'

'Forget it.'

Rachelle turned and went back inside. He wondered what was happening. He decided he lacked an understanding of

121

women. In all those years with Arlette, he knew he had never understood her. She would say one thing and mean another and he could never keep up. His present companions seemed no different. François shrugged and went out to his outhouse to cut a joint of venison. He found a rough cloth and cut a piece, wrapping the meat in that.

'You're going?' Shirley said.

'Yes, you need a radio. I'll go out this afternoon to the farm where the partisans get their food, and I hope I can find them.'

'If they survived.'

'They seemed young but not stupid. I wonder how the Germans found out about the drop. Arnaud had no opportunity to tell anyone. Maybe they saw the beacons and realised what was happening."

'I need you to find out.'

'It's a worry, but patience is a virtue. I must go.'

Rachelle and Shirley watched as he cycled down the unmade road towards town. He glanced over his shoulder as he turned right into the main road and he could see the two women standing, side by side, at the door to his little house. The thought that it was not now a 'house' but a 'home' seemed to warm him somewhere deep inside. It was as if, after long years on the outside, banging on the door, someone had finally let him in. It was exhilarating but painful too.

2

François knocked on the door of the Rosbif house; then he remembered the bell-pull. The faint sound deep in the house amused him. It was a throwback to olden times, when such things were commonplace. Most houses had heavy door-knockers but he pictured the maid, with her little up-turned nose, reclining in the kitchen and starting as the bell rang out. Then he pictured her staring down at the Colonel's bald pate moving between her legs and he grinned at the image. He had finesse, his old Colonel.

He waited. He shuffled from one foot to the other and looked over his shoulder. There was no one about since it was early. He rang again. The door swung open. It was not the maid, but the lady of the house, Mme. Arnaud. She wore a green dressing gown wrapped tight around her ample frame, and a red nightcap. He likened her to a Christmas tree, green and multi-coloured. Her blue eyes however, were red-rimmed and he knew she must have been crying.

'Madame, if this is a bad time...'

'No,' she said, 'come in. My husband left a message.'

'He has gone out perhaps?'

François knew what had happened. She had caught them. She had found her husband with the maid and he had run away with her. It embarrassed him. But he admired the old man too. He would try to support him through this if it were possible.

He followed her to the kitchen.

She sat down and reached with unaccustomed awkward-ness, under the table. What was she doing? Her behaviour was strange. He wondered if he should leave.

'I brought some venison. It has hung for almost a week.'

'Shut up you silly man.'

'I was only...'

'You don't understand. They were here in the night. They took him.'

Her mouth tightened as she spoke. He could see anger in

123

her face now, determination.

'They searched the house and took away things...'

'Who came? Who searched?'

'The SD. That filthy little slut of a maid, she worked for them. She reported him and they took away his radio. It was an old thing, just a keepsake from the war.'

'The SD? What did they want with him?'

'What do you think? He is a Colonel in the Gendarmerie. They said they had questions. They took him to the Mairie.'

'Questions? But what about?'

'He told me about you. He said you could be trusted. Here then. He wanted you to take it to Inspector Ran's house.'

'The policeman? You are mad.'

'No, he said you can trust Ran, he isn't one of the partisans yet, but he wants to protect Jews and is on a knife edge.'

'May I see it?'

'What?'

'The message.'

'Oh, yes. Here.' Mme Arnaud passed him a piece of paper, torn from an envelope. He read it and his heart began to thump against his ribs. His mouth became dry and a tremor appeared in his hands.

'What does it say?'

He read it aloud.

Auguste, I am compromised. SD officers are searching for me as I write this. I have given it to Marquite and she will see you get it. I will say nothing. Is there anything to say in any case?

Colonel Andre Arnaud.

124

He looked up when he finished. Their eyes met. Her blue-red eyes became moist. Tears began to make their troublesome journey down her cheeks. He reached down and placed a hand on her shoulder, patting in a gentle, reassuring way, but he had no words now. He knew they would torture Colonel Arnaud. They would find out everything and they would arrest even François, the town drunk. The smelly old town drunk. It was laughable in a way. How could anyone think he was a resistance fighter? He was just a drunk. He knew he needed to act and act now.

'At what time did they come?'

'About four in the morning.'

He had difficulty understanding her through her tears.

'There may still be time. I must go. Can I do anything for you?'

'No. I won't need the venison.'

'I will leave it here. It is my reason for coming.'

'Oh. Yes. Yes, you go now.'

He turned to the door feeling desperate. He felt like a man on fire running towards the cool waters of escape. He knew the Colonel would talk. He knew they would come for him and he had to return and warn his two women. Behind him, he heard gut-wrenching sobs. Those bitter sounds spurred him on as the door slammed at his exit.

He had seldom cycled so fast. A passer-by might have wondered if he was in a race but there was no one around to witness how his legs flew in his desperation. Would he be there in time? He had to be. He would fight if the SD were there already; he would kill as many as he could before they got him.

Chapter 12

Let's go, let's go,
Step on it,
Let's go, let's go,
Come on, get going.
– from *Paroles* by Jacque Prevert

1

His bicycle clattered to the cobbles as François jumped from it at the front door. The momentum of his arrival threw him against the peeling paint. He burst in and found no one there.

'Rachelle. Rachelle,' he screamed.

Shirley appeared from the back yard. She frowned when she saw him.

'What on earth?' she said in English.

'The SD may be coming any moment. You must both get away. Where is Rachelle?'

Calm and slow, Shirley sat down on the tattered couch, where François used to sleep before she came. It was Shirley's bed now and François slept in the shed outside.

'She is in the woods. What's happened?'

'They have arrested Colonel Arnaud. He will talk; we have to leave.'

'But where to?'

'We will go to the partisans. If I can leave you hiding with them, I can maybe come back and find out what is happening.'

'I'll get her. She was only walking and said she'd be back soon.'

'We have no time.'

François scrabbled under the couch. He withdrew his Mauser.

He said, 'You can use one of these?'

'Of course I can.'

'There are only two bullets in the magazine. I used the others.'

'Practise?'

'Sort of. Come, we have no time. I will pack what food we have and anything else of use. You must gather your things.'

'I don't have any bloody things do I? Have you forgotten?'

'You have my Christmas present.'

'A coat? A coat is hardly a wealth of belongings.'

'Well, you will need it. It's cold outdoors this time of year.'

'How long do we…'

Rachelle appeared at the door, followed by Cognac, a flurry of tail-wagging and grinning teeth. François frowned as their eyes met.

'It has happened. We must go. Gather your stuff.'

Rachelle looked at him. One moment frozen, a few seconds later, running to the bedroom. She emerged within a minute, her rifle slung on her shoulder and a small canvas bag containing the little she had accumulated since her stay began. They set off on foot into the forest, heading towards Fontaud.

2

'Two women in tow,' he said to himself. 'How can any man manage like this?'

The late winter afternoon darkened around them as they approached Fontaud. A covering of snow entombed the field at the edge of the forest. It had rained the day before and the water freezing on the snow made the surface icy and firm. Walking through the forest, François wondered what he could do now. It seemed he had no choice but join the partisans. Returning to Bergerac involved a risk he was unwilling to take. His problem was how to find the partisans whom he had met before and whether they had survived the ambush, the night Shirley arrived.

'Sure you know where you are taking us?' Shirley said.

'I met the partisan group near Fontaud. The farmer there used to feed them. I have it in mind to ask him where they might be.'

'If he knew, would he tell you?'

'Maybe he can get word to them, I don't know. Anyway, Arnaud's capture will put him in danger too, I have to warn him.'

'So you think Arnaud will talk?'

'Arnaud? Yes, he will talk. Not because he is weak but because they all do in the end.'

'Uncle,' Rachelle said, 'is he not strong? I know he is old but he is famous for his bravery in the old war.'

'It works on anyone. They all know they can't be rescued. No one will come for them and they face long days and nights

128

of pain all alone. Can you blame anyone for talking? I saw it in the war. No, it is not his weakness but the inevitability of the suffering, my little friend.'

Rachelle shivered and came close to him. Inured to his odour, she took his hand as they walked. He glanced over his shoulder. Shirley, who followed behind smiled. François knew she understood.

'There,' François said and pointed across the white meadow towards the farmhouse. 'This is Fontaud. You two wait here and I will walk down to see if the farmer can help us.'

He walked forward but before he cleared twenty paces, a shot rang out in the silence of the forest. He hit the snowy ground and in his mind, checked himself for a wound. There was none. He realised the partisans had found him and he drew a grey, stained handkerchief from his jacket pocket. Tying it to the rifle barrel, he waved it above his head. Silence greeted him. François lay there, waving his truce-flag but not daring to stand. Nothing happened. He called out. No answer. He lay still in the end, waiting. They would come, he was sure. It occurred to him it might have been the Germans shooting at him but he calmed when he analysed the situation. No Germans would fire without shouting afterwards—it was their nature. No, it was a partisan or some of them. He wondered whether it was the girl Josephine or maybe one of the two men.

François wondered whether his two women were safe. He reasoned they would be, unless they showed themselves. As his toes began to numb in the cold, he thought his life was in a process of change. He felt like a man keeping his balance on a slippery slope, his feet moving fast in the hope of arresting his descent. He knew he had landed on his backside this time, but as long as Rachelle and Shirley were safe, he would allow the partisans to do whatever they wished with him. He knew they might suspect he was a traitor; after all, everything in which he involved himself with the partisans seemed to have gone wrong. They would have to be stupid not to suspect him.

'You.'

The voice came from his right. It was familiar but unrecognised.

'I'm François Dufy. I seek a friend.'

'A friend? What friend?'

Feeling more confident because he realised the Germans would never ask him such a simplified question, he said, 'I'm looking for Josephine. She knows me.'

'Josephine? How do you know her?'

'Who are you?'

'No. Who are you? Remember I have a rifle pointed at your position.'

'My God man, this is no game. Let me stand and identify myself and I will explain.'

'Then leave your weapon on the ground. You think I can't recognise a German weapon when I see one? Stand up, hands in the air. Now.'

François stood. It was his best chance but he had no great cares about the outcome. He had long since ceased to care about what might happen to him; he only cared about Rachelle. The thought struck him as he stood and the understanding of his attachment to the girl hit him hard. Where was she? Was she safe?' The insecurity gripped him and he wondered about running back to the tree line.

The figure approaching through the gloom of the spring dusk surprised him. The man was tall and broad with a straggle of unkempt brown hair, in places long enough to reach his shoulders. A few yards from Françoise, the man stopped and said, 'Why are you looking for the resistance?'

'You? I thought everything was going well for you? Inspector Ran was looking after you.'

'I told you, he and I fell out over the persecution of my people.'

'Where's your yellow star? Faded away in the sunlight?'

'Ha. You think to make a joke of it?'

François said, 'No. No joke. You've joined them?'

'Yes. What are you doing here?'

'I thought you had a daughter?'

'I have. Monique is safe.'

'Look, I don't know if you knew it, but Colonel Arnaud has been taken by the SD. They will find out about Fontaud, about the meeting place and about the farmer's cooperation with you. He has to be warned and my position is now unsafe. I need help.'

'Josephine suspects you are a traitor. She said you are one of our targets.'

'What?'

'Yes. She figures you set them up. Her friend Josef died at the drop.'

'I am a Frenchman. I would die for France and would never betray my own people. If Arnaud was around, he would have vouched for me.'

'It makes little difference. She and Jules may want to kill you anyway.'

'Look, Pierre, I found the British agent. She is with me. I have kept her safe now for three months. You think if I were a collaborator, I would do this? She can vouch for me.'

'Where is she now? Captured?'

'No, she is…'

'Right behind you. Don't move. I have a rifle pointed at

your back. I mean it.'

Shirley stood behind Pierre. Her outline in the fading daylight made her look ethereal to François, as if she had appeared from nowhere; appeared to save him, like some guardian angel.

'English?'

'Put up your gun,' she said.

François noticed she smiled as she talked as if this was all some kind of joke to her.

Pierre Dreyfus slung his gun onto his shoulder and putting his hands in the air, turned to face the English girl.

'You don't need that,' he said.

'You didn't need to fire at François either.'

'I didn't. If I wanted to kill him, I would have placed the bullet between his eyes. You think I'm a novice? I've been hunting and shooting in this forest since I was a child. How do I know you are who you say you are?'

'I haven't said anything yet. I am from SOE. I need to contact your group and begin setting up a partisan group. My explosives were lost when I landed and I have no way now of contacting London. I have marked time like a holidaymaker here and if it were not for François, the Germans would have found me long ago. You owe him a lot.'

'I have only been in this group for a week. I know François from living in Bergerac. It doesn't mean I trust him.'

'You know Arnaud has been arrested?'

'No. That is a problem. He was our main contact with London.'

'Take me to the others.'

François said, 'They killed Josef? That night of the drop I mean.'

'Josephine and Jules said so. Although they lost one man,

they recovered some equipment I believe.'

'Josephine said that?'

'Yes, but she doesn't even trust me. I don't know all of it; they just sent me here to pick up some food.'

François said, 'this place is compromised. Arnaud knew about it so you must assume the Germans do too. We need to warn the farmer.'

'He's not there. I've been camped here for three nights and there is no sign of activity at the farm. Maybe they have picked him up already.'

'It may explain why Arnaud was arrested,' Shirley said.

They were silent and Shirley slung her rifle on her shoulder. Rachelle appeared out of the gathering darkness at the tree line.

François tried to motion her away. She ignored him.

'Uncle?' she said.

'I'm alright,' François said.

She came to his side, holding onto his arm. He thought how, without him, she would be in danger here with these dangerous people. Without him, there would be no one to look after her.

Looking at Pierre, she said, 'I wish to join your group. Before you object you should know, I am Jewish, my parents have been taken away, and I can shoot a gun.'

'Rachelle. What are you saying?' he said.

She stepped away from him and Pierre moved between them, his back to François. He looked her up and down. He smiled. 'Jewish, eh? You think it means I can trust you. I trust no one. We'll see how Jewish you really are when we get back.'

He turned. 'Let's go,' he said.

A long trudge began. They crossed fields, the deep snow

frozen on its top layer, but hard enough to take a man's weight. Every third step they sank to their knees in the snow and the going seemed to François to be exhausting. Entering the forest seemed almost a pleasant relief and after three hours of this footslog, they were all relieved to reach their destination.

The trees thinned and the first they knew of the camp was a challenge from a deep throaty voice. Pierre stepped forward and François could hear a muted conversation. The lookout glanced once over Pierre's shoulder and they continued talking. Minutes passed and he felt Rachelle's hand squeeze his but he was unsure whether it was giving or asking for reassurance. Pierre turned and gestured them to come forward. They followed him into a small clearing where a fire glowed and crackled and François recognised faces. He sighed; he would have to justify himself all over again and he was finding it tiresome. This time he had nowhere else to go and he knew it. His biggest concern was he wanted his old life back. It was one where he could move unfettered in the knowledge that no one would hinder him. It was a life where he was free. All that had dissolved with the arrival of a young Jewish woman and a Briton, and now he was homeless. He felt manipulated, not by the women who entered his life, but by fate. The force of that fate drove him on now; he needed to convince the partisans he meant them no harm and to take over where his Colonel left off. To facilitate, to foster and to show by example.

Chapter 13

It doesn't give a damn,
The earth.
It turns and all living things set up a howl,
It doesn't give a damn.
– from *Paroles* by Jacque Prevert

1

Darkness began to descend as François and the others entered the clearing. Josephine and Jules stood near the fire. They both glared at him as he entered the circle of light. A thin downpour began as he did so and he shuddered from the drops running down inside his collar.

François held up his right hand.

'Before you say anything,' he said, 'You need to know a number of things. First, Arnaud has been taken by the SD. His wife told me that. Secondly this…' he gestured to Shirley, 'is a British agent who has been hiding with me since the attack at Cazenac. I have nothing else to say to you. The facts speak for themselves. It is not possible for me to have betrayed you, Rachelle will vouch for the fact that Arnaud made me leave to meet you as soon as he told me about the drop.'

'You expect me to believe you?' Josephine said.

'Ask them. They will tell you.'

Josephine turned to Rachelle. She took the girl aside and questioned her on the far side of the camp. François could see the strain on Rachelle's face as she defended him. It came home to him again how much she cared for him. He watched as her brow wrinkled, as her mouth tightened and her hands gestured. It kindled anger. Who were these silly people to question him? Who was Josephine that she felt she had the power of life and death over them?

'Look,' he said, raising his voice, 'either you kill us now or you stop this stupidity. Don't you think the Nazis would have a good laugh if they knew how we fight each other? I have stayed alive in this stupid war by being careful. You must all be the same. I said careful, not stupid. It is stupid to ignore the obvious and foolish to ignore advice when it comes from those who know. You must move your camp. Arnaud will talk. He will do so unwillingly but all the same, it is beyond human strength to experience torture and not give way in the end. We can't get him out of the Mairie; we can't rescue him. He knows that and I hope he will hold out long enough for us to escape. Yes, I said we. They will be after me too.'

Jules stepped forward.

'The only other way the Germans could have learned about the drop would have been from my brother. They tortured and killed him. He would never have talked. They could only have learned about the drop from you.'

'If you are really as stupid as that, you might as well kill me now. There would be no future in fighting the Germans alongside someone so foolish. Have you heard nothing I said? If your brother was taken, he will have talked. It is beyond human endurance to suffer torture alone, knowing no rescue will come. Can't you imagine it in your head?'

'I know what they did to him. I don't have to imagine.'

'Then you will understand. They all talk.'

'And if you are right,' Josephine said, 'what chance do we stand?'

'Simple. We move camp and we regroup. Shirley will become our go-between. She needs a job, maybe in the railroads and I need to find out if it is safe for me to return. Look, I'll help you and I will kill Germans but I want you to keep Rachelle safe, you hear?'

There was silence then. Josephine looked at the ground and Jules put his arm around her waist. The rain intensified, as if the heavens opened up above them to express its own emotions.

'I still don't trust you,' Jules said.

'Do I care?' François said. 'Frankly, it is of no consequence. The fact remains, we all need each other and the longer we delay the closer we come to being discovered. I need to return to Bergerac. I will need to find out how much Arnaud has said and I have a message to deliver.'

'Message?' Josephine said.

'Yes, Arnaud passed me a message to deliver to Inspector Ran of the Vichy Police.'

'But why?'

'Here,' François said, taking the scrap of paper from his pocket.

Josephine read it. She frowned then looked up from beneath her brown beret.

'Why is Arnaud communicating with a policeman? He says there is nothing to tell but he clearly trusts the man. Is he on our side?'

Pierre said, 'Auguste is a man with second thoughts. His wife has taken my daughter in and will protect her. I don't know whether there is more to tell. It sounds as if Arnaud has persuaded him to cooperate in some way.'

'If that is so, he might be useful to us,' Josephine said, 'You think he can be trusted?'

Pierre said, 'Yes, but he will struggle with acts of violence. I've known him a long time. He's very religious too.'

François said, 'Look, the Vichy police force has interned and persecuted the Jews here in large numbers. They do the dirty work for the SD. Even if he has suddenly changed, he is still guilty of terrible things. I think we can use him but we cannot fully trust such a man.'

Jules said, 'So suddenly you talk about 'we' as if you are one of us. I can't trust you either until you prove yourself.'

'Prove? How?'

'We will give you a mission. If you do as we ask, we might trust you.'

'I will do what I can but Shirley is the one to decide in the long run although she has no way to contact London now. We need to either get in touch with other groups or send some kind of request for a radio.'

Josephine said, 'We have a radio. We salvaged one packing case from that disastrous drop of yours.'

'It wasn't my drop. I just brought Arnaud's message.'

'You have a radio?' Shirley said. 'Why didn't anyone tell me?'

'We didn't know you were here. We didn't trust Arnaud after the drop went wrong. We've been working on our own.'

'You've contacted London?' Shirley said.

'No, we couldn't work the damned thing. It receives but it won't send.'

'I'll fix it. It's part of my training. Let's move from here. The farmer in Fontaud is sure to have been arrested. He will direct the Germans to you even if he only knows the vague direction of your camp.'

The partisans dismantled their encampment with speed. Within an hour, the group was on the move. They headed towards Bergerac and the forest south of the town. Excluding Pierre, three others had joined the band. Jacques and Amos were brothers, who like Rachelle, were hiding from the SD. Philippe was in his twenties, a carpenter by trade, who sought to avoid the authorities sending him to a work camp in Germany. They all followed Pierre and he seemed to know with precision where to go. He knew the place well and seemed certain they could hide in that area without being detected.

François noted how, as they walked, they kept him and Pierre in front. He felt their mistrust was foolishness, but how could he blame them? It was a sign of the times that no one trusted anyone else, yet he was about to deliver a message to a Vichy policeman whom he might one day need to rely upon.

2

A cold sun rose above the snow-clad trees all around the new camp. François and Rachelle stood at the periphery. He looked down at her and smiled. She clutched his shoulder, tremulous hands grasping and gripping him. He found the conversation painful but it all needed to be said.

'If you leave me here I will be all alone.'

François said, 'No. You will be with the partisans and you can shoot a rifle as well as any man. They will protect you and as long as you avoid the Germans, you will be safe.'

'I don't want to avoid them, I want to kill them.'

'I know,' he said, touching her face with a gentle hand.

'Will you come back?'

'Yes, of course.'

'What if you get caught?'

'I won't be caught. I have to deliver Arnaud's message and then who knows? Maybe I'll come back here. I do need to find out whether I am in danger or not. If Arnaud talked, and I'm sure he will have, then there will be no going back and Cognac and I will have to join these young fighters. Not a very comfortable time for an old man.'

'You're going then.'

It was Shirley. She approached behind him and he spun around in surprise.

'I… Yes. I'm going to deliver the note to Ran. It was Arnaud's last free act. He seemed to think this was important. I don't know if Ran can be trusted but if Arnaud thought he could, then maybe he will be useful to us.'

'Yes, maybe. I need some kind of job to establish my credentials.'

'Please come back,' Rachelle said.

He reached for her and gave her a parental hug, his hand patting her back.

Shirley said, 'Don't worry Rachelle, I will be here and you and I will see him when he returns.'

'You sound as if you will miss me too.'

She looked at him then. A quizzical expression crossed her face as if grasping for some thought only now surfacing.

'François. You are right. I will miss you. I won't miss the odour, but yes, I will miss you.'

He grinned and turned towards the path leading from the clearing where the partisans camped. He was silent but the thought that Shirley would miss him too came as a shock. She was a cool one that. He never saw her betray panic or anxiety but the thought she might regret his going had failed to cross his mind, until now. He wondered why she occupied so much of his thinking, as he stamped through the light, melting snow. He was heading towards Bergerac and heaven only knew what was in store for him.

Pierre had given him directions. The Inspector's house stood at the edge of the forest so François had no concerns about any casual passers-by seeing him. Besides, it was Sunday and most people would be in church anyway. Tramping the path, his boots slipping now and again on the ice-covered tree roots, he identified the tall pine where Pierre had described it. He had fifteen minutes more to walk. He stopped and listened. There was silence all around him and he felt reassured by that as he lit his pipe. Watching the smoke drift in a slow-moving haze to his left he began to wonder what he was doing with the partisans. He felt too old for this nonsense now. He had exacted his revenge with the killing of the SD officer and the two German bullies who beat Rachelle with such viciousness. It was not enough for the partisans. They wanted blood on blood and then more. It was obvious he needed to keep an eye on Rachelle however. She was only sixteen and he admitted to himself he still felt protective of her. If they exposed her to real danger, he would never forgive Josephine or Jules for that matter.

The tree line ended at a short field and he saw the house fifty yards away. A road passed by on the opposite side at the front of the dwelling. A ruined outhouse, half its bricks missing, stood close to the main building and he made for that. He wanted cover and he wanted no one to spot him.

Gaining the road, he sauntered up to the front door trying to look casual. There was no answer when he rang the doorbell. He knew it would look strange if he loitered. The lock presented no challenge and he forced it with his knife. He needed to wait inside or risk someone seeing and recognising him. He still had no idea whether he was in mortal danger or whether Arnaud had kept silent so far.

He pushed the door open. The house was silent. He walked through the vestibule and crossed the hall towards the kitchen. It was a typical farmhouse kitchen with a big oak table, overhung by a wooden frame with pans and strings of garlic. There was a black range on the opposite wall and he headed for that to warm himself. It was then he heard a noise. It was as if someone tiptoed on the landing upstairs. It made him shiver. Then he recalled how Pierre had described leaving his little girl with the Ran family and he wondered whether the mouse-like sounds might have been the Jewish girl. It seemed clear Auguste Ran had something in common with the old drunk.

The front door stood ajar as he left it, so the returning family would know he was there. It would be a shame after all, he thought, if the police inspector entered and began shooting at intruders. He had not long to wait. As he looked out of the window towards the tree line, Ran's car came to a halt outside. Taking his hands from his pockets, he placed them where Inspector Ran would be able to see them. Then he waited.

The Inspector appeared, moving with care around the doorjamb. 'Who is there?' he said.

François said, 'Oh, Inspector. I am sorry. The door was open and I knew you would be in church, so I thought you would not mind if I waited here in the warm kitchen. It is so cold outside.'

'Dufy, if you came here to steal, I will arrest you and let Judge Dubois deal with you in the morning. Empty your pockets at once.'

The Inspector pointed his weapon at him. François emptied his pockets under the poignant threat of the pistol.

Ran examined the contents. From one, François produced a button, a Laguiole knife and a few francs; from the other a soiled handkerchief and the folded piece of Manila paper.

Ran poked the note with the barrel of his gun.

'What's this? You can write?'

'Naturally I can write, Inspector. It is the reason I am here,' François said.

'What, writing?'

'No, to deliver a message.'

'Push it across the table.'

Ran took his eyes from François only long enough to pick up the scrap of paper. He read it. The Inspector's face changed. The look of shock would have been obvious to François even if he were a fool.

'Where did you get this?'

'Well Inspector, I was delivering some beautiful trout to Madame Arnaud and she asked me to bring this to you without delay. I was delayed however, but it is here now.'

'You have read it?'

'Inspector, I am a poacher, you know that. I have been to your prison, you know that too, but I have not sunk so low in the scheme of things to read other's correspondence.'

'François, you do not speak like a poacher. Who were you before the war?'

'I was as you see, a man who enjoys living off the land.'

'The truth.'

'I was a school teacher in St Cyprien. But you know how, if you like a drink, they condemn you out of hand. It was most unjust.'

'What do you know of this matter? What happened to Colonel Arnaud?'

'Why, the Germans took him. I am sure he will be released.'

'Sure?'

'Well what would they want with such a man?'

'That is for me to know and you to keep quiet about. You understand?'

'I am in touch with certain people whom I come across in the woods from time to time. If you require me to pass the odd message, it is no problem.'

'Who have you been speaking to?'

'Speaking? I don't understand.'

'Why would I want a message passed?'

'Perhaps it is good to stay in touch with old friends. My mother often said you should always care about small cuts and old friends.'

'Damn it man. Speak plainly.'

François whispered, 'Plain can be dangerous. Just remember, if you need a message sent, François could perhaps be of service.'

'I don't know what you mean.'

'Of course you don't Inspector. My lips are sealed. May I go?'

'Yes, go. Next time don't break in, wait on the stairs.'

'Perhaps it would be unwise. May I use the back door?'

'Go.'

The door closed behind François and he made his way back to the forest where Cognac waited in the snow, sitting with the patience of a priest. He called her to heel and joined the path, then cut to his right, making for his house. He would have to be cautious. He did not trust the inspector even if Arnaud did. Anyone who could collaborate with the SD had to be a traitor. Even if the Colonel thought he was turning him around, the inspector, to François' mind, had such a long list of crimes behind him to make his future trial a long one. Such men in François' opinion should be shot when the war ended, if there was any justice to be relied upon.

It took an hour to reach the belt of forest behind his house. He checked in the snow around the building with care. There were no footprints and it reassured him. Using a key, hidden behind an old paint pot, he let himself in. The place was undisturbed.

He wondered at that. Even if Arnaud was still holding out, he could expect the SD to arrive at any time, as soon as the old Colonel broke. At least no one had come since the three of them had left the day before yesterday. He wondered if he dared risk going into town but he decided against it. If there were even a suspicion, the SD would pick him up. No, better to sit quiet for a day or two and await events. If the SD came, Cognac would warn him and he could be away into the forest before they even knew he had been there.

François entered his outhouse. He cut a slab of meat from the remains of a deer's carcass and began cooking it on his stove. He had delivered the message but he wondered why he promised to take messages now for Ran. It occurred to him it might have been something to do with the little Jewish girl he knew must be hiding in Ran's house. He was clearly becoming "maudlin", as Shirley would have said.

He poured himself a tin cupful of good, red Bergerac as he waited for the venison to fry. Sipping the wine, he realised he had not thought of Jean-Paul for some time. Was it always like this? The pain remaining absent as long as he was distracted? Yes, he knew the pain was the same but less frequent. If the lad were here now, what would he say of his father? Had François become both soft and unfaithful to the memory of his son?

He tipped a little wine into his frying pan and watched as it bubbled. The venison had a texture of rubber but François ate it anyway and then picked his teeth with a wooden toothpick he always carried. After two more cups of wine, he felt sleepy and he locked up, preferring the safety of the shed, where the hatch at the back would allow him an escape route, if anyone came. Dusk descended and with grudging sluggishness, sleep came. The last sound he heard was Cognac at the end of her tether, sniffing around his door, but he held no inclination to admit her. She was a working dog in his opinion, not a damned pet as Rachelle seemed to think. Damn these girls.

Chapter 14

They are at table
They eat not
Nor touch their plates
And their plates stand straight up
Behind their heads
– from *Paroles* by Jacque Prevert

1

François felt close to despair. He sat in the shed clutching a bottle of Bergerac, taking sips now and again. Wiping his mouth on his sleeve, he leaned his back against the rough wooden wall behind, trying hard to figure his next move. The light was fading and the patch of sky showing through the grubby window of the shed became red and purple as the sun set. Two days passed yet he was no nearer to any of his goals.

The first day, he hunted in the snow. He took two rabbits at the edge of the forest but saw no geese. He felt lucky since the scarcity of game in the winter often made his forays unsuccessful.

On the second day he reconsidered his caution and ventured into town, only to find no one was after him, but all the same he seemed no closer to finding work on the railroad for Shirley and he gleaned no intelligence worth reporting to his partisan friends. He scratched his armpit and wondered how he would be able to help get the resistance movement started, but no ideas came to mind. Frustration loomed and he felt a rising dissatisfaction with himself. He continued to drink and ponder the short foray into town in the afternoon, which had been so unproductive.

He had first gone to the shoe shop. Wandering up the alleyway, he found it closed down. Police barriers stood across the doorway and it seemed clear no one had been there for a long time, perhaps since the shooting. He wondered then whether Lucille had become a casualty of the resistance, some kind of collateral damage to which he would need to adjust in the longer term. If she was hiding at her nephew's house the SD might still trace her, and she would expose him, he was certain. But it occurred to him he had no knowledge of a longer term. He was already risking his life by the simple act of being there. Perhaps his long term would be very short. He stood looking in through the window, but what he expected to see apart from the empty shelves, puzzled him. It gave him no satisfaction to think Lucille might even now be languishing in the Mairie, broken and beaten, and all because of him and his wish for revenge. It made him wonder whether all the resistance acts would have consequences and attract reprisals. He reassured himself that, as Stalin once said, one has to break eggs to make an omelette. The Germans would take reprisals for everything acted out against them, but he knew there was no other way. To resist meant the partisans had to be strong: they could not cave in and give themselves up for a shopkeeper, a farmer or a baker. No, he would keep his nerve and he recognised he needed to work harder to establish Shirley as a normal citizen of the town, so between them they could glean enough information to pass on to the partisans.

Drinking wine in the gloaming became soporific and unproductive and in the end, he decided to sleep again. His eyes closed as he lay on his striped mattress, behind the fastened wooden door. He trusted Cognac to keep watch for him, chained to the post outside the door as she was; she would keep him safe.

He became aware he had slept several hours, when he heard the dog bark. He heard a vehicle pull up outside the house. He prepared to exit his shed through the hatchway in the back-wall. Then he paused. A car door slammed outside. A single car. SD travelled in numbers and it seemed to him it was too soon to bolt. François used all his woodcraft as he slipped, silent and unseen, in the dark at the side of the house. His shotgun was loaded and he knew how to use it.

A man stood at the front door; he wore a warm, long, wool coat and a flat police hat. François recognised him but remained where he was, uncertain whether to step into the faint light emanating from the streetlamp fifty yards down the street. He watched.

Auguste Ran, for it was he, stood uncertain since there was no answer to his knocking. François sidled to his right keeping in the shadows, his footsteps muffled by the snow.

He cocked his shotgun.

Turning, Ran said, 'François?'

Silence. François waited.

'François? Is it you?'

François, a shadowy figure, stepped into the faint light and relief spread across Ran's features as he recognised who it was.

François said, 'What do you want? You're alone?'

'Yes. I need some help.'

'Help? What can a man like me do to help the police?'

'I need you to pass a message to the partisans.'

'You are sure no one followed you?'

'In the fog? I would have seen the lights.'

'Perhaps if I was following I would not have betrayed my-self by putting on headlights.'

'We don't need to play this game. I need something from you, that is all,' Ran said.

'And you come here? You are incriminating me.'

'No one followed, I am sure.'

François grunted then turned, breaking his shotgun and heading towards the back of the house.

Ran followed around the side of the house. He swore as he stepped on a pile of dog excrement and François smothered a laugh. The Inspector wiped his boot on the snowy grass and followed to the shed. Cognac, chained to her post outside, snarled at Ran and he took a small detour to avoid her quivering snout. François called to her and she sat, head cocked to one side, eyeing the policeman as if he was some kind of unusual fish. François almost said she had wonderful taste in people, but he resisted the temptation and opened the door.

He lit his oil lamp where it swung from a string looped onto a hook on the ceiling. François thought it illuminated the place well enough. Ran wrinkled his nose as if the damp smell offended his sensibilities, but François noticed nothing, he was used to it. He realised it was obvious he lived here and not in the house. He wondered if that knowledge was something for which it was worth killing the policeman. If Ran told the SD, they could surround the place and be in the forest before even Cognac reacted to their presence at the front door. It would be easy to trap him then. In a split second, the thought disappeared. He knew Arnaud trusted this man and it was enough. Despite his underlying suspicion of the Colonel's competence as a spy, he still respected his judgment of men. Too much water had passed under that bridge for him to abandon his loyalty to his wartime hero.

Ran said, 'You sleep here?'

'Yes, it is safer. My dog warns me if anyone comes to the house. The SD are not after me as far as I know, but things can change anytime.'

François looked at Ran and smiled. He said, 'No one is immune from arrest, even you. And they all talk in the end.'

'You need have no fear of that. I know nothing. It is safer for everyone concerned.'

'Yes, times have changed. Now we communicate less, because we know the more we share, the greater the danger. Once the opposite was true, is it not so?'

'Yes.'

'What message?'

François stood close to the Inspector. The man wrinkled his nose and stepped back. It was as if the odour of the older man was enough to make men flee. It amused François. It was his disguise, his alter ego and he was proud of it.

'I have a list of five names. These men must be taken out and hidden.'

'Traitors?'

'No. Local farmers, men with families. If they remain, the SD will hang them as a reprisal for Linz, the SS officer the Maquis killed.'

François had no knowledge of a dead SS officer, but he remained impassive. He was determined to give nothing away to this man. He said, 'They will only pick five more.'

'I have a plan. I can't tell you what it is. The less you know...'

'Very well. I'll take your message, but if there is an answer, how do I deliver it?'

'Just stand in the market square and sell your goods. I will send a man to arrest you.'

'What?'

'If we arrest you it will look like your usual spell in the cells. Oh, by the way, if you are in my office, you cannot speak freely. They are listening.'

'Even you?'

'Brunner.'

'Maybe old Arnaud talked.'

'No it was before they arrested him. Besides, I think he died before they learned anything. I think Brunner was worried in case I could prove he murdered a girl in our town.'

'Who?'

'Never mind.'

'If the SD come tonight, I will know you have set me up.'

'I was with them once, but I have realised who they are. They are messengers from Hell. I serve only France. I needed to see it that was all.'

'Then long live that. I will have to go now if I am to deliver your message. If I'm successful I will be in the market square.'

'Good luck.'

François waited until he heard the sound of the car's engine fading into the night. It was late and he felt doubtful whether he could find the partisans in the darkness. Even if he did he would have to be careful, or they might shoot first and worry about the identity of their target later.

He whistled to Cognac and released her from her tether. Gathering his belongings, he set off into the dark.

So the old soldier was dead. To François it was the end of another chapter in his life. Arlette, Jean-Paul, Alma and the rest, the pages turned and he could never read them again. He would not miss Arnaud; the man was never part of his daily life, but Arnaud had grown in his consciousness like a legend or a myth and become larger than life. His maid and lover betrayed him. François thought she might be his next target, but he put that thought away for the moment, there seemed to be more important things to do now. He wondered how the old soldier had died. Had they tortured him? Ran seemed to think he died before he talked but such luck seemed too much to expect. Suicide perhaps? No, weakness of that kind was never part of the old Colonel's life and François knew it. It was a puzzle.

Yet, although Arnaud's death was news to him, it was also in some senses the lifting of a burden. If Ran told the truth, then there was a good chance the SD were not after him. He might be free to move, to gather information, and perhaps with the right opportunity, to act. He recognised a feeling of relief mixed with optimism. It was as if he looked forward to the chance of fighting back against the invaders. The thought he would be doing it with a German rifle brought a smile to his lips. Turning their own weapons against them, would be amusing. He pictured Meyer's face as the man looked up towards him. The German could not have seen him and François wondered whether there was some kind of divine intervention at play, but he dismissed the thought as soon as it came to mind. He had rejected God and all the trappings of the church. He was not Job. He was François Dufy, sniper, hunter and dare he think it? A partisan.

2

It was late at night by the time he reached the partisan camp. The temperatures had risen and the melting snow left damp, muddy paths and areas of dirty white beside them. The moon was full and François saw the lookout before the man spotted him. He called out in a soft voice, cautious lest the man reacted by loosing wild shots at him.

It was Amos. Hearing the sound of François' voice, he hit the ground and his rifle barrel glinted in a dull reflection of the moonlight.

'It's me,' François said. 'François Dufy.'

'Advance.'

'Amos, you fool, would the Germans call you? Don't shoot. I'm alone and I have news.'

François stepped from behind the protection of the pine where he hid. He held his hands up, shotgun and rifle slung over his shoulder.

'You startled me,' Amos said.

'If you were startled you weren't doing your job. You should have seen me long before you heard me. Amateurs.'

'What are you then? A professional?'

'I am a schoolteacher. If a schoolteacher can sneak up on you in full moonlight, what do you think the German SS could do? You need to sharpen up; you know it.' He grinned, and said, 'Take me to your leader.'

'Very bloody funny, you old poacher.'

They both smiled and François entered the camp unmolested. Amos followed behind.

154

'Amos. If I were a traitor, would not the Germans be behind me? Yet you follow me as if there was no further threat. My arrival has not removed all the Germans in the Dordogne Valley has it?'

The boy looked uncertain. He stopped in his tracks, then he smiled and said, 'You know, one day if you irritate me enough, I might shoot you.'

'Then none of this will matter to me. We are better directing our bullets towards the Germans though. Where is Jules? I have news for him.'

'Over there,' he said and indicated a tent at the north end of the tiny encampment.

'Very well, you go back to your watch and for the love of St Michael, keep your eyes open.'

François heard Amos muttering to himself as he walked away and left François wondering whether his news was urgent enough to wake Jules. In the end, he decided the boy had nothing better to do than act upon the information he was bringing, so he knocked on the tent pole with the butt of his shotgun.

'Merde.'

'It's only me,' François said.

Jules was the first to appear. He emerged braving the cold, wearing a vest and trousers pulling the braces onto his shoulders as he stood up. Behind him, François could hear Josephine scrabbling in the dark, no doubt searching for clothes.

'What on earth are you doing here in the middle of the night?'

'I have a message and it won't wait. You want to fight the Germans, well here's your chance.'

'We've been busy doing just that old man.'

'Linz?'

'You've heard?

'I heard a man called Linz, an SS officer, was killed. Was that your group?'

'Of course it was, who else? We are the only ones here.'

'Inspector Ran came to see me.'

'Oh? I thought…'

'He needs some farmers and others to be removed.'

'Killed?'

'No, he says they are on the German's list for reprisals, because of what you did. They need to be hidden.'

'Hidden? Here?'

'Look, I don't give a fuck where you hide them, you can stick them in the tent with you and Josephine for all I care, but they need to be hidden. I told him the Germans would just select another five but he seemed certain he could prevent it. We need to act now, or as soon as possible at any rate. I take this man seriously because Arnaud trusted him, I don't know why.'

'Arnaud told you?'

'You saw the note.'

Jules said, 'Oh, yes. Arnaud was a fool. He should never have exposed himself in the way he did.'

'Exposed?'

'Well he must have done something.'

'He had a spy in his home. She betrayed him.'

'His wife betrayed him?'

'No of course not. It was a maid they employed. She was working for the Germans. Look. I'm just delivering messages. Do what you want, but my advice is…'

Jules said, 'Advice? You think we would take advice from you again?'

'You are very stubborn sometimes. Do you really think if I

was a collaborator I would be here once more, and the Germans would not be behind? Think man. Ran may be a boon. We can use him. He must have plenty of information and if he is softening, we can use him and his knowledge of the German forces. Think.'

Jules remained silent.

Josephine stuck her head out of the tent. 'It's you,' she said.

'Where is Rachelle?' François said.

'Over there.'

Josephine pointed to another tent.

'She'll be asleep. Don't wake her.'

'And Pierre?

'Who knows? I'm not his keeper. Why have you come back?'

'I need to talk to Shirley.'

'She's with Rachelle.'

François said, 'You killed that SS officer?'

'Jules did. I was keeping watch. Why?'

'The Germans will seek reprisals and everything will be locked down. Ran asked me to pass a message hoping you and Jules would cooperate.'

'So? You'd better go and do it.'

'He wanted an answer. You will do as he asked?'

'What does he want us to do?'

'Jules knows. I'm not telling it all over again.'

'François,' it was Pierre.

François turned and he was surprised at the relief he felt seeing the Jew.

'I spoke to your friend Ran.'

'There is news?'

'Ask Jules. In the morning, I will go back. I have things to do. Have you any food?'

'Food? Yes a little. The farm is still shut up. They must have got the farmer.'

'We need to make some plans here,' François said.

'If you think we are sharing our plans with…' Josephine said.

'Look,' François said, 'if you want to become successful at this and to stay alive, we all need to trust each other and be able to rely on each other, particularly if it comes to a fight.'

Pierre said, 'I trust you François. I know why you fight; the others, I think, don't understand.'

François remained silent then. In his mind, a question arose. He too wondered why he was involving himself. For a moment, he almost said it was for France, for his country. Like in the First War. The words were on the tip of his tongue but a sudden doubt struck him, a revelation.

Pierre looked at him. He frowned. 'What?'

'If you know why I am in this fight, then you know more than I do. I hate the Nazis, yes. But that is not it.'

'I know this.'

'Oh, you do?'

Josephine said, 'What are you two babbling about? I thought you were going, Dufy.'

'No. Not yet. I will sit by the fire for a while; it was a long trudge through the snow. I will eat and wait for Shirley to awaken. You won't mind?'

'Do what you wish. You talk about trust. Do you trust us?'

'I do, but if I am being truthful I wonder about your ability to do this kind of work. I should tell you Arnaud, for all his appearance of bumbling, was a fine soldier. When I was under his command, he ordered me to work as a sniper and take out German officers. I did that many times and what was worse, I always believed I was right. Now I'm not so sure.'

'Don't worry about us. We are fighting for our lives. We know the right of it.'

'Then we all have a common goal,' Pierre said handing François a small package.

François turned and found a place by the dying embers of the campfire. He unpacked some smoked sausage and bread from the package and began to munch, deep in thought.

'May I sit?'

It was Pierre.

'Of course, it's your camp,' François said indicating a seat at his side.

'You mustn't judge them too harshly. They are good people.'

'I have never doubted it. I just think they need to learn their trade and they take advice badly.'

'It will come with experience.'

'When you said you knew why I was fighting, what did you mean?'

'Isn't it obvious?'

'No.'

'You have deep feelings for Rachelle. It is clear.'

'She calls me Uncle. It is a friendship.'

'I fight because of my daughter. I want her to grow up in a world where she will be free. I think you fight to keep Rachelle free. Perhaps you feel more than you recognise for this girl.'

'Of course not. I have a responsibility to her, I found her when her parents were taken. Someone has to look out for her.'

'What about the Rosbif woman?'

'What about her?'

'I see the way you look at her.'

'She's just a young woman. I am almost an old man. Can you not let an old one have his fantasies? If I was ten years younger perhaps things would be different, but it is not so.'

'No, but this is thin ice on which you skate. You may get wet.'

'No, not me. I am light of foot and carry no baggage.'

'Sometimes we carry more than we know or care to admit. I bid you goodnight. There are still some hours before dawn.'

Pierre left François by the fire. The dull red glow through the grey ashes shed a faint light on François' boots. He turned up the collar of his coat and drew it around his neck staring into the remains of the blaze. To him, the fire was like his life, once bright and cheerful and now reduced to greying embers. Perhaps Rachelle coming into his life kindled a flame for a while, but how could that remain lit? François understood then, though perhaps he had known it all along, that Pierre was right. It was Rachelle and his feelings for her driving him on to fight and protect her.

He glanced over his shoulder and realised he was alone, Jules and Josephine having gone back to bed, and although he could hear Amos skulking across the far side of the encampment, he felt isolated. He chewed the bread in his hand. No, he had finished with love. Enough of those deep painful feelings. Jean-Paul was dead and he had taken all that remained of François' love with him to the grave. He shrugged. What did any of this - what did Shirley call it? - "maudlin" thinking? - achieve? No he admitted to himself no feelings for anyone, only a kind of deep numbing pain, but a pain so strong it would sustain him through this war and his chance to avenge himself on the killers of his only son.

François lay down and patted his canvas bag into a semblance of a cushion for his head and his eyes closed. He thought of Shirley and the way she smiled at him when he spoke English, the way she brushed her hair. He shook his head. These were not good thoughts. What was happening to him? Was it Alma all over again?

3

A foot prodding at his shoulder awakened him. It made him jump at first. He looked up. It was Shirley.

'Good morning Mon Ami.'

He looked up, bleary-eyed and sleep-enmeshed.

'François. It's me,' she said.

He smiled. It was involuntary and related to his dream but the reality of it produced a kind of embarrassment.

'Shirley?'

'Yes, it's me.'

He sat and looked up at her. The pre-dawn light brought its mystery of faintness and softening and it made her seem like an angel to François' tired eyes. He struggled to his feet.

'How... how are you?'

'Well I'm fine, just frustrated to be so inactive.'

'No. I mean, how are you? They have treated you well?'

'Of course. I just meant...'

Another female voice interrupted her.

'Uncle. Uncle, you came back.'

Rachelle ran to him. Her youth and her eagerness overcame his usual formality. He took her in his arms and the pleasure of that greeting surprised him but brought out a kind of embarrassment. He did not want his feelings on show any more than he wanted to acknowledge them himself, but the strength of the emotion took over and he responded, patting her with a gentle hand on her back in that familiar gesture to which he had become accustomed.

She drew back a little.

'Uncle, I was so afraid they might have got you.'

'Me? No. I don't even think they are looking for me. The police told me Arnaud died before they could get any information from him. And you? You are well?'

'Yes Uncle. Shirley is showing me how to be a partisan, a Maquis.'

François frowned. He looked at Shirley but she shrugged and turned away.

'Lorna Doone,' he said.

'Yes?'

'I have much to tell you, though I spoke to Jules last night.'

He recounted his news to the two women.

'So you trust this man. Inspector Ran?'

'Well, he's taken in Pierre's daughter and is hiding her. He has as much to lose as any of us. Besides, Arnaud...'

'Yes, so you said, he trusted him.'

Rachelle said, 'What will you do now Shirley?'

'As long as François is free and the Germans don't know about me, I'll be free to move. I've been in touch with London.'

'London?' François said.

'Yes, I have orders to get close to a man called Schultz.'

'He's SD. They are not nice people to get close to.'

'I know what I'm doing, but I will need you nearby so I can communicate. Will you find out a little more about him and his habits? Does he drink? Does he womanise? Where does he go when he is on his own? That kind of thing. I can't

162

follow him myself, but maybe you can, if Ran was correct.'

François held her gaze for a moment he felt an uncomfortable irritation. He did not understand why. He said, 'Surely you want to get to know Brunner. He's in charge, after all?'

'No. London was specific. This man Schultz is known to them and they advised me to stay away from Brunner, I don't know why. They also want a job doing, which would make Brunner useless to them for information. Didn't Jules and Josephine say anything last night?'

'No. What are you talking about?'

'They need Brunner out of the picture. They think Schultz will be promoted if he is gone. If Schultz gets friendly with me before Brunner is out of the way, then it makes me more plausible.'

'They seem to know a lot these SOE people.'

'It's their job. Maybe they know who you are too.'

'I'm flattered but I think all anyone knows is that I'm the town drunk.'

'You'll do it? Follow Schultz and remove Brunner?'

'Kill Brunner?'

'Yes.'

'What about the little group of children here in the woods? Will they pick flowers while I take all the risks?'

'No. I will keep them busy. One load of explosives was saved and it is possible to steal dynamite from the quarry according to Pierre.'

'What about Rachelle? I don't want her taking any risks.'

'Uncle, I am free to do as I wish. I want to fight and help the Maquis. Amos will look after me—he said so.'

'Amos? What does he know? He's only a boy with as much craft as a child in a nursery.'

'He's nice. Besides he does know what he's doing and he

said he would watch my back.'

'Yes, while you undress I suppose. Look Rachelle, don't get too involved with these people, you are young and any of them might die anyway.'

'You're not my father. It's up to me.'

François looked skywards and clicked his tongue. After all he had done for the girl, she was fighting him. It was Jean-Paul all over again.

'Look, you've managed to stay alive so far. If the Germans catch you, they will shoot you. You are too young for all this.'

'Yes, Uncle and you are too old. Maybe we should both go back to Bergerac and shut ourselves up in your house until the partisans have won the war for us. Then we can emerge into the new free world and count the corpses of the Frenchmen who died to save us.'

'That's not what I mean and you know it.'

'I'm staying. They said I could stay and if they need my help, I will give it. I can shoot and I know how to lay a mine. I am sixteen but you treat me like a child.'

She stormed away to her tent and François had no inclination to follow. He looked up at Shirley. The appeal in his eyes made no impression.

'She is right you know,' Shirley said.

'About what? A sixteen-year-old girl facing death with a group of incompetents?'

'They are not incompetent. They are going to blow up trains, ambush troops, and do what they can to hamper the German war-effort in France. If it's any consolation, I've already talked to Jules and Josephine. They've promised to keep Rachelle as safe as they can.'

'It's not much. I don't want to mourn her. I've invested a great deal of time and effort in keeping her alive.'

164

'So she's just an investment of time to you?'

Her eyes smiled as she spoke and he understood the barb.

'Maybe you're right, what do I care?'

Inside, he felt he was betraying Rachelle with those words, and a subtle guilt feeling took him. He turned and gathered his bag, slinging it over his shoulder.

'I'll need more ammunition for the Mauser.'

'I'll get you some. They took plenty from the soldiers when they killed Linz. Reprisals?'

'Yes, of course. The ever necessary price we pay for the work we do.'

'You'll do as I ask? About Schultz, I mean.'

François turned and walked towards her. He placed his hands on her bony shoulders.

'Lorna Doone, do you know what you are doing? You would give yourself to such a man?'

'I didn't say that. It will be enough just to lead him on a bit.'

They walked to Shirley's tent and she stooped, entering. Emerging moments later, she handed François a leather pouch. 'Bullets,' she said.

He smiled and walked away past Amos, into the wood. He whistled as he walked. His mind whirled with emotion. Rachelle. Had she a death wish? He realised he was angry but he recognised the same powerlessness as when Jean-Paul had gone to war. What could he do about it? She was not even his daughter, yet he felt responsible for her.

And Shirley. He wondered why her role in the cause ran-kled so much. He had no rights over her and even less right to disapprove of the plans sent by London. So, he had to help her. Help her in what way? Aid and abet her in socialising with SD officers? He hated that. Given the chance, he would have shot the lot of them.

An oystercatcher called, off to his left, and he could smell the pines surrounding him. The forest waking around him on the winter's morning forced him into the present. He looked up at the sky and its blue, hidden now and again by white cloud, raised his spirits. He might end by joining his son and his wife, but for now he was alive and it felt good.

Chapter 15

And all the Guardia Civile capering around a stretcher,
Where a dead gypsy still dreams.
– from *Paroles* by Jacque Prevert

1

A hazy moon shed a faint light onto the cobbled street outside the Bon Auberge restaurant. The night was still and the snow, fallen the night before, thawed in patches, leaving areas of ice and slush. François loitered. He hated the idea of being obvious but no alternative suggested itself, so he stood outside the restaurant late that night, watching the customers entering and leaving. Schultz entered the place around eight o'clock and he remained inside; at least François had not seen the SD officer leave. No one spared the old man a glance. He was careful to appear drunk, clutching a half-empty bottle of eau-de-vie, and when anyone looked, he stumbled or swayed and the diagnosis should have been obvious to anyone.

He was not a happy man. He spent the previous day in the police cells after his arrest by some of the Vichy-French police. He smiled as he recalled how he engineered it. He stood with his barrow close to the prefecture, selling trout. Every time he shouted, he drew laughter and in the end, a crowd formed. They laughed too at his antics as he called at the top of his voice, 'Buy some nice trout. Not as fat as Gőring. Fat trout, but not as fat as Gőring.'

It took only half-an-hour before the police came and carted him away. Even they smiled when they arrested him. One of them, a man called Roland, explained he was sorry to arrest François and he sympathised with his feelings, but it was as much for his own safety as it was for the breach of the peace. François smiled in return and in the back of his mind, he noted the man's name. He might become a sympathiser if he could put him under the right pressure.

It was late in the afternoon when they released him. They took him up to Ran's office first. He was tempted to speak but the Inspector put his fingers to his lips and François recalled how Ran told him about listening devices in the office. The greatest surprise came when Ran stood and shouted. He smacked his fist into his open palm and pretended to have hit François. Next, Ran grabbed him by the elbow and dragged him down the stairs. He realised the policeman was drunk.

The Inspector wanted him to arrange a meeting with Pierre. François gave it low priority because at first he thought the man was mad. The risk for Pierre seemed enormous. There was also the distinct possibility it would be a trap. He took the message anyway, but unaware of the outcome, he continued with his wanderings, following Schultz, noting Brunner's movements, and freezing in the cold. He felt threatened, hunted. He still suspected Arnaud could have talked and the SD might be playing a game with him. He checked to see if they followed him whenever he went into town, but never saw signs of anyone dogging his steps.

François wished he had a pistol. He felt uncomfortable to be out in the open anyway and the thought nagged him throughout the days. On one afternoon, three green-clad SS soldiers followed him and he noticed he sweated despite the cold and his heart drummed against his ribs as if his arrest might be imminent. He stopped to look into a shop window and although they passed him by, his anxiety showed no signs of abating. He looked over his shoulder as they walked past and he wished he were holding his rifle. He analysed whether he could have killed all three without them returning a shot but he knew it was all a foolish daydream and he put the thought out of mind.

The partisans insisted he should kill Brunner and he decided he would, but it would take time. He understood the risks. On his own, he would stand a better chance than if he were part of a group. He remembered Meyer and it encouraged him. Tonight however, he followed Schultz.

The German, a tall, thin serious-looking man seemed to go out often, eating and drinking with other officers. This time however, François followed him to a restaurant with a small bar and a scratched-out sign advertising live singing. It was cold enough for him to wear two pairs of gloves as he waited in a doorway opposite the restaurant. He felt like a man whose wife was in a shop and he elects to stay outside, but regrets the choice, even though he knows, he would hate the alternative and feels he cannot change his mind.

Within an hour, he observed Brunner, the SD Major, the man in over-all charge of the local SD entering the eatery. François wondered which one he should follow when they came out. He had never seen Schultz out of control; the man seemed humourless to François and never expressed a human side when he was out in the town.

François removed his gloves, placing them in his armpit. He took out his pipe and tobacco. He placed the pipe in his mouth and reached into his pouch. Drawing out a leaf of the flake, he rubbed it between his thumb and fingers. He loaded his pipe as if it was a gun, deliberate and carefully. Packed just right, he perched it between his teeth and lit a match. Puffing on the pipe, he felt warmer, as if the red glow of the contents made a difference to the numbing chill surrounding him.

He coughed. The cold became oppressive. A picture came into his mind. It was of his mother, scrubbing the front step of the house in which he grew up. He smiled to himself as he witnessed again, her generous posterior wagging as she wielded the scrubbing-brush. Her flowery dress and the scarf on her head brought a feeling of nostalgia. She turned and looked over her shoulder at him. He recalled her face, round and ruddy, the smile on her lips and her pleasant chuckle. He had loved his mother so much and the bitterness he felt when she went, struck him anew almost as if it was a recent event. It created a feeling of longing within him, a wish to be back in those 'old days' when there was nothing to cause worry; a time when he could rely upon others like his parents to shoulder his burdens, taking the pain and the weight of life away.

The Two SD officers emerging from the restaurant brought him back to reality. They left together then split up and he still wondered whether he should follow Schultz or Brunner. An idea came to mind however, and so he remained stock-still in the doorway. He recognised he had something to do here, besides following the Nazis.

François glanced at his watch. He knew he was getting drunk. The alcohol was not warming him either. The watch was his father's and given more time, might have awakened more nostalgia but as it happened, the owner of the restaurant emerged and began drawing down the shutters. When the chore was almost complete, François crossed the street. He cleared his throat.

The owner startled at the sound behind him. He was a short stocky man wearing a greying apron. His bald, shiny head betrayed moisture at the exertion of pulling down the roller-shutter and he seemed a little unsteady on his feet, perhaps drunk François thought.

The restaurateur said, 'Who are you?'

'Ah, pardon me. I saw you closing up and wondered whether you might have a job?'

'A job?'

'Oh, no. Not for me. For my niece. Her parents died in the bombings in Paris and she came here to find me. It is a very sad business. She needs work. I can't support her you see. I just wondered whether you have a job available. I'm sure she would do any kind of work.'

'Who are you?'

'Me? I'm François Dufy. I sell things. Mainly game, you know, rabbits and venison and geese in the winter. Fish too. I could supply you if you want. I just wondered…'

'I've seen you in the market. You drink too much my friend. Didn't Ran's men arrest you the other day? Made me laugh.'

'Well, I like a drink.'

'I was tempted to say I like a man who likes a drink but your personal hygiene is…is…'

François smiled and he put his bottle, still half-empty, into his pocket.

'Don't suppose you have any decent wine?'

'We're just closing. Sorry.'

'Come on, I fought in the last war. I would still fight if I wasn't an old one. You would turn away an old soldier, injured for France?'

'Hmf. Perhaps for an old soldier then. You've heard about

the old Colonel?'

'Yes. He was my commander in the war. A terrible thing.
You know something about it?'

'Come, I will tell you what I've heard. Dufy? Is that an
Irish name?'

The restaurateur, who moved like an inebriate, indicated
the door and both men entered. François wondered why the
man was so compliant, but he could smell success here as well
as alcohol and he entertained no notion he would fail. He
thought Shirley would be on the first rung of her ladder. He
felt like a man holding it with trembling hands looking up,
expecting her to fall. The realisation he felt something for her
came into his mind and he tried to shrug it off. He was endangering her and he knew it.

2

The restaurant, empty now, could seat forty at the small rickety tables. Chequered tablecloths showing spills and stains
adorned the table tops, and each table bore a bottle with a
candle perched in the top. The restaurateur blew out several of
the flickering flames and indicated for François to sit.

'I'm Bernard,' the restaurant owner said, stretching out a
moist, sweaty hand.

François took it and looked around the restaurant as he
shook hands. They were alone.

'Nice place you have here.'

'Yes, but before the war it was better. I used to make money. Now? The Germans use it as a source of free food and en-
tertainment. Well, only food now. My singer was murdered.
She was a beautiful girl, voice like an angel. Inspector Ran is

investigating, but you know the Vichy police, not much good unless they're arresting Jews or homosexuals.'

'Homosexuals?'

'Yes. They don't even have to be real criminals and they cart them off to Drancy.'

'Is that where they take them? Even the Jews?'

'Yes. I don't know what the country is coming to. Damned, damned Germans.'

Bernard looked over his shoulder as he spoke, as if someone would be there to write down his comments and charge him with them later. His face changed, like a man sobering up after a long night's drinking.

'You could be a spy for all I know. You won't tell anyone what I said?'

François laughed. 'Me? A spy? I might spy for France but those days have long since gone. No, my friend, I am just a poacher. You can give my poor niece a job?'

Bernard stood and padded round to the back of the little bar. He produced a bottle of wine.

'Last one this. I've been protecting it from the Germans. They don't understand wine, you know. It's a living thing to be nurtured and cared for and when the day comes for it to be born in the glass it must be admired, praised, and appreciated. It is like a christening every time you open such a bottle as this. Not like these Germans. They drink it down like it was beer. It's an infamy.'

'Ah,' François said, 'you understand.'

'Understand?'

'Yes. It is a basic thing in life. Wine is life. It is a microcosm. Inside that red liquor, there are microscopic heroes, giving up their lives for us; yeasts expressing their fineness, their finesse.'

François hiccoughed then continued, 'We are honoured to share that with the little fungi. They should almost be worshipped for the pleasure they bring.'

He hiccoughed again, slurring his speech. He rambled on, 'Little at a time, not glassfuls swallowed like German beer. What has happened to France? I almost wish the little yeasts could rebel and jump up and choke the bastards.'

'For that fine speech, you will be rewarded by a wine so sumptuous you will never taste its like.'

'Here let me see.'

François read the label out loud, 'Chateau de Fieuzal, 1932. I don't know what to say. For years now, I've drunk cheap Bergerac until it is coming out of my ears. A good Graves like this makes me wish I could do something for you in return.'

'But you can. Did you not say you are a poacher?'

'It's true.'

'Then if you can get me haunches of venison, I will consider this a fair trade.'

'And the girl's job?'

'Can she sing?'

'But if she can't sing, she can wait at table, can't she?'

'Well I can't pay wages unless she is very good and anyway, I have a waitress.'

'She is a beautiful girl, and the kind of wages a waitress earns makes no difference to a man like you. Santé.'

François sipped his wine.

'If she is as beautiful as you say, perhaps she will attract custom. Send her along tomorrow.'

'Day after. She's gone to visit her aunt.'

'Well day after then. The wine?'

'It is like dying. One might reach one's destination and only realise one is in the right place when one smells an aroma like this. It is a triumph, formidable.'

'You talk like an academic. You aren't just a drunk are you?'

'And you are just a restaurant owner? We all have a background.'

'Yes. Arnaud and his wife were here once and he said something similar.'

François sniffed the glass. He placed it on the table and swirled it around. He sniffed again then drank.

'The old Colonel was a card, was he not?' Bernard said.

'Eh?'

'One for the women?' Bernard said.

'I don't know about that. I was his subordinate in the war. He was a great man.'

'Here's to him then. So sad.'

'You heard what happened to him?'

'Yes. Brunner was full of it. I heard him talking in his loud German accent.'

'He said?'

The restaurateur pulled his chair closer to the table and leaned forward. They had become conspirators.

'They arrested him for a spy. Of course, we all know it was nonsense but they took him to the Mairie. Apparently he died of a heart attack on the doorstep.'

'So they never tortured him? I'm glad about that; he was a good man. A Frenchman who believed in our country.'

'As we all do.'

'Then what would you do to help our country?'

'You sure you're not a spy?'

'Don't be silly. Do Nazi spies understand wine?'

'I would do anything for my country.'

'Someone may one day ask you to do something. If you speak truly, it will be no hardship.'

'Who are you?'

'Me? Just a poacher who believes in our country. I look for people who feel the same. One day…'

'I don't trust you.'

'That is an excellent start. May I have another glass?'

On the way home, François checked over his shoulder with a frequency convincing him he was becoming paranoid. He had found a job for Shirley and perhaps secured an ally. He did not entirely trust Bernard but in this strife, who could be trusted anyway? He sensed something in the man. It was a kind of patriotism he too felt and he was desperate to find others who shared his burden of anger. It was that very desire making him feel perhaps, this Bernard would be a useful contact.

Later, in his shed, as his head hit the pillow created by his boots and his coat, he had begun a journey from which there would be no turning back for Shirley or for him. He hoped she could sing too.

Chapter 16

Of a world dead on its feet,
Of a world condemned,
And already forgotten.
– from *Paroles* by Jacque Prevert

1

Pierre faced François, a frown expressing his feelings. They stood on the edge of the partisan camp. The partisans moved the camp often and this time they were close enough for François to find them within an hour of leaving his house. Rain filtered through the pines above them and François drew the upturned collar of his black woollen coat around his neck. He longed for the summer months when life was easier.

'I think it would be unwise,' he said.

Pierre said, 'He is sheltering my daughter. I owe him for that. Besides, we were friends all through our childhood. I can't ignore his request.'

'He is a strange man. I told you he was drunk when he released me. If he's so close to cracking up, he may be unreliable. Why don't you take Amos with you so you have some back-up?'

'No. Auguste may be on the wrong side, but I know he hates what the Germans are doing, now that he knows for certain. I do trust him.'

Rachelle interrupted them. She wore baggy brown trousers and a man's shirt. Her brown jacket and beret added to the appearance of untidiness. François wondered whether she looked like an effeminate man or a masculine woman.

'Uncle are you coming or not?'

François said, 'No my little friend. I have to talk with Shirley. I may have found her a job.'

'A job? She's leaving?'

'I don't know yet do I? Anyway, I'm too old to go chasing after trains. You will be careful?'

'Amos will look after me.'

'Amos. Amos. It is all you ever talk about now. Amos the fighter, Amos the lover I suppose.'

'What's wrong with you? Anyone would think you were jealous.'

François shrugged off his irritation and turned back to Pierre.

'Brunner will be a difficult target. He lives alone; there are no guards on the street, but the house itself is secure. The iron fence outside and the high wall at the back make it a difficult prospect. It will be impossible to shoot him at the Mairie too. The guards are all around there and the only good view is from the shoe shop and that avenue is closed since someone shot Meyer from there and the owner fled.'

'Think about it though, will you? London wanted him dead and Schultz milked, but they didn't say why. Surely they will just be replaced?'

'Maybe the Rosbifs have an agent in the SD who might get promoted. Who knows?'

Pierre patted the older man's shoulder.

'Good luck my friend. I'll go to meet Ran alone despite

what you think.'

François and Rachelle walked towards the tents. She entered one in front of him and he followed. He smiled when he saw Shirley. She sat on a wooden box brushing her hair. An uncomfortable feeling crept over him then. It was an emotion he recognised. There was a tension in his neck and his heart seemed to skip. For a moment, he found words elusive.

'François. You have news?'

A moment passed before he found his words. 'Yes. I may have found you a job.'

'That's a big step forward. Doing what?'

'Can you sing?'

'What?'

'Can you sing?'

Rachelle giggled next to him.

'You want me to be a singer? I can't sing a note. Tone deaf, my teachers used to say. Where is this singing job?'

'La Bonne Auberge. It's a well-known restaurant in the town. The owner might give you a job as a waitress if you can't sing. You may need to charm him though. I told him you are my niece and your parents died in Paris from bombing.'

'There were no bombs in Paris. Didn't you know?'

'Well Bernard doesn't know that then. He said nothing about it.'

'What's so special about this restaurant?'

'Both Schultz and Brunner go there regularly.'

'We seem to be getting somewhere at last. I will need to clean up.'

'I'll take you there if you like.'

'No, we can't be seen together. If he gives me a job I will need to contact you from time to time.'

'Yes, I'm going to supply him with venison. He seems a good man. A patriot.'

Leaving the tent, François noticed he was sweating. Seeing Shirley unnerved him, and he understood why. Try as he might, he could not shake off this feeling of excitement when he was with her. It was laughable for a man of his age, but he recognised it all the same. He needed to hide the feelings. She would be sure to laugh at him if he expressed his thoughts anyway. Best keep quiet. Best keep away from her, he thought.

His business concluded, there was no reason for him to stay and there was no one to say goodbye to either. He began to feel isolated as he left the camp. He was a part of them yet somehow also apart. It was not like a military unit. There seemed to be no hierarchy, no lead. Jules was in charge but at times, François felt Jules' hold on the others was slim. If it came to a real fight, he worried how they would cope. Did he care? He knew he did and he cared about Rachelle, caught in the middle with her dreams of revenge, so angry yet so very vulnerable.

2

The mute, icy street, as quiet as a dream, with its frosty cobbles and thawing snow, glistened silver in the moonlight. Not even a cat stirred and the only sound was an owl hooting somewhere far off in the gloom of the late evening. Flakes of snow descended, and with remarkable accuracy, as they always seemed to, a few found their way into the gap between François' neck and his collar. He shuddered. The house in which Brunner lived, stood away from the street and a tall iron fence with spikes protected it from intrusion. On the opposite side of the street a ten-foot wall prevented anyone from seeing into the SD Major's commandeered home. François knew however, there was a way. He had spent the better part of three days looking for a method to circumvent the wall and he knew now he could do it.

There was an open space beyond the wall where apple and other trees grew. The orchard belonged to the Church and it adjoined the churchyard. From one of those trees, he could get a good enough view into Brunner's house, he was certain. The rifle, fully loaded, hung beneath his black coat and he wore a beret pulled down over his eyes in an effort to make his face less recognisable if any passers-by were to notice him. To-night he would kill Brunner. Tonight was a night of dark revenge and he savoured the prospect.

It took only moments to climb the graveyard wall and find his way in the dark to the tree he had selected the day before. It was a tall elm, leaf-bereft but with a good thick growth of branches and he was certain he would not be up there long. It was not the nearest tree; he would have been too easy to spot in those. This tree, tall and strong, stood back from the road-way, an unwelcome visitor no doubt among the apple and plum trees around it. He smiled as he climbed and he questioned why the Church gardener left it to grow. He reflected that perhaps the man had not the heart to cut it down. François was like that himself sometimes. More than once he had sighted on a doe in the woods and let her run, rather than kill the creature if he did not need the meat.

He found a perch twenty feet up in the tree and sat down on a branch, which was horizontal enough to be comfortable. He took out a leather strap from his canvas bag and looped it around himself and the trunk. If he went to sleep, he would not fall. It might be a long night after all.

It would be a difficult shot from this tree. He would have to support the rifle freehand without anything to lean on. He knew he could do it. He had done it before. His mind went back to a day in the First War, when he perched in another tree, another place. The memory of that day was as fresh in his mind as if he was witnessing the event unfolding before him now. The difference was, this time he held no fear. It was funny. His nerves were calmed, his hands steady, despite his drinking. François wondered if it mattered to anyone whether the Germans caught him or not. Rachelle? Well, she would be happy with Amos no doubt, stupid dopey boy that he was. Shirley? No, she did not care for him the way he now recognised he cared for her. He even wanted her. When he went to sleep at night, he understood the meaning of the tumescence next to his thigh, stimulated by his thoughts about her. It had become a nightly event. Too old. Too close to the end of life, that was the problem. So, if no one else cared, why should he?

The sound of a car pulled him from his reverie. It parked at the left e..d of the wall and he could only hear it, not see it. He wondered whether it would drive on, when he noticed a man approaching Brunner's house. The man stood outside for a few minutes as if hesitating, then yanked the bell pull. François did not hear the jangling bell but he watched as Brunner came to the door. The man wore a dressing gown and slippers. The two talked for a few moments and after a slight delay as they decided who would ascend the stairs first, they both went in. François recognised the visitor. It was Inspector Ran.

Thoughts raced through his mind. It put him off his shot. Lowering the rifle, he thought about the scene he had watched enacted below. So, Ran visited Brunner at night. He could not be trusted. Perhaps he was working for the SD all along.

There was a solution however. If François could take them both out of the equation at the same time, he could eliminate a great deal of risk. He sighted through the metal sight of his weapon. He saw Ran from the back in the window. He could see Brunner too. They both stood still. He wondered whether one bullet would be enough to get them both. He smiled as he began to squeeze the trigger. He stopped.

Brunner stepped back. Ran had something in his hand and they seemed to talk, with Ran backing away and Brunner stepping forward. A few moments passed and François felt as if he was watching a stage play. The German struck Ran on the chin. He disappeared out of sight. Next Brunner disappeared too. Moments later, he heard the muffled sound of a gun firing. François realised he had been sitting stock-still, fascinated by what had happened. One of them had fired a shot. Perhaps there was now only one to kill.

He analysed the situation. If Brunner killed Ran then it suggested Ran was not the traitor he had thought. If Ran killed Brunner, François thought, he was still not a traitor. Minutes passed. In the end, François saw Ran emerge wearing a leather coat, with a bundle under his arm. He paused in the doorway and bent down. He came out of the house clutching a bottle; wine from the shape of it.

Ran drove away and François was about to climb down when he heard the siren. Four vehicles arrived. Three green military vehicles and one black Mercedes. He dared not move. If they saw him, the chase would be short. He sat still. He swore under his breath. If any of them looked his way, he felt they could not fail to see him. He felt so exposed in the tree; he drew himself towards the bole hoping to be as inconspicuous as possible.

François watched as soldiers slid from the vehicles. They

invaded the house. François thought it looked like a miniature version of what they had done to France but he could do nothing but hide now. He recognised his hatred for them. He knew also how hatred creates bitterness and he reasoned with himself how he did not hate the individuals, only their leaders, and a system which made them into the cruel invaders they had become.

Presently, two men staggered out carrying a black bag, which they loaded into one of the trucks. Soldiers patrolled up and down the street and still François dared not take the risk of being seen climbing down. He knew it was Brunner's body in the truck and François smiled to himself, knowing Ran had done his job for him. There was a certain satisfaction in that. He wondered what the Inspector would do now. He would have to run. If he ran, he would take his family and Pierre's daughter too.

It was several hours before he dared leave his perch. He waited until the soldiers seemed stationary and he did his best to climb down the opposite side of his arboreal refuge. He skittered across the graveyard reflecting how the night had been fruitful. More than that, Ran had eliminated his target for him. Even though Ran was a man in whom he had no trust, his actions had put him out of the picture too. And what was even better to François was he had not wasted a single shot.

Chapter 17

And he says to him,
'Good morning Uncle Grésillard,'
And then he wrings his neck,
And he ends up on the scaffold at Quimper,
After eating two dozen crépes,
And having smoked a cigarette.
– from *Paroles* by Jacque Prevert

1

François and Rachelle walked side by side in the forest. High above them, the sun shed its cold splintered rays through gaps in the grey clouds. It was a clear week since Pierre had left and they often talked about him, wondering how he fared with the Vichy-French policeman and their families. Pierre had fought with Josephine over that one before leaving. François heard all about it from Rachelle.

'I thought he was going to hit her.'

'And where was Jules?' François said.

'I don't know Uncle. They seem to do what Josephine says now. If you ask me, she's the real leader. She's the one who ordered this mission.'

'Yes. Maybe that is the safest thing. Jules is inexperienced and he doesn't take advice. Josephine is more malleable.'

'Amos would be a good leader too.'

'Amos? He's as wet behind the ears as my son would have been.'

François heard himself speak but as soon as the words emerged, he fell silent. It dragged it all up in his memory; how the boy argued with him and how he had said the same things about him as he said about Amos.

'Uncle?'

'What?'

'Why are you so nasty about Amos? He is a good Jewish boy and he is here out of the noblest motives.'

'You think avoiding hard work in a German camp is noble?'

'You told me they were death camps.'

'Well, yes. He is fighting for his life though not out of nobility, you know.'

'I don't care. I love him.'

'What?'

'I love him.'

'At your age love comes too easily. Try sharing some bad times with him and expecting him to give things up to feed you and your children and you'll soon see what love is.'

'Why do you always denigrate love?'

François said nothing.

'I love you too Uncle. You saved me and you risked your life in hiding me. I will never forget that. Let me have a life though. Amos is a good man.'

'He's a boy.'

'Yes, but he will become a man and I believe in him. He's Jewish too, like me.'

'You are too young to have such feelings. Life is long. You don't understand how long it is at your age.'

186

They became silent and trudged on, each isolated in their own thoughts. At the edge of the forest a steep bank descended before them and the railway line could be seen stretching for miles to left and right.

Jules, who followed close behind, almost bumped into them when they stopped. He carried the explosives. François had no first-hand experience of their use, but Shirley had taught the group well and Jules and Jacques were the 'experts' in the methods of setting explosives.

Jules said, 'Jacques, you get down there and set the charge. The rest of us will wait and cover you.'

'I'll go with him,' Rachelle said.

'No, stay here,' François said.

She grinned over her shoulder at him, her disobedience an obvious pleasure. She slid down the bank with Jacques and François watched as they began to dig a small pit under one of the sleepers. He observed them setting the explosives and the detonator. They rigged it so the pressure from the train's wheels would depress the tiny plunger. It needed only millimetres of movement. They scrambled up the bank.

A movement on the opposite side of the tracks caught François' eye and he looked up. At least twenty men moved towards them. The nearest threw themselves down and raised their rifles. They lined the embankment on the opposite side of the track. François unslung his weapon, lay down in the thicket, aimed and fired. The shot echoed as it rang out.

In an instant, there was chaos. Men shouting, rifles barking. All the time, François was looking for enemies aiming at Rachelle. He saw one man sighting his Mauser. A single shot and the German lay still. François placed the headshot below the brim of the helmet. It must have penetrated the face but it took off the helmet, leaving a grisly gap in the man's skull.

Rachelle was up, Jacques behind her. Shots crackled all around. On the crest of the bank, the young man flew forward as if he jumped from a trampoline. He lay still. Blood leaked from the front of his chest. With one glance, a mere second, François knew he was dead. Rachelle, hidden now behind the embankment, knelt at his side. Amos came away and joined her.

François shouted at him.

'He's dead, get back up here.'

Stunned for a moment, Amos seemed too shocked to move. François shouted again, never taking his eyes from the railway line and the soldiers. He was searching for another target. Some of the Germans crossed the line to his right. They were out-flanking. He fired a shot and slithered backwards down the slope to where Rachelle, tears in her eyes, sat next to the dead boy.

'They're coming round down there,' he said.

She did not react so he shouted up to the others.

'Pull back, they're circling round. We must go.'

'But Jacques? We can't just leave him?' Rachelle said.

'Come on. He's dead. No time.'

François grabbed her arm and pulled her away. The others, Jules, Amos and Philippe, backed away from the embankment, and after a few yards, they all turned. They ran. They ran tripping, sometimes falling. Their breath came in gasps, their chests heaved. The low branches snagged them. They were cut and bruised. A battered group of rag-tag failures, running for their lives. François looked at Rachelle. The tears streamed down her face. He let go of her arm. Holding onto her had been a reflex. He knew what she felt. It troubled him how he felt so little himself, but he knew also they would be lucky to escape. The Germans must be in pursuit. They might have dogs.

A mile further on, they stopped to catch their breath.

'One of us must stay to delay them and allow the others to escape.' François said. 'Any volunteers?' He smiled then. 'I thought not. I'll stay. I'll find a place where I can see them and meet you all back at one of the rendezvous we arranged. You know what to do.'

'Who put you in charge?' Jules said.

'No one. I'm not in charge. Do you think you can do a better job at delaying them? Are you such a good shot?'

'Uncle, I won't leave you.'

'Rachelle, I will be fine. You must run. Go now. No arguments.'

He took her arm again and pushed her towards Amos. 'Protect her,' he said. 'I'm sorry for your loss but you must run now. You must use your wits.'

The partisans exchanged glances and then as one, they turned and ran. François followed them at a walk, looking around for a suitable spot. Within a hundred yards, he found it.

2

The forest tree line came to an abrupt end and a meadow, wintry and cold, stretched before him, like a huge clearing. On one side, it descended to the Dordogne and on the right, towards the further outskirts of the forest. To François, it seemed as if it was a killing ground provided by some divine providence. For him it was ideal. How often had he stood, backed by trees and hidden away, watching game of all kinds scampering, awaiting his bullet? He ran now, gaining the trees and he heard dogs barking behind him in the misty woods. It seemed clear they would follow his trail across the bare, freezing mud and turf.

He checked his pocket. He had twenty-five bullets and five in the rifle. If there were only twenty men, it could be enough. He intended to delay them. A single shot might do that but the dogs were a worry. They could follow a scent with ease even in this cold. There was little else to distract their nostrils here. He found a gnarled and twisted willow trunk fallen long ago and lying behind it surveyed the scene. Nothing.

He glanced to his left then his right. Their instinct would be to spread out and outflank him perhaps on both sides at once. To avoid them entrapping him, he needed to plan his moves. To his right was the river, with its brown, cold waters, but welcome if he needed them.

A dog bayed at the tree line opposite. He looked through the sight. Two dogs. Beautiful brown and black Alsatians. Their leads shone silver and fierce as they strained, tugging at the men who held them. François saw the two handlers bend forward and release their charges. The Alsatians began to run towards him. These dogs were not stupid and he knew it.

He took the first one in the chest and its whimpering lasted barely a second. The second, he killed with a headshot at ten yards. It made no sound as its limp body collapsed in the mud. The game was up; his enemies knew where he hid. Keeping low, he backed away from the trunk and sidled down out of sight to his right. He stood behind a pine and peered around it at the meadow.

As he predicted, they fanned out. He saw one group of five or six split away and run, stooping and hiding behind bushes for cover away to his left. They would take five or so minutes to reach the safety of the trees on his side of the open grass.

He aimed standing and supporting his rifle with his left hand. The shot bumped his shoulder but he saw one of them fall. With a grunt of satisfaction, he sidled on to his right, heading for the river. He knew what he had to do now.

This whole escapade gave him a feeling not of fear, but elation. It was as if he had come alive. He experienced an exhilaration he had not felt since he was a young man. The Germans hit the ground as soon as he fired and he waited for another target. They lay within his killing range; in fact, he could kill them at twice the distance. He knew they were crawling, keeping low. He moved again, always silent, always out of their sight. It was a deadly game of cat and mouse. If they reached where he stood, he would be further away and drop one or two of them. He kept the fallen willow trunk in sight. It would be the first place they reached.

It took them longer than expected but a man appeared with unexpected rashness by the tree-trunk. It took a second only to fire and that man fell too. François continued his flight. The scene repeated itself three more times until he felt they had learned their lesson. This time they stayed out of sight and he moved, backing towards the river, his river, his Dordogne.

Waiting almost half an hour, he heard a twig crack to his left. A shot rang out and he felt a thump on the outside of his left arm below the shoulder. It twirled him like a dancer and he fell, accompanied by shouts from his adversaries, who came running. They began to search the thicket as he crawled. He heard two others calling as they ran. His left arm felt heavy but his hand moved despite the trickle of red smearing it. He stood with the speed of a striking snake. He fired the gun from his hip and the man who had shot him fell. François levelled his rifle at the other, who did the same. François was quicker. The German cried out as the bullet entered his chest and threw him sideways.

François ran. He sprinted as fast as his injury allowed. Shots rang out. He kept running. Reaching the bank, he jumped. It was a bend in the river. The bank fell away towards it in a steep descent. He hit the mud with a faint splash and launched himself into the icy current. With his boots and coat on, it was hard to stay afloat. He turned onto his back in the numbing cold and saw the soldiers reach the bank. They opened fire. François saw the waters around him boil. He let the current drag him down.

Once past the bend, he surfaced, treading water hard, and struck out for the opposite shore, clutching his rifle in his left hand, the strap wrapped around his wrist. He struggled to stay afloat, let alone swim, but François Dufy was not a man to quit. He would not give up. Light-headed, but still conscious, he crawled out onto a muddy, flat, bank; hands and legs numb as a dead man's. He lay there, close to exhaustion, breathing hard, thinking air was in as short supply as the goods in the market. He smiled at the thought.

It was hard, but he managed to belly-crawl first, towards a mixed wood above him. Gaining the top, he crept on all fours. Reaching a tree, he pulled himself up. He looked around. He recognised the place. There was a small canal ahead, parallel to the river and beyond it, the main Sarlat road. Trees stood over its far side. He had to hide and lie low. Flexing his arm brought pain but his grip was strong, so he knew the bone was unbroken. The icy canal robbed him of the little restored circulation in his legs but he stumbled onto the opposite bank and forced himself to walk across the road and into the woods on the far side. He knew the place well and as the ground began to slope upwards, he used his rifle like a walking stick.

Keep moving, he thought. Keep moving. On and on. He must have plodded for an hour or more before he stopped and rested. There were no sounds of pursuit and he stood, leaning against an elm tree. Looking around, he slid down, cold, wet and damaged. He needed to get back, but how?

3

François was drenched, cold and happy. He realised he felt good. It was, despite all his sadness, good to be alive. His boots squelched as he walked and it was only the hard muscular effort of his progress keeping his body temperature high enough for him not to freeze. The pain in his arm began to increase but still he did not care: it was no more to him than a child's angry pinch. A little of his flesh between its index and thumb on his upper arm, squeezing and kneading as he walked. He would shrug it off. There was a certain satisfaction in his newfound injury. It confirmed he was alive and it felt good.

It was late by the time he reached the outskirts of town. The evening was cold, cloudy, and moonless and despite the frigid spring breeze and his soaked clothes, he sweated as he slunk from doorway to doorway. The streets were silent, not even a rat scuttled by, as he made his way towards town. François hid his rifle in a rubbish dump on his way, marking the spot with a rusty oil-drum.

He reasoned the Germans would have to be stupid not to guard the bridge across the Dordogne, in case he did make it to the far bank. They would search the forest, but he knew it would prove fruitless for them. His only chance now, was in town and he knew where to go. He had prepared the ground.

La Bonne Auberge nestled in a small cobbled alleyway near the prefecture, between a Charcuterie and a small alleyway, opposite a clothes-shop. François slid in silence into the doorway opposite the restaurant. Pushing into the gloom of the alcove, he flattened himself against the door, hoping to be invisible. All seemed quiet enough, but he waited all the same. Now he was stationary, he shivered in the numbing cold. Once, a military vehicle drove past, four soldiers inside. Satisfied they had not spotted him, he ran to the alleyway on numb, frozen legs. Finding the back door to the restaurant, he hammered on it. A light came on in an upstairs room. Bernard stuck his head out of the window.

'Who are you?'

'François Dufy.'

'Who?'

'François. You know me. The venison man.'

'Are you mad? At this hour? You think I want meat now?'

'No, Bernard, I need your help. Something has happened. Life and death.'

'What's wrong?'

'Life and death.'

'I can't let you in, it's too late. Come back in the morning.'

'Let me in. They'll kill me.'

'Who?'

'Let me in, you shit-faced son of a hog.'

The window closed. Minutes passed before he heard a key turn and a bolt drawn. Presently, the door opened. François pushed past Bernard.

'The Germans, they're hunting me. I need somewhere to dry out and to hide for a day or two.'

'You can't stay here.'

'I've nowhere else to go. I told you, one day someone

would need your help for the cause.'

'Cause? What cause?'

'The resistance you fool. Didn't you understand? You are up to your neck in it now. They had better not find me or I'll tell them you've been sheltering me.'

'But what if they come? They'll torture me. You have to go. Here, you go now and we'll say no more about it.'

Bernard tried to open the door but François raised his foot and slammed it shut. He grabbed Bernard by the lapels of his dressing gown. He leaned into him, scowling, aggressive.

'Look, you. You think you can sit here earning money from these German pigs while the rest of France starves. They torture and kill our people, they kill our young men and fuck our girls and you want to be neutral. Are you Swiss? Swedish? Well?'

'I…'

'No you're fucking French. You will live and die here and you will fight one way or another. Last week, do you know what I saw? Shut up, you mouse. I saw a boy, no older than ten. He stood beneath a German sign. It said, *Rauchen Verboten*. You've seen them?'

François was close enough now to kiss the man, who wrinkled his nose at the stench of the older man's breath.

He continued, 'I saw him reach up with white paint. No brush, just his little hand. He painted out the letters until they read "RACE VERTE". You understand what that means? Well, mouse? Well?'

'I… It means green people.'

François let go and threw up his hands in exasperation.

'No, no no no no! It means he was expressing a kind of resistance. That little boy can't hold a rifle. He can't kill German Nazis. But he resists. He fights. He is a hero.'

He struck his open palm with his fist; he threw a punch in the air.

'That child is what the resistance is all about. Each of us must do what we can do. No one expects you to become a soldier. What use would a fat innkeeper be against the Hun? Not fighting, but resistance in every way, subtle or obvious, it doesn't matter. Resist, object and show it, then die.'

He calmed then. He felt almost bashful. The vehemence of his words, the aggression, seemed out of place now and he wished he had expressed more control. François reached forward and smoothed the lapels of Bernard's dressing gown.

'Sorry… sorry. I lost my temper. A man should always keep his temper. I apologise. Where's the wine?'

Confused, Bernard stepped back with a look of fear mixed with a strange respect.

'You're bleeding,' he said.

'This? A scratch. I need a drink. Where is my niece?'

'Claudine? She went out. With that German, Schultz.'

'Er… yes, Claudine.'

François realised he had forgotten Shirley's pseudonym.

'I don't have any special wine, only Bergerac or Cotes du Rhone.'

'I don't mind. I will even pay for it. Look, I need a place to sleep and some hot food. I don't want to be shot on an empty stomach. Seriously, though, I had hoped you would be one of us. You said you believed in France.'

'I'm scared, that's all.'

'We're all scared. No one wants to die but if we have to, well…'

'Let's not talk about that. You need to dress that wound. It's still bleeding. You'd better take off your coat.'

They sat in the restaurant where the only illumination

came from the hallway. He eased his coat off as Bernard scrabbled behind the bar. He took so long François wondered whether he would pop up with a bottle, a first-aid kit or a shotgun.

He began to relax. He felt sleepy. It was as if the entire gruelling experience had kept him strung tight as a violin until now, and he felt a sleepiness descend as the tension passed away. The bottle arrived, two glasses were plonked on the table and as François looked, he realised Bernard held a roll of bandage and a bottle of iodine in his hand.

'I keep these for when we cut our hands on broken glass. You can't be too careful. Here.'

Bernard helped the older man off with his shirt.

'You've been shot.'

'Yes, a flesh wound.'

'Looks bad to me. My mother was a nurse. She taught me what to do but I never saw such a big hole.'

Bernard, with uncharacteristic mildness began to clean the wound with the iodine. He mumbled to himself as he did it. Françoise noticed the pain but remained calm and sleepy. He drank wine and soon Bernard's bandage held the wound closed, snug and firm.

'You do a good dressing.'

'You need a doctor.'

'Oh yes? And which doctor do you trust? I don't trust any of them. Better to drink my health. Santé.'

By the time two bottles and a chicken breast disappeared, François needed sleep and a change of clothes. Bernard worked and François watched. He ascended the stairs with his head spinning, wet boots, soggy socks and a belly full of wine. He was too exhausted to ponder. His eyes closed and as sleep took him, his last thought was of Shirley. Where was she?

Chapter 18

He's a prisoner,
He's cornered by his promises,
He's called to account,
Facing him.
An accounting machine,
A love-letter writing machine,
A suffering machine,
Seizes him,
Hangs on him,
Pierre, tell me the truth.
– from *Paroles* by Jacque Prevert

1

François felt confused as he awoke. He opened his eyes and for a few moments, he thought he lay in bed in the house in St Cyprien, and any moment Jean-Paul would enter and tell him to get up. His thoughts cleared. The pain from his arm reminded him of the day before and he experienced a deep resignation. No Germans had come in the night. No SD had arrested him and, he analysed, it meant Bernard could be trusted. He lay back on the pillow wondering how long he should remain here. He stared at a crack in the ceiling, running the length of the room. It was like the crack running through his life: soon the whole thing would be laid open for all to see if he did not guard his feelings better.

He pondered his situation. The Germans might patrol the bridge for weeks. He had to get his rifle and find his way to another bridge, even if it meant walking all the way to Bordeaux.

The room looked sparse but clean, a single picture hanging on the wall. It was a view of the market square, milling shoppers painted in oils, looking blurred and vague. No recollection came to him of climbing the stairs to this attic room. François frowned as he peered at the window jutting out from beneath the eaves, boasting a view of the town and the cobbled alleyway below. It looked an uninviting escape route. In one corner of the room, a dresser stood, battered and brown. The pitcher and bowl standing upon it seemed to François to have seen better days too. Next to the door, stood a heavy wardrobe and he noticed his clothes, folded neatly on a chair. They would still be damp, if not wet and he did not relish the thought of putting them on.

It was not long before Shirley appeared at the door. Her damp hair looked tousled, hanging in straggled locks about her shoulders. Even without make-up, he thought she looked as beautiful as his memories of her. He propped himself up on the pillow. His naked chest embarrassed him. He pulled the sheets up. She smiled.

'Quite the patriot these days I hear,' she said.

'Eh?'

'Your speech to Bernard last night. He's full of it.'

'Full of shit. What did he say?'

'You made a speech about the resistance. I thought it was out of character.'

'Why?'

'You never expressed strong feelings about the resistance before. I always figured you didn't care too much.'

'You don't know me.'

'No?'

'I fought in the last war. I lost a son to the Fascists in Spain. I hate them. Mme. Arnaud persuaded me. Arnaud convinced me too. You think I'm a fool? I will fight. I had to rough Bernard up a bit; he would never have let me stay otherwise.'

'He might have.'

'He knows who you are?'

'No. he suspects, but he would never give me away. In a childish way, perhaps I trust him.'

'Shirley, you can't trust anyone. If they catch you, all will end for you, maybe even for the little group of young people in the forest. Where were you last night?'

'You don't need to know that.'

'Where?'

'Well I went to a party with Schultz.'

'Party?'

'Yes. All the SD were there. It was a useful event. I noted who was there and I managed to get a little information. Schultz talks to me. He is unwise.'

In English, he said, 'I suppose they drink Champagne and listen to music. Dancing too.'

'Well?'

'You debase yourselves with these swine. I thought you came here to kill them.'

'No. I came to gather intelligence. I am authorised to do anything which will get me into Schultz's confidence.'

'Even sleep with him?'

'How little you understand us women, about life.'

'You are going to sleep with him aren't you?'

'What's the problem François? You aren't my father any more than you are Rachelle's.'

They were both silent then. François thought he knew what she meant. He was of her father's generation maybe. He was too old for her. It only underscored his own fears. He stared them in the face; he was almost an old man to her. He glanced at the window, Shirley looked down. She sat on the edge of the bed.

'I'm sorry. All I meant was that if it comes to it, I will do anything to get information, anything.'

'But...'

'Look François, I'm an agent. I have a job to do. My feelings are secondary to what really matters - intelligence. If you must know, he makes my flesh crawl.'

'I don't understand the idiom.'

'I hate it when he touches me.' She reached out and touched his bandage. 'How were you shot?'

He smiled, lapsing back into French.

'With a rifle.'

'François, what's happening to you? You seem different.'

'I don't know. A year ago, I had nothing to live for. Now...'

'The resistance?'

It was on the tip of his tongue. It was like a hair in his mouth. The words he wanted eluded his tongue, but not his mind. When they came, they were the wrong ones.

'Yes, yes. That's it.'

He looked away. He felt annoyed with himself.

There was silence then and François wondered if he had disappointed her. Had she wanted him to say something else? Did she care for him? No. It was ridiculous. An old man and a young woman. He looked at her.

'You are thinking what?' he said at last.

'Oh, just… Nothing. I'll leave you to get up.'

'Would you ask Bernard if I can borrow some clothes? Mine will be wet.'

'What have you been doing? Swimming in your clothes? I will need to know what you were up to yesterday.'

'I'll tell you when I'm dressed and come down. Jacques is dead.'

'Oh no. How?'

'Let me get up and I'll tell you the whole story. We may have serious problems now. It is possible they have an informer, these Maquis adolescents who roam our woods with their rifles and explosives.'

'Poor Amos. He will react badly.'

'Rachelle too.'

'Yes. Well, I'll leave you to it, I'll get you some clothes, and we can talk.'

She got up to go, walked to the door.

'Lorna Doone.'

'Yes,' she said, turning.

'What information is so important for the Englishmen?'

'I can't tell you that.'

As she left, he pondered her words. He began to feel he understood nothing. The depths of it all eluded him. He felt like a man who embarks on a journey without a map and discovers the distance is much greater than he imagined. He had forsworn God, which was easy. He had isolated himself from humanity and when he first came to Bergerac, he had been pleased not to commune with anyone. Withdrawing into his solitary world, he sat and looked out; all the events of the war meant nothing to him then, it was incidental to his grief, his very existence. Once Rachelle came into his life things changed and he knew he was changing too. It was as if he had come alive. His feelings were deeper now than they had been for years, and he knew he had a role to play in the resistance. It meant much more to him than he had ever recognised before.

A mental picture of old Mme. Arnaud on her bicycle came to him, her gestures, her words. She had shamed him into caring. The Colonel too, accusing him of being on holiday while his fellow countrymen died, had pushed him, launching him into the place in which he saw himself now.

Meanwhile, he was trapped in bed, without clothes. He closed his eyes. It was a long time since he had slept in a bed. Life was not so bad after all.

2

Even his underwear was on loan when François entered the empty restaurant. Shirley and Bernard sat at one of the tables, coffee cups before them and he noted there was a pile of croissants on the table too. He poured coffee and ate. No one spoke for a while until he finished. The smell of fresh coffee brought back memories to François as it always did. Recollections of childhood, his and Jean-Paul's. He could not understand why it failed to upset him today: his mood was one of optimism, which seemed out of place and exaggerated.

He described the events of the previous day but he did not embellish his role, he stated plain facts and no more. When he stopped speaking his companions stared at him. His matter of fact description was not a false modesty, it was a natural reluctance to say more than was needed.

'You think the Germans were there because of a tipoff?' Shirley said.

'I don't know, but if it was, then your position here is unsafe and you are both in grave danger.'

Bernard interrupted, 'Oh thank you both for ruining my life. I didn't ask for any of this. If you're right, we can expect to be arrested any minute.'

'That's why I think you are wrong. They would have arrested me long ago if there were an informer among the partisans. Schultz would have me in that Mairie and be questioning me now.'

'He could easily be watching you instead, to find out who you mix with. Better to get a whole group, leader and all, instead of just one agent.'

Bernard said, 'Agent? You mean you're a spy?'

'Bernard, you knew quite well I was not just a waitress.'

'Yes, but a spy? What am I to do now? My goose is cooked. If the Germans don't arrest me now, they will, as soon as they catch you two.'

He got up and paced the room.

François said, 'Why are you so reluctant? You are a patriot, it is obvious. There will always be some risk but as long as we support each other…'

'François, it's all right for people like you. All I have is my restaurant. It is my living, my life.'

Shirley said, 'There are more important things in life than restaurants.'

'Not for me.'

'Bernard, Bernard,' François said, 'we are all in this together. I told you someday someone would ask for your help. You helped me. You still are helping. It makes you one of France's heroes, a resistance fighter. Is it not a good thing? Yes, we all risk our lives, but it is for a great cause. For France.'

'And you? What do you risk? You go hunting. You sell meat and get drunk. What are you really risking?'

The vehemence in his voice struck home. François reflected he might be right. What was he risking? His was a useless, selfish life. All he had invested in, his family, his career, had dissolved like suds in a drainpipe. Now he fought for France, but it was a fight without meaning. His personal struggle was not the partisans' or Maquis' fight. It was deeper than that. It was a fight to love. A desperate desire to find that which mattered most to him deep inside. It was a hard admission and not one he relished ever expressing to another.

He looked at Shirley and he knew what he really wanted now. He wanted her admiration, her adulation no less, yet behind that thought was an island of common sense. The facts seemed to fight with his fantasies and he was well aware of the conflict. He knew it was not a reality. It could perhaps never be. He looked at his coffee cup, swirled the contents and finished it. He stood.

'Look, both of you. I have sunk into this as a ship sinks in a sea. I had little enough to keep me going when the war started. Now, I have the Nazis. I'm grateful to them. They provide me with a reason to go on. I fight for France but really, I fight for François Dufy. Perhaps it will reclaim me I don't know, but it will be a grand battle and one I will never be ashamed of.'

It was as if he had made a speech again. Both his listeners stared at him. Shirley knew it was the most he had betrayed of himself since she had met him. For Bernard, he knew, it was a continuation of the confusion and consternation born of the ranting the night before.

He looked at the restaurateur. 'You think I'm crazy. I'm

not. I just believe in our country, and anything I can do to free it from Nazi and Vichy rule is right and justified. I don't think you believe anything else but you're scared. Who could blame you? Remember this though. We all have to die, it is what we leave behind that matters. Perhaps they will one day erect a monument in the market square to us. Perhaps the Germans will catch us and torture us, but we will die as heroes. It is a good thing.'

'François,' Shirley said, stirring her coffee and looking down, 'speeches are fine. Underneath all this fighting and killing of Nazis in France, there is more at stake than you know. I can't tell you the whole of it, but I have much to do. I need your help and Bernard's too. Undermining the Germans is going to be the key to the survival of my country. I, like you, seek revenge, but I have more to do than such simple motives would allow. I have to get information and disrupt the German war-effort. Bernard, I trust you even if François has doubts. I see how you react to the Germans in the restaurant. You can't hide it from me.'

'I hate them, but I'm as scared as anyone else. What can I do anyway?'

'Scared? We are all scared. We all have much to lose, don't we? Sheltering me is a start. Helping François is a start. There is much you can do if it's asked of you. I need you.'

François knew Shirley could be persuasive. He read the signs on Bernard's face. Is there a Frenchman alive who would not support a woman who needed help? He thought not, and he realised the Rosbifs were clever in that. He realised in his own case, he was no different from the bald restaurateur. It seemed to him it was all about Shirley. He began to wonder if it had not been so, ever since he first met her, in that field near Beynac.

Chapter 19

One stone,
Two houses,
Three ruins,
Two grave diggers,
One garden,
Some flowers.
– from *Paroles* by Jacque Prevert

1

François stopped in the forest. He looked down at a crocus sprouting at his feet. Spring seemed to come early this year despite the preceding cold winter. Above him, it began to drizzle but it held none of winter's wrath. The rain felt gentle to him and pleasurable, as if the tiny sloping drops would cleanse him and bring him renewed into another spring, another time of beauty in his beloved Aquitaine forest. He knelt, examined the emerging flower, and smiled. He had not many reasons to do so, but there was a simple pleasure in such a gentle, soft adornment of life—a gift of nature. This was the first time for years he had felt in tune with his surroundings in this way, and it made him feel good. The elation was akin to the feeling he experienced after fighting his running battle with the Germans in the forest a week before. He knew for once, why he felt this way. Yet, when he analysed it, he felt foolish; it was all because of one kiss; a gentle kiss on the cheek from Shirley when he set out to cross the river and find the partisans. He felt even more foolish when he thought about his age and the absence of any sign of true affection from the English woman, his Lorna Doone. Yet in a strange way, it did not matter to him and he questioned whether love ever needed to be returned. He knew how brotherly love and paternal love were inviolable and so mutuality in its exchange was unnecessary. Love for a woman was something different to him.

He had only loved Arlette before. It was true he had been infatuated with Alma, but he knew also, this was, in all likelihood, symptomatic of reaching out to someone, as a kind of sexual analgesia. He retained no illusions about it. They both needed each other then and although he knew it might have developed, losing her was not comparable to his loss when Arlette died. And now? He had feelings for Shirley, but he remained realistic. He wanted her. He knew that a fox, looking up at the moon with loving eyes, had a better chance of reciprocation, yet it did not frustrate him. He put it down to the contentment of middle age, despite the fact he was barely fifty years old.

François walked on. Perhaps fifty was not so old. Perhaps Shirley might come to love him. He stopped short. Damn. I'm becoming a fool. I'm fantasising about a young girl almost half my age. Damn, damn, damn.

The reality came to mind then. You stupid old drunken duffer, he thought. This girl is a foreign agent; she is here because she has a job to do. She has not come to France to find romance with an ageing drunk.

The feelings began to hurt. They were real. He preferred his fantasies and lapsed into visions of Shirley in his arms, in his bed.

Then he heard the gunshot.

It broke the stillness of the early spring morning like a stone shattering glass.

He stopped. He listened and there it was: the loud cracks of rifle fire about half a mile away, southwards. It could have been the partisans or the Germans, he could not tell anymore. They all used the same weapons now after all. There was a rat-tat-tat of a sten-gun and then more rifle fire and he walked at a brisk pace, maintaining stealth despite the speed with which he moved.

He came to a gulley, a road running through it, and guessed it was the forest track leading to Bazet. Looking down from the embankment above, he saw an open military vehicle, a Schwimmwagen, lying on its side, and four uniformed SS soldiers lying beside it. The shooting ceased. Silence encompassed the scene until he heard a shout to his right. It was Josephine.

'OK, they're not moving. Keep your weapons ready and approach with caution,' he heard her say.

She came first, followed by Amos, Philippe and a tall blond man whom François had not seen before. The last to emerge was Rachelle. She held the Mauser he had given her all those months ago. The weapon, steady in her hand, smoked a little from the barrel and she pointed it at the dead Germans.

François whistled. It was the tune of a song, the song of the partisans, which no German would whistle. Rachelle looked up to where he lay on his stomach watching the scene below.

'Uncle? Uncle, is it you?'

He stood up and said, 'Yes, it's me. You've been very busy here.'

The girl beamed when she saw him.

'I told you I would kill Germans. I told you.'

He frowned then when he realised she was right. Inside, he noticed a feeling of deep regret, almost a feeling of grief for Rachelle. He taught her to shoot and this was the consequence. However much he hated the Nazis, to know Rachelle enjoyed killing them brought home to him what this war meant. The conflict was robbing this child of her childhood, thrusting her into a world where death and wounding were commonplace and children wielded guns. For in truth, she was still no more than a child to him.

'François. You always seem to turn up too late to do anything useful,' Josephine said, looking up at him.

He descended the bank and looked at the bodies, ignoring her comment.

'These are Waffen-SS,' he said.

He prodded one with his foot and turned him over. The neck-flashes and the shoulder badges showed he was an officer.

'There will be a price for this. This one is an officer.'

The blond man said, 'Who are you?'

'I am François Dufy. I take messages and I save these young people's lives. Who are you?'

'My name is Seppo Latinen. I am Finnish.'

'Long way from home?'

'Yes. I was travelling north when Germans attacked my brothers and friends. They killed my brothers, two of them. I have been fighting ever since. I was in the south before. Now I am here.'

'And this was your idea?'

'No. Josephine wanted uniforms.'

François looked at Josephine. She understood the question

in his glance but said nothing.

Amos said, 'We need to sink the car in the river.'

'And how do you propose to do that?' from François.

Josephine shrugged. She removed the magazine from her sten and peered at it, then removed the bullet from the chamber of the gun and said, 'We'll drive it to the deepest part and push it in, of course.'

'Oh? You realise it is an amphibious vehicle? It's a Schwimmwagen, designed to float. The doors and the hatches are waterproof and contain cells of air to make it buoyant.'

'What?' she said.

'It will float whatever you do to it. I know it isn't your fault, how could you know? The SS use these. Maybe they planned to use it near the Dordogne since my escape.'

There was silence then. Josephine frowned.

'Your choice is to blow it up or bury it.' François said.

Seppo laughed. He was a big man and his wide shoulders shook with mirth. He had a broken nose and a high forehead. The humour was infectious. In seconds, Rachelle began to laugh and the rest followed. François stared. He felt no humour about the dead Germans and the difficulties ahead clearing up the mess. Worse still, he disliked Rachelle's involvement in the killing. The war was changing her, fragmenting her heart. It was what war had done to him, destroyed his feelings, his capacity for love, until he met Rachelle and later Shirley.

Shirley. What would she have to say? He realised then he did not know her well enough to answer his own question. Still, he stared at his companions. The laughter was like a knife. It cut him to the quick. He reached down and began removing a uniform from a corpse near him. It was a Waffen-SS Oberst. The bloodstains and holes might make the uniform useless if it was inspected close-up, but it could prove useful all the same. From a distance, once they washed it, they could perhaps use it. They hid the amphibious vehicle in the forest and buried the bodies. They kept the uniforms and the German weapons.

2

Morning found him in the partisans' camp, damp and ruminative. The spring sunshine did nothing to assuage his feelings. François didn't feel his normal self. He felt like a man who took a sharp about turn on a road and found himself wondering why he now travelled in the wrong direction. Nothing he did gave him relief. He was searching, but until he knew what he was seeking, how could he be successful? Shirley's arrival had overwhelmed him emotionally.

He watched as she sauntered into the camp and the others flocked around her as if she was some deity they wished to worship. He held off himself. It was as if he refused to show his feelings for the young SOE agent. He knew he was infatuated with her but it was so contradictory to his normal emotional being, he refused to give in to it. It angered him.

'François,' she called as soon as his dishevelled figure came into her line of sight. She waved above the others' heads and he had no choice but to acknowledge her.

'Why are you here?' he said.

'I have news. There is a munitions train crossing Aquitaine and we need to destroy it.'

'Why?' he said as if he did not understand.

'They are on their way south, heading for Marseille. The Germans will ship the contents to North Africa. It will help our lads in Africa if we can destroy it.'

'We have enough explosives?' he said looking at Josephine.

The partisan smiled, 'We have a pile of dynamite from the quarry. Don't worry about that.'

Seppo slapped François on the back. The blow landed like a pile driver. François stumbled forward. He glared at the Fin.

'Well my little French hunter. What do you think of that? We're blowing up a train.'

'Look you Russian idiot, if we are going to blow up a train, we do it my way. Last time, Jacques got killed, ask Amos. This time we do it with more stealth and care.'

Seppo's raucous laughter irritated François though he did not know why. His shoulder blades ached every time the man slapped his back. He decided he hated the Fin. His jollity and his constant laughter rankled to the extent François would cheerfully have put a bullet in his brain had it not been for his obvious sincerity when he was serious.

François often wondered if the man could be trusted. He came out of nowhere and his story was a strange one. He claimed to be a migrant worker who became trapped in Marseilles when the Germans took over. He said he hid with his brothers and they travelled home together, but on the way, a German military patrol attacked them. In anger at his brothers' deaths, he joined the partisans in the south. When a traitor infiltrated the group and destroyed it, he moved north and came to Josephine's band.

They made plans. François felt it was time to take a firmer stance over the mechanics and no one seemed to object. It was a project they could ill-afford to bungle. Even Josephine listened as François described his ideas.

When Shirley left, he walked with her and they spoke English.

'It is going well with Schultz?'

'He's eating out of my hand. He's starting to talk. Mainly about the weight of his responsibilities and too little detail yet, but you know, they trained me to get information slowly.'

'As a lover?'

'Whatever it takes. It is too dangerous to be prissy.'

'Prissy?'

'Scruples about how to get the information. I've managed to keep him at arm's length but I may have to give in at some stage. If I get the information I need, I can ditch him.'

'I can put the bastard in a ditch for you whenever you like.'

'No I mean stop seeing him. Your accent is improving.'

The brightness of her smile seemed to light up the darkness of the forest shade. The look in her eyes was untroubled and François began to question whether she told him the truth. He felt jealous and he knew it. He also knew he had not earned those feelings and he had no right to feel as he did. By the time they reached the road where they would part, he began to feel angry with himself again.

'You will take care?'

'Naturally,' she lapsed into French. Her change of language seemed as natural as changing her clothes. It was as if she became French as soon as she neared Bergerac.

'Working tonight?'

'Yes.'

'Bernard will look after you.'

'I'll need to look after him I think. He's running scared. He sees Germans in every corner now, even under his bed.'

'Reliable?'

'Yes. Just scared. He thinks he loves me.'

'He said that?'

'Yes.'

214

'And you… You like him?'

'Don't be ridiculous. He is a plump restaurant owner in a small town in rural France.'

When they parted, she kissed both his cheeks in friendship. As he walked away, he felt as if she slapped him instead. It was not what he wanted and her scorn at his suggestion about Bernard seemed to make it clear: she could never return the feelings lurking beneath his own thoughts. He shrugged and forced it out of mind. There were more important things to think about. They expected the train in two days and they needed a dress rehearsal.

Chapter 20

I put my cap in the cage,
And went out with the bird on my head,
So,
One no longer salutes,
Asked the commanding officer.
No.
Replied the bird.
Ah, good,
Excuse me, I thought one saluted,
Said the commanding officer,
You are fully excused—everybody makes mistakes,
Said the bird.
– from *Paroles* by Jacque Prevert

1

François felt his past life was coming back; he felt like a schoolteacher. He was not an explosives expert but he understood how to blow up a train. He saw many such things in the First War and now he was here; ready to do the same again. It was a different war, a different philosophy, but the same brutal aim pervaded everything. He wanted to kill, maim, or disable his enemy and the hatred he felt when he rode away from Guernica burned in his mind as no other emotion could have.

He still wanted revenge.

François had taken them through their rehearsal the day before. They dug holes beneath sleepers; they set mock charges and covered them up. They practised using the electric boxes and plungers and they trained at keeping watch.

Today, he was lying on his stomach looking down the embankment. The afternoon sun stabbed spears of light though the fir-trees across the space between the embankments, either side of the railway line.

It had to go like clockwork. It needed to be a perfect operation or they would all be at risk. Capture, torture and a firing squad were all a reality and he knew if the Germans took any of them it would be a disaster.

He looked at Josephine who lay next to him. Her profile accentuated her long nose and her beret did nothing to soften her features. François watched as she stroked a wisp of errant brown hair back under the cap's edge and she turned and looked at him. She caught his stare so he glanced away. The look on her face was one of bitter determination. Rachelle too, on his other side stared down at the railway line, her concentration manifested in a frown as if the very furrows on her forehead were there to prove her unbroken attention. He looked again to his right. It was the first time he took in how pretty Josephine was. Her curly brown hair, swept up now beneath her beret and her skin, which seemed to shine with a kind of glow he never noticed in real life, in a camp where all they had to look forward to was the next meal or the next flight to another camp. François reflected how adversity brought out the best in some people, and he learned now it was not only a mental best, it could be a physical one too. Josephine was more alive than he ever imagined her. Her vibrancy became infectious too. François could see it in the others.

They all seemed wound up like the spring on a hair trigger. Today would be a good day and he could feel it.

They waited.

François checked his watch. Five minutes to go. He looked down the line of Maquis again. Amos was there next to Rachelle and Jules beyond Josephine. Philippe lay further down, his rifle at his shoulder, ready. They sent Seppo across the line to scout out any German troops. After their last experience, it seemed a reasonable option for someone to keep a look-out.

The waiting began to fray his nerves. He thought about his first day as a teacher. He was young then, maybe early twenties, wet behind the ears. He recalled his dry mouth, the tendency for his tongue to stick to the roof of his mouth and the faint echoes of a desire to pass water. He even remembered the faces of his would-be pupils. The lesson started well, but when he wrote on the blackboard, the children laughed as soon as he turned his back. It was not until the end of the class he discovered how they stuck the sign on his jacket. It read 'Cochon Nouveau' and he felt it too when the headmaster removed the note in the corridor. The recollection made him smile.

'What's so funny?' Josephine said.

'Oh, nothing. I was thinking about an incident when I began working as a teacher.'

She was silent. It meant nothing to her. She continued to stare at him until he looked away again. She was a strange one this Josephine. When she laughed, it lit up her face like the fireworks on St Stephen's day. It happened so seldom however; it made him feel she might only have a sense of humour once a year.

'Uncle,' Rachelle said. 'If the explosives don't go up, what do we do?'

218

'If they don't explode, we have failed. We go home. What else? We start again and there will be other trains, my little one.'

'Shirley will be angry.'

'Yes. Her mission is to damage this train. Since the Rosbifs beat the Germans in North Africa, I don't think this is such an important train, but we must do what we can. France needs us too.'

'Can you hear it?'

'No. What?'

'The train. I hear it.'

'You have young ears. How wonderful it must be to hear everything.'

'Uncle. I hear it.'

François called down the line. They took up their places. There would be no mistakes and no sudden German attacks this time. François was determined for it to go well, not only for the partisans, but for Shirley's sake too.

He heard the train then. It must have been about five minutes away. His heart beat fast, which surprised him. There was no reason to feel anxious, he thought. We blow the train, leave and it is done. There are times in any man's life when things go well either through planning or just plain luck, and today, François was certain, things would work out in their favour. Had he not planned the whole thing himself? There could be nothing left to chance here and he knew it.

His first glimpse of the train came as it rounded the bend a hundred yards from where he lay, looking to his right. There was comfort in the sight. Preparation, that was the key and God knew he had prepared for this.

They kept their heads down, out of sight. An alert guard might see them and bring the train to a halt in the wrong place. When it happened, it all went fast. The loosened section of track gave way as if it was pre-ordained, exactly as they predicted. The wheels drifted onto the gravel and the whole train came to a sudden halt. The strain on the couplings must have been considerable but only the engine dislocated. The trucks behind remained on the track. François raised his hand. When he was certain they could all see him, he brought it down - like killing a rabbit, like an axe.

He saw Rachelle pushing down the plunger. He found himself praying the current would flow. There was a short second of silence. He wondered if it took God time to hear prayers, then he dismissed the thought; there was no God. Then it went up. The third carriage down, exploded like an erupting volcano. Flames, sparks and fire rose in the air. The partisans kept their heads down, this time to avoid the debris, flying and flaming all around then. Then the second charge blew. Then the third and fourth, almost together.

The ringing in his ears felt almost unbearable. He looked up and saw six of the trucks reduced to wreckage. They had done it. Fires raged in the remaining two trucks and he knew they would burn until there was nothing left. He heard the staccato cracks of exploding munitions. Dense acrid smoke was everywhere. As if in response to an order, they all backed away. They stood on the forest floor and looked at each other. The smiles and the backslapping began, despite Seppo's absence.

And then they ran. Helter-skelter they fled. Through the forest, over tree-stumps and green grass, across fields and back into woods. Seppo knew where to meet up and they had no worries for him. He needed to cross the railway line further west to avoid the Germans who must be on their way. The explosions were so fierce and noisy it was inevitable. Out of breath, panting and laughing like children, they stopped in a clearing. François, hands on knees, trying to catch his breath, smiled as much as the others did. He caught himself laughing and stopped. This was no time to relax. Half the German troops in Bergerac and the surrounding countryside would be on their way. They must lie low now and he knew it. Rallying the others, he found the track leading south. The partisans followed. They broke into a jog and he found Josephine next to him.

Panting and breathless, she said to him, 'I'm sorry.'

He looked sideways at her then back to save a trip and a fall on tree roots.

'I know… what you are going to say… it's alright.'

'No you don't'

He grimaced, trying to smile but it went wrong. He found his breathlessness competed with his facial expressions.

'You know now, I am on your side.'

'Huh,' came the curt reply.

They ran on in silence. There was a tall elm-tree, a landmark, and they veered left into the denser woods. The camp was several miles distant but no one cared. They could run all day, if their mood stayed. The joy and satisfaction spread with the ease of a wave when one throws a stone into a pond. Even Amos, grieving Amos, smiled and laughed between breaths.

François felt as if he was a wolf. A wolf that, after years alone as a rogue, finally joined a pack and belonged. He felt accepted.

2

The sun began to fade as they approached the clearing where their tents stood. Cold winds cooled them, but they were beaming and worn. François reflected how happy and tired was a hundred levels above unhappy and tired and he thought of Jean-Paul. How the boy would have loved to have been here. This was what the boy should have been part of, not some foreign civil war. François might have coped if he had lost his son in this part of the war. The boy would have fallen a hero, fighting for his country, not a stupid foreign legion in a hot indolent country where bombs fell and women died.

The first shot hit him in the thigh. He stumbled and flew before understanding came. There wasn't much pain, just a dull thump twisting him to his right, as if a giant hand had flicked him away like so much chaff into the bushes. He thought they must have found the camp and now it was the partisans' turn to take the punishment. François found he could still move and he released his rifle from his shoulder strap. He tried to roll, but his leg denied him. Dull pain, like a heavy weight, pressing on his mid-thigh told him what was happening. His head swam and he thought he must be bleeding. He sat up. Keeping low under the cover of the thicket, he took a scarf from his pocket, tying it tight around the hole in his quadriceps muscle. Satisfied the bleeding was slowing, he looked around. They were a hundred yards from the camp and he heard the crack of rifle fire in front and to his left. He was angry. His hatred burned and he thought of Rachelle. Where was she? She was running behind him when the shot hit him. Had she escaped? Where were the others? All he could hear were shots fired, some behind and some in front. He thought the partisans were returning fire but he couldn't help, he was unable to stand and it made visibility impossible. He crawled. There was no option but to snail his way as far as he could, and escape the inevitable German search line. They wouldn't leave a partisan lying in the thickets to fight again.

He estimated it was twenty minutes before the firing began to recede. It didn't cease, it drifted away into the distance, and he crawled again. He continued on this molluscan journey until he thought he might be safe, and then he stopped to see what damage the Sauerkrauts had done him. He sat propped against the bole of a tall pine, looking at his thigh. A neat hole adorned the front of his trouser leg. He looked behind the hole, craning his neck. The bullet, which entered at the front, seemed almost to have travelled skin deep before exiting at the back, making a bigger hole. He realised the bone couldn't be broken, so he attempted to stand. The scarf dripped blood and he wondered whether some major vessel might have succumbed. His head was clear. He wasn't breathing faster than his running and crawling might have required, and he checked his pulse. A hundred and twenty. He knew the signs of shock and realised he would survive.

His leg still took his weight so he tried to walk, but it gave way and he fell sideways. He had to get away. What of the others? If the bastards hurt his Rachelle he would find them, kill them. Nazis. Fascists. The hatred rose in his mind as a bitter acid might rise in his throat, and he stood again. This time an iron determination kept him upright and his mind began to focus.

François cut away to his right and forced his way through the hazel bushes and the over-hanging branches of the pine trees. Grey-brown fingers and hands reached out for him, grabbed at him, and scratched at the scarf tied about his bleeding thigh. He wondered where to run. Town would be too risky now. He felt he couldn't jeopardise Shirley again. Last time he was desperate, this time he felt he knew what to do, but he needed help first. He needed a doctor.

He had never felt he needed a medical man before. This time he did, and he knew it. If the bleeding from his wound did not stop, even the alcoholic poacher understood there would be consequences. Where could he go? He remembered the veterinarian who helped him when Cognac became ill the previous winter, but he lacked confidence in seeking help from an animal doctor. He knew where Dubois, the pathologist lived, because he had delivered fish to him many times. Anyone in town could tell you the old drunken doctor cycled into town from the outskirts, twisting and turning in an inebriate haze every morning, on the way to the hospital. François wondered if a pathologist was a real doctor or not. Sewing up a corpse with a wide rough stitch was one thing but diagnosis and surgery were something quite different.

There was nowhere else on this side of the river, so he adjusted his demands to necessity. Perhaps the pathologist would give him up. Maybe he would be true to his name. He was a Dubois, linked to the local judge and the law courts. Such a man would turn anyone in if he thought they were terrorists.

Could he not rely upon the man's Hippocratic Oath? Would he not do his best? These were imponderables. He puzzled over them for only a brief moment as he hobbled towards the southwest stretch of housing around the town. He knew he had to take the chance or face the likelihood of bleeding to death.

Chapter 21

There are great puddles of blood on the world,
Where's it going all this spilled blood?
Is it the earth that drinks it and gets drunk?
Funny kind of drunkenography then.
– from *Paroles* by Jacque Prevert

1

Dark was descending when François rapped on the door with his rifle-butt. So what if they saw him? He became reckless in that. If the neighbours saw him, they could report it, and then what? He would not go without a fight. He would gladly die thinking of Jean-Paul, Arlette, and everyone else who went before. He felt like a man who has come through a plane crash and survived. Having grabbed his mortality in such a moment and faced it, what was there now to fear?

A faint voice sounded behind the door.

'Who is it?'

'I need your help,' François said.

'What do you want?'

'I'm wounded.'

'Wounded you say? I'm not a medical doctor. Go to the hospital. I'm no use to you.'

'Auguste Ran sent me.'

There was a moment of silence. François heard a bolt drawn. The door opened a crack.

'Ran?'

'Yes. He told me if I needed help to come here,' François lied.

'But he has gone away. What do you want?'

'I've a wound in my leg and I will bleed to death without your help.'

'Go to a doctor. I'm no good to you. Anyway I've had a few drinks.'

'I like a man who likes a drink. Anyway, even you could patch me up for Auguste Ran's sake, now he has left for Switzerland.'

'Switzerland, you say? You knew him well?'

'Please. I cannot stand much longer. You will face the prospect of me lying on your doorstep.'

'Who are you?'

'François Dufy.'

'Not that drunk who sells over-ripe game? Are you drunk?'

'No. Just damned well in pain and losing blood on your clean doorstep.'

'I…'

'Please help me.'

The door opened and the small, round, plump pathologist stood looking at François. There were beads of sweat on the balding forehead and a look of fear in the grey eyes.

François said, 'Well?'

'Here,' Dubois said, reaching forward towards François. He looked from side to side out of the doorway, checking to see if anyone witnessed the scene.

François for his part remained undecided whether to threaten with his rifle or not. There was an odd tiredness in him though. He did not wish to fight, to struggle. This was all too much. He felt faint but he knew he needed to walk. He reached out for the pathologist and the world began to fade. He retained faint recollections of Dubois catching him and the feel of plump hands and arms supporting him. He saw nothing more until he awoke on a couch. It was a couch in a long room, with lamps burning and a fire lit in the hearth, then all went black.

2

Dubois stood over him when he awoke fully. The round face and the balding pate made him look cherubic to François, who felt as if he was landing upon a cloud on his journey to heaven and here was a plump seraphic figure ready to escort him away. There was an inexplicable air of kindness in the pathologist's face and François realised there was nothing to fear here. He relaxed and laid his head on the bolster behind him.

'Here, drink this,' Dubois said, proffering a small glass of clear liquid.

'What is it?'

'Calvados. I don't have any cognac. Happily the Germans don't seem to understand its beauty.'

François took the glass and drained it. The raw spirit burned in his mouth and throat and he grimaced a little as he swallowed.

He said, 'Good stuff that. Look, I need some stitching on my leg; I haven't even had time to look at it yet. Would you sort it out for me?'

'Germans?'

'Do you really want to know?'

'Well I would like to know if I'm dealing with a hero or a man so clumsy he shot himself in the leg, so yes.'

'Some Sauerkraut bastard shot me in the forest. I crawled and limped here.'

'But why me? I can't help you. I'm a pathologist. Maybe if you die during the night…'

'But you're a doctor aren't you?'

'Look Dufy, the last time I touched a living patient was almost twenty-five years ago. I deal with the dead. I investigate and I create a portrait of their death as far as it can be proven by medical science. Besides, I have no medical equipment, no bandages or probes, sutures or anything else. All I have is a little Calvados and a few bottles of wine. We can get drunk together while you bleed to death maybe, but that is all the use I am to you.'

'You must have stitched a few wounds as a student? Don't they teach you anything like that in these great Medical Colleges in Lyon?'

'But if it goes wrong? What if it becomes gangrenous and you lose your leg because of me.'

'I trust you.'

'Have another drink. I can't help you. Not that I don't want to, I just…'

'Look, Doctor. Can't you just look?'

'No,'

'Please.'

'Well, I suppose…'

'Please. It won't be your fault if it gets septic, I know that.'

'I need antiseptics and sutures. I have nothing here. I could telephone a proper doctor.'

'Who would you trust?'

Dubois paused. He shrugged.

'You are right. I suppose I could go to the hospital and get some things. There is a risk, you know. Someone might follow me.'

'Is there no one you trust there?'

'Trust? No. There are some I can rely upon perhaps. Sister Gaillard maybe. She has a soft spot for me.'

'Look, I have to be on my feet by the morning. Can you go tonight?'

Dubois grunted. 'Here, take the bottle but leave some for me when I get back. My access to hospital supplies will not extend to anaesthesia so you'd better be drunk by the time I return.'

François smiled. He said nothing, but watched as the pathologist pulled on his galoshes and raincoat. Dubois left without further argument, placing his hat rather askew upon his head, leaving him alone in the room. François realised the doctor must have been drinking already. The Calvados bottle was, after all, only half-full.

He looked around the room. Along one side, were bookcases full to bursting with books and he caught himself wondering what books a man like Dubois would read to collect such a large number of them. He shifted on the couch. The pain from his leg became exquisite but he put it out of mind. More blood dripped onto the floor as he hobbled towards the books. It was as if he was developing a burning desire to see them. He always thought you could learn a great deal about a man from his books and he wanted to know Dubois, otherwise he could never trust him. For all he knew the pathologist was contacting the authorities even now. If he found a copy of *Mein Kampf* he would know.

Holding on to the first bookcase, he stood on his good leg

and read the titles. They were mostly medical books. The life of Freud. A biography of Jean-Paul Marat. What was this here? The complete works of Shakespeare? So, the old sot liked Rosbif plays?

The rest were medical books and François realised the amount of reading such a man would need to understand his work. He finished with this bookcase and hobbled to the next. This was better. Baudelaire, Zola, Balzac, the latter represented by *Le Père Goriot*. Quite the literary student, François thought. He continued to look at the books. It was a goldmine of literature, French, English, even American. He picked up *Tom Sawyer* and thumbed its pages. In the half-light, he sped through the first few paragraphs, gaining pleasure from his familiarity with the writing.

Then real joy. Nikolai Gogol's *Dead Souls*. François had not read this book since he was a student. He took it out and limped to the divan. He looked down at the floor when he reached his seat. There was a blood trail all the way to the books and he realised both that Dubois would know what he was up to and that he was still bleeding more than was safe. He needed to distract himself. He opened the book at the chapter in which the main character walked through the double doors of a dining room and stood examining a huge spread of food, including a roast sturgeon and all manner of fine meats and other food. It made him as hungry today, as it did when he first read the book. On that occasion, he was a starving student in Lyon. He had hardly two *sous* to rub together and the description of the sumptuous Russian feast made his mouth water. He took a sip of the Calvados and chuckled to himself at the memory.

He read for a few minutes and put the book down. So, Dubois had good taste in literature. His eyes meandered around the room. There was a portrait of an old man, whiskers adorning his grim and serious face, and from his dress, a well-off man in the eighteenth century. A relative? His eyes continued to roam around the room. On the mantle, an antique clock ticked a soft chorus and next to it stood the photograph of a young woman, in a silver frame. She was smiling, with a small child on her knee. François found himself curious who the woman could be. A wife? A sister? He realised he would in all likelihood never find out. A sabre hung from the wall next to the mantle and further along, a shotgun lay suspended horizontally on two long nails, driven deep into the wall. Was Dubois a hunter too? Perhaps. There was a moose head on the wall above the gun and he wondered whether the doctor once acquired a trophy sometime in his life.

The arrival of his host interrupted his thoughts.

3

Dubois held an armful of bandages, bottles and strapping. He put them all down on the low table at François' side and began to empty his pockets. There was a scalpel, scissors, forceps and curved, wicked looking needles. From another pocket, he took out a bottle containing catgut sutures, languishing in spirit. He smiled as he ordered his equipment on the table.

'So you've been on a little journey around the house, have you? I could track you easily.'

'I looked at your bookshelf. I used to be a teacher and the range of your reading interested me. Sorry about the blood.'

'No matter. My housekeeper will take care of that. She, at least, is discreet.'

'You trust her then?'

'Her son ran away to join the Maquis months ago. She has no love for our Wagnerian Heroes. I'll help you remove your trousers. Here…'

François undid his belt and drew his trousers down with Dubois' help.

'I usually cut garments off with scissors when I do a post-mortem examination. Not appropriate this time I suppose.'

'Is that meant to be funny?' François said wincing as the rough cloth scraped the entry wound on the front of his thigh. Dark blood welled up and Dubois held a lint pad to it. François wondered if it was more to prevent further damage to the furniture than to staunch the wound. The pathologist spread a clean, white, towel underneath. François thought it looked cold and clinical. Dubois poured antiseptic over the area, pressing with a firm hand. François lay back, his head swimming, gritting his teeth against the sharp pain.

'I have some Novocaine. It may help. Brace yourself.'

François said, 'You're enjoying this.'

'Wouldn't you? After forty years, I have a live one to practise my skills on.'

Dubois exhaled a chuckle.

'Oh God in Heaven. It smarts.'

'Sorry. Just a pinprick. It will stop hurting soon.'

Dubois picked up the scalpel.

'What's that for?'

'Am I the doctor, or are you? Look, the wounds are ragged. I can't sew up edges that look like bunting on a feast day.'

'Sorry. You just don't inspire confidence. Your hands shake.'

Dubois worked quickly.

He said, 'My hands shake with accuracy. Calm yourself.' He hiccoughed.

Time passed for François as if it were infinite. The local anaesthetic dulled the pain and his pathologist and surgeon seemed to be happy with the result. He had a habit of emitting faint laughter as he sewed up the wounds. François could understand why the man became a pathologist. He had no bedside manner.

At last, Dubois said, 'Look here my friend, you have a problem. The bullet passed clean through but the shock wave passes through the muscle and over the next day or so, the muscle fibres will die off. You can estimate how long ago a corpse lived by it. The nuclei become pyknotic.'

'What?'

'It means there will be a lot of dead tissue inside the stitched area. If it turns septic, you will be in trouble. You need to rest it and you need to be in a hospital where proper doctors can examine the wound every day. Ideally, you need sulfa-drugs.'

'What's that?

'Never mind. More Calvados?'

François held out his glass. The last drops burned as much as the first swig but he enjoyed it all the same. 'I suppose if I'm pickled in this stuff it might preserve me?'

'Naturally. It is like Eau-de-vie, preserving everything for the future. Some wine? I have a good Bergerac and even good glasses to drink it out of.'

'Then don't delay my Doctor. The night is young, though neither of us can make that claim.'

The session began then. Four bottles passed by, without either of them noticing the quantity. They talked about books. They discussed authors and they debated the value of allegory. François began to slur his speech.

'So who is the beautiful angel in the picture?' he said, gesturing towards the mantelpiece.

'Ah, my wife and daughter.'

'Dead?'

'Ha! No, not dead. My daughter is studying history in London, at a University there. I sent Marie, my wife, to join her in April two years ago. I didn't want her to be here when the Bastards came.'

'But you stayed?'

'Naturally. I am a Frenchman. I do not run away.'

'Ah, because your brother is the Judge.'

'No. He is a poor pathetic creature who does as the Germans tell him. I have lost my respect for him. He dealt with Brunner, you know, the dead SD Major.'

'He did?'

'Yes. He tried to sell out Auguste Ran to the Germans.'

'Bastard.'

'Yes.'

'This man Ran. You liked him?'

'It's true. He was a good man underneath it all. He had a conscience. Not just religion: he felt for people. That girl who was murdered for example.'

'The Leclerc girl?'

'Yes. You knew about it?'

'Yes, he told me.'

'I think he went there and killed Brunner for that. He couldn't stand the thought of Brunner escaping justice. I think it's why he ran away, he had to escape the SD.'

'Perhaps. But he allowed many Jews to be deported and he arrested many who were not criminals.'

'He was a little weak, that is true, but his heart was sound.'

'No. No man who betrays others to their death has a good heart. We wouldn't help him escape, for that.'

'Oh?'

'No. Pierre Dreyfus went with him anyway. They were childhood friends you know.'

'Yes, I knew that. You have always been a partisan?'

'No. I became one when I awoke to what the Sauerkrauts are doing to our country. Arnaud was my Colonel in the last war. He insisted. They killed him.'

'Yes. I did the post-mortem.'

'He had a heart-attack?'

'No. Who told you that?'

'Never mind. So they tortured him?'

'Yes. His face was unrecognisable and there were burn-marks all over his body.'

'He must have talked then?'

'Who knows?'

'He was a strong man. Even so, we know they all talk.'

'When they released the body, the Germans were full of the fact they did nothing to him, but I knew.'

'He will have talked then.'

'Perhaps.'

'If you know so much, are you not in danger?'

'They don't have the imagination to realise what I think of them. They think I cooperated to ingratiate myself. The death certificate said it was a heart attack. I could hardly put tortured to death, could I?'

'No. Perhaps not. Look, I'm very tired. Can I stay here to-night?'

'My old man, of course you can. Do you think I, as a doctor, would send you out with that leg? Anyway you are now a monument to my expertise, I can't let the Germans destroy a work of art, surely?'

'I'm grateful.'

Dubois helped him up and found François a mattress to sleep on in the hallway, next to a cellar door.

'If they come tonight slip out this way.'

Dubois indicated the cellar.

'Get down the stairs and the hatch maybe won't be guarded. It opens out on the alley behind. It's all I can do.'

'Doctor. I'm very grateful for this. You've saved my life.'

The pathologist smiled.

'You won't say that when the Novocaine wears off.'

As François closed his exhausted eyes, he could hear Dubois chuckling to himself as he ascended the staircase. He wondered what it meant and he gripped his rifle tight. It occurred to him, if Dubois told the truth, the Germans would know who he was. Surely, Arnaud would have told them? They might even know a British agent was coming.

Chapter 22

At each mile,
Each year,
Old men with closed faces,
Point out the road to children,
With gestures of reinforced concrete.
– from *Paroles* by Jacque Prevert

1

Five days after the shooting in the woods, Dubois allowed François to leave. Before then, he insisted he stay to the point at one stage, of locking the front door and standing in the way of the back door. François for his part accepted the doctor was in charge and felt a strange reverence for his advice. It was as if the repair work on his leg kindled his respect. Their relationship changed during those five days too. François, who forced his way in with his rifle, began to feel more and more like a patient, a restless and petulant patient, but all the same, a man in need of treatment. He felt torn too. He wanted to know how the partisan group fared but possessed no means to find out. Most of all he worried for Rachelle. Dubois said he had heard nothing and it could have meant they got away or it was because the Germans wanted no one to know.

Shirley too was unreachable. He knew any attempt on his

237

part to let her know he was safe would bring new risks. In the end, he settled for hiding, worrying and drinking. He spent the days reading and when the pathologist returned from the hospital, they ate, talked about books and drank wine, ever more wine, until one of them slept, not from boredom but intoxication.

On the fifth evening, the last one, Dubois said, 'I left a message with that silly restaurateur.'

'What? Bernard? You went there?'

'I am a doctor. I can go anywhere, especially now since I falsified Arnaud's death certificate. The Germans seem to think I am one of them. I can sing Wagner and quote Schiller and they believe anything I say. They really are the most stupid, indelicate nation on earth.'

'Don't underestimate them. If Arnaud talked, the SD will know everything about the partisans and that means me too. It may not be safe for me to stay in Bergerac any longer. If he held fast and kept his mouth shut then I am free to move. I will have to find the remaining partisans.'

'Yes, there is much in that. You should be able to walk tomorrow. Your wound is healing well. A tough old bird, eh?'

'It seems to me, whenever I am in need there are Frenchmen who come to my aid. It's as if our whole country is ready to resist, fighting and doing whatever they can, to defeat the Hun.'

'We are a Nation. Many did not understand they had the power to resist. We all do our little bit. A tiny stone thrown on the rock-pile drags down another and soon it is a landslide. This is the nature of things my friend.'

'I am very grateful to you. You saved my life. I will not forget.'

The plump pathologist looked up at François. He smiled

and said, 'I must say I was not confident I could patch you up. I am as proud of myself as if it was a major operation but truly, it is I who am grateful to you. Of course, I did a lot of surgery in the last war but it was a long time ago. You gave an opportunity to do something myself for the resistance. I wish you God's blessing. Kill them all and I shall be well rewarded.'

'I may have need of your skills again sometime.'

'I don't think it should become a habit. You've drunk me out of house and home.'

The handshake was firm and brief. François turned into the night and disappeared into the light mist of the evening. The street was silent. Not even a dog barked. François kept his ears sharp and his eyes open for any sign of pursuit. There was none, and he retraced his steps towards the area of the old camp. He moved fast for a man with a limp, ignoring pain. He knew he needed to reach one of the other camps where they had agreed to meet if the Germans ever attacked. Contingency plans meant much to them. A stray thought brought a picture of Seppo into his mind. The attack came when the Fin was absent on the other side of the railway track. He wondered whether there might be a connection. Seppo could be working for the Germans. It would explain how the Germans found the camp. He put that idea out of mind however, thinking he was becoming paranoid. Perhaps the pathologist's wine made him over-cautious. At least now, he could find Rachelle, unless the Germans had taken one of them. It would mean the rendezvous points would all be compromised. He knew he needed to be cautious.

2

Dawn began to thrust a faint light through the canopy of branches above before François found the remaining partisans. He waited at the edge of the camp for minutes trying to assess whether they were there or whether it might be a trap. Next, he circled the camp in a wide sweep to be certain no one hid in the surrounding thickets. Today he could not trust anyone. He reflected on the stupidity with which he approached their last camp. Usually he whistled to Cognac and hearing her bark or whine would tell him what was happening. He neglected all his cautions last time; he did not intend for the Germans to catch him in that way again.

He whistled. It was a short quiet, high-pitched sound. Listening with care, he heard Cognac bark in recognition. It was faint and strangled but he knew her. Still he could not bring himself to enter the clearing. He waited, hiding behind the wide bole of an ancient pine. Presently, he saw Amos emerge from a tent. The boy stretched and poked at a dying glow with a stick. He built up the fire and walked towards François, unzipping the fly of his brown corduroys, unseeing.

'Amos.'

Amos looked around for the origin of the voice.

'Here. Straight ahead. Is it safe?'

'Safe?'

'Is it safe?'

'Yes. François? It is you? François? What are you doing here? We thought they shot you. I'm glad you got away. Come, I'll make some coffee, I need to talk to you.'

Something about the way he looked at him, made François wonder what was coming. He followed him to the kindled blaze and sat on a box. He stuck his leg out for comfort, and could feel the relief as the pain from his healing wound began to ease.

'Where is Rachelle?'

Amos avoided eye contact. He poked at the fire.

'Well?'

'François, I don't know what to say.'

A familiar pain hit François as hard as the bullet in his leg when it struck. He felt time slow and looked at the lad in front of him.

His voice low and slow, he said, 'Where is she? They shot her?'

'We... we don't know.'

'What do you mean you don't know? They shot her, they caught her, or she escaped. Did she know to come here?'

François stood up. The pain in his leg made him wince. He stepped round the fire and grabbed Amos by the lapels of his brown jacket, pulling him to his feet. It was a grip like iron and, struggle as he might, Amos could not get away. When Jean-Paul died, François had no one to blame but himself. Today he had Amos, he had the whole group. He reacted with real anger this time; he wanted to fight, to remonstrate and argue. Someone would pay for this. Where was Rachelle?

'Where is she? If you left her I'll kill you.'

'I... I can't breathe. Let go. You think I don't care? I loved her.'

'Love? You don't know what love is. If you loved her, you would stop at nothing to find out where she is. Did she or didn't she know to come here?'

'Yes... no. She knew we would make another camp. She

241

said she would return to your place if we ever got separated. She thought she could hide out in the forest nearby.'

'You've checked?' François said, relaxing his grip and Amos breathed deep with relief.

He said, 'I've been there every day. I've been frantic with worry. There wasn't a body, you see. I can't find her. She must have lived.'

'Then they've got her. We won't be safe here. Rouse the others.'

François turned to shout into the nearest tent but was pre-empted by Shirley, who emerged, half-dressed hair awry. She stopped, staring at him for a moment, then she stood upright and ran to him. She threw her arms about his neck.

'François. You're safe. I thought you were dead.'

He patted her back and squeezed her.

'I thought you knew. Only yesterday, the doctor told Bernard I was safe. He was looking for you, to tell you.'

'But I haven't been there in days. I thought they might have captured Rachelle. If they did, then the SD will know I'm S.O.E. and there would be no escape.'

'Rachelle will have talked and you cannot go back now. We have to move from here too.'

François held her to him; he felt tears moistening his eyes and he blinked them away. He did not want her to see them.

'I didn't know where you were. I was so worried.'

'You were?'

'Naturally. What did you think? You think I don't care?'

'No. Not that. I...'

'François. Rachelle has gone. If she still lives, she is in the Mairie. You are right, we must all move and keep moving.'

'I want to try to get her back.'

'Get her back? Impossible. There are more than fifty soldiers in the Mairie. There is nothing we can do. She understood the risks. We all know what happens if we are caught.'

'We could kidnap Schultz. They might exchange him.'

'They won't. Believe me. I've thought about it. They will know about me so I can't now use his infatuation for me to find out about Rachelle. We have to write her off.'

'François. You are still alive?' It was Josephine, followed in close order by Seppo, Philippe and Jules.

He turned. 'Yes, alive. What happened to you?'

'We fired some shots and scattered. You know about Rachelle?' Philippe said.

'Yes. There must be something we can do.'

Josephine said, 'Do? No. Nothing.'

François wanted to scream. He felt like assaulting someone. He rounded on Seppo.

'And where were you? You disappeared so very conveniently after we blew the train. Why weren't you behind us?'

Seppo, for his part, smiled. It was a wistful smile, without humour. There was none of the usual bonhomie or repartee. He said, 'You are upset. I can see that. Perhaps you wonder if I am a traitor and told the Germans about the camp? You will wonder if everything I said was a lie. I understand. What can I say? I cannot prove I am innocent, nor can I convince you except by dying. If I need to die to show you, I will gladly do it to get that girl away from the Germans. Understand this: they killed two of my three brothers. I hate them. I will help you in any way I can.'

François calmed. The logic and emotion together in Seppo's words stung him hard and he realised the truth of it. It was not until a man lay bleeding in front of you, you could convince yourself he could be trusted. Everyone in this stinking war could be a traitor. The SD could put pressure on anyone, threaten families, torture people to give away information but they can never take your heart. More correctly, he thought, they cannot take your mind. You can say things; you can betray, but it would not mean you were a traitor, only you were in pain. It was an unspoken rule among the Maquis: if they catch you, hold out twenty-four hours so your brothers and sisters have time to shift, to hide.

He sat on the box. He stared at the fire. There had to be something he could do. Five days were gone, wasted. Rachelle was in the Mairie, they would have tortured her, beaten her and maybe worse. She would be screaming, crying, alone; no one to come to her aid, and what was François Dufy doing? Nothing. Whingeing about a sore leg, getting drunk with a pathologist and now, ready to take it all out on the partisans. And still she was suffering. There had to be something he could do.

3

The sun sank in a crimson explosion visible from the tree line as François and Shirley stood on the edge of a field looking into the deepening dusk.

'Shirley, have you slept with Schultz yet?'

'None of your business.'

'I need to know. How does he feel about you?'

'He is desperate for me. I haven't gone to bed with him and it seems to be a major irritation to him. Now he will know who I am, so it doesn't matter. He would have me arrested on sight.'

'But if he thought he could turn you against your country? What would happen?'

'I don't know.'

'But if he thought you were useful, he might tell you about Rachelle.'

'Rachelle? You're mad. He won't tell me anything if he wants to turn me. All he will want is to control me and make me pass information. It's daft. Besides, they will have shot her or sent her away by now.'

'No. I don't mean a long-term thing. If you can once persuade him how you want him and show him that, he might tell you. You are trained in this - an expert. I have to know. I need to know what they will do with her. Whatever it is I will do anything I can to stop it. I…'

He stopped short of saying what he felt for Rachelle and Shirley did not press him. She seemed to understand. In the silence following his plea, she sat down by the tiny track and put her head in her hands. To Francois, it all seemed so hopeless and her reaction made her feelings obvious to him. He put a hand on her shoulder and when she looked up at him, he smiled.

'You know, my Lorna Doone, before I met Rachelle, I had no reason to live. My wife, my son, both dead and what has a man left to exist for after that? Arnaud persuaded me to fight. He told me off for being on holiday from life and he was right. I had retreated to a place inside myself, a way of escaping the real world. I did not even read a newspaper and it all passed me by until this young girl, her face swollen and bruised, came into my life. She taught me to love and she taught me to hate. Yes, it is strange, something like the duality described by Rosetti. Good and evil. They are the same but different facets of the same coin. They exist in us all. I don't care if I die in the attempt. I will rescue her. I love her you see. No, not like that: as a father, as a friend. If she died, if they shoot her, my life is as nothing. I will have nothing left. Nothing to live for. I need your help.'

Shirley looked up at him. Her eyes moistened and it was an odd sight for François. He had never imagined those eyes, beautiful, sharp and clear, as eyes expressing the emotions of pain. He did not understand what it meant. He realised then however, that somehow, he confused her with some timeless and adamant icon of strength and he understood too, his reading of her was wrong. She was, like anyone, as emotional and soft inside as the words he threw at her and he began to regret what he was asking her to do.

'François?'

'Eh?'

'You're a good man.'

'Good? I…'

'Yes. I will help you. It is not what I am here for, but it is something I cannot deny. If there is any way I can find her, I will do it. What do you need me to do?'

François explained his plan. When he finished, Shirley shook her head.

'It won't work. It's stupid. You're expecting too much of Schulz's feelings for me. What makes you think he will not arrest me on sight?'

'Human nature. You said yourself he is desperate for you.'

'But this is not about infatuation, it's about war and espionage and work. It's my job, his job. He is a professional soldier. If I were him, I would simply have me arrested, tortured and then do as you suggest.'

'No. You underestimate the power of sexual attraction. Baudelaire had much to say about it'

'You know, schoolmaster, sometimes you talk rubbish. I'll do it, but I will need back-up.'

'And what else are partisans for? I will speak to Josephine. I will be there. I will make sure no harm comes to you and they will not capture you while I am alive.'

'But if you aren't? It's very risky. I don't want to be tortured. Mind you, I have an escape route if they do catch me.'

'You have?'

'You don't want to know.'

'I do.'

'It's called the cyanide holiday.'

'Eh?'

'I have a capsule. I can keep it close. If they take me, they won't have time to question me. We all have one.'

'We?'

'SOE.'

'Silly Old English?' he said in English.

'François, if you call me a Rosbif again in front of the others, I will shoot you.'

They both smiled and walked back to the camp. It was a tiny, narrow forest path and full of slips and trips. When François, limping from his leg wound, stumbled over a tree root, he fell towards her. She turned and held him. For one solid, tense moment, he felt temptation, but it dissolved in his lack of confidence, born of age and a lack of courage.

'You know,' he said, 'I have to free her or at least find out what they have done to her. If they kill her I will kill every man in the Mairie.'

'And how will you do that?

'With anger and hatred. It's stood me in good stead since Jean-Paul died.'

'Jean-Paul?'

'My son. He died fighting these Fascist bastards in Spain.'

'I didn't know. I knew he was dead but I didn't know...'

'Why should you?'

She reached forward and placing her hands on his shoulders, she kissed him on the cheek. For François, it was electrifying. He held her at arm's length and stared at her eyes; he wished he could recoup the last twenty years. It was a foolish thought. He knew what she felt for him and he knew too it could not be a sexual passion. As anyone else at his age would, he understood it was the youthful kiss of a close friend. In many ways, he found it reassuring. There was no responsibility coming with the physical contact. He did not need to pursue the sexual dream whether he wanted to or not. He was honest about it. What could a man, almost fifty years old, offer a woman half his age? The more he thought about it, the more the notion repulsed him. No, he was not a monster; he needed to control his feelings. It was as if the loss of all those who truly mattered in his life diverted him towards his adolescence, his formative years, in an emotional sense, and he rejected those feelings. How could a man like him ever dream of love with a woman like Shirley? It was ridiculous.

Chapter 23

One shouldn't let intellectuals play
With matches
– from *Paroles* by Jacque Prevert

1

By eight-thirty, François was close to giving up his plan. He stood in the drizzle at the corner of the Rue Picard waiting for some sign of the Sauerkrauts arriving. Schultz came every other night to eat and drink the wine. Perhaps he was looking for Shirley. François hoped so. Behind him was the alleyway and the side-door into the restaurant and ahead, the empty cobbled street. Seppo, a sten-gun behind him, propped up against the shop door, waited in the dark doorway opposite and the others were already inside, dining or drinking.

François pondered that if it came to a fight, whether the group would perform better sober or drunk. He swore to himself. All he wanted was to hear those few words from Schultz, and it meant endangering the entire group. Yet, they consented to risk their lives. They valued Rachelle too it seemed, not in the way he did, but in their way. Perhaps it was their loyalty to each other bringing anger with the whole war and its effect upon their lives. François wondered whether their rage was a simple part of why they became partisans and resistors, in the first place.

And why did he hate? The Fascists and Nazis robbed him of all he held precious before the war, but there was more to it than that. He never wanted to get involved until he found Rachelle, and now she represented to him a reason to care, a reason to live and to love. He wished at times, they had taken him instead. The world would not notice whether he occupied the few square feet of his body-space or not. But Rachelle? She had a whole life ahead of her, maybe children, and a future. Her life was worth more than his was, in the worldwide scheme of things, and he knew it.

He heard the car arrive before he saw it. The quiet diesel hum of the Mercedes seemed unmistakeable to him and he backed away towards the door behind him. He recognised the car as it shot past the alley entrance and felt a sudden rush of adrenaline. Schultz was here. If he read the man right, Shirley would entice him to use her as a double agent and François would know everything.

Know what? Know if Rachelle was alive or dead; know whether they would shoot his loosely adopted little girl, or whether there might be a chance of salvage. He bit his lip. His hatred for the Germans swelled, out of all reasonable proportion. He wanted so much to save her. At that moment there was nothing he would not do to get her out of the Mairie; nothing he would not give. He knew he risked his life, but he did not care. There was no God. No Heaven. All he believed in at that moment was either salvation for Rachelle or revenge for her loss, and he was desperate to be her saviour. If it were too late, revenge, a poor second, would do instead.

François slipped in through the side door. A nervous Bernard greeted him.

'What the hell are you doing here?' François said.

'I waited for you.'

'I told you. Business as usual and wait and see what happens. You are deaf? Should I shout until the Germans hear me? Stupid.'

'With half my customers demanding free meals and wine, you say business as usual? That couple in the corner, they ordered the best wine in the house and then said they are with you. My God, it's a disaster. A debacle.'

François smiled.

'Your country needs you Bernard. What's a few francs in exchange for freedom? Just do what I told you and it will all be fine.'

Bernard turned, wiping sweat from his forehead and pushing aside the cotton drape, he re-entered the restaurant. François, using as much discretion as possible watched, pulling the drape aside a fraction.

He could see Shirley. She walked up to a table and began chatting with a smile on her face. She seemed cool, relaxed. As he continued to observe, he saw Schultz enter, accompanied by two SD officers, both strangers to François. Shirley's expression changed and she eyed the Germans as if they were more important than the other customers. She made a beeline for Schultz. François watched as she kissed him, first on the cheek, like Judas, then, as the German warmed to her, he kissed her on the mouth, in front of everyone as if he possessed the power over her, to do this. François wanted to kill the man there and then but he knew it was not a serious possibility. It was cat and mouse, hunter and prey. He did not intend to reverse the roles and become the mouse, so he let the moment of anger and jealousy pass, and he watched, calm and concerted. The Germans took a table near the door.

A conversation began between Shirley and Schultz. There

were smiles and gestures then Schultz frowned. He turned towards one of his companions and placing a hand on the man's arm he leaned towards him and spoke into his ear. The man nodded and Schultz stood up. Shirley turned and walked towards the drape behind which François stood. She glanced over her shoulder and Schultz followed. François, turning, mounted the rickety stairs and climbed to the top, to the little room where he had awakened on that spring morning which seemed, so long ago. He sat on the bed. His leg ached from the strain of climbing the stairs, but he ignored it. The wound was healing well.

Fifteen minutes passed, feeling to François, like an hour, and he began to get restless. He stood up, then sat down. He drummed his fingers on the dresser and noticed a bead of sweat running down the side of his face. Checking his watch, he said aloud, 'It must be time. Damn this waiting.'

He waited another five minutes and checked under his jacket. Yes, the gun was there, yes the knife too. François opened the door and crept in silence as any hunter can, down the first flight of stairs. The door to Shirley's room was shut and he approached as quiet as a cat stalking a sparrow. He placed his ear to the thin wood of the door and listened.

Voices, muffled and indistinct were all he could hear. He had not reckoned on being unable to hear their conversation. Had he left it too long or was he early? Neither prospect would fit his plan. So far, it had gone well and the German behaved as Shirley predicted he would, but he needed to allow enough time for her to get the information he needed. François waited, listening. They were still talking. There was a sound behind him. He jumped, drawing his knife as he turned.

It was Bernard. He whispered, 'What's happening?' What

are you doing?'

'Shut up you fool. I nearly killed you. Sneaking up on me. Crazy.'

'Where is Shirley?'

'Bernard, go back downstairs and see to your customers. I will be down soon and will tell you what to do.'

Bernard muttered to himself and descended the stairs. François turned back to the door. He heard nothing now and he sweated, thinking maybe it was time.

Then it came.

One word.

She called him.

'Now.'

He heard her voice, distinct, a shout rendered unmistakable and clear to his straining ears through the thin wooden door. He stepped back a pace. Forcing his shoulder onto the door it burst open. Knife in hand, he stepped fast to the bed. The German lay on top of Shirley. François reached out. He grabbed him by the hair. Leaning forwards, he put the blade of his long Laguiole hunting knife against Schultz's throat.

'Get up,' François said, his voice a harsh whisper.

As the German rose to his knees, Shirley, extricating herself from beneath, slapped Schultz hard in the face. There was venom in that slap.

'Bastard,' she said.

There was a faint smile on the German's face, perhaps an expression of confidence but François reflected it might have been resignation.

'My men are downstairs and my driver is waiting in the car. He can radio for help very quickly.'

François noted he spoke perfect French. He could have admired such a man for that.

'Not quick enough to save you. Believe me. Now shut up,' François said.

Shirley dressed as fast as she could.

'He told me. We don't need him now.'

François reacted fast. Drawing the knife across the German's throat took an instant. He held the man down on the bed by his hair. The struggles ceased within a few minutes. There was still blood pumping from the severed arteries when he let go. He looked at the German's face. The eyes stared wide. The pupils were huge and black. Like a dead rabbit, a fresh kill. The crimson stain spread on the sheets. Blood dripped onto the floorboards. He spat at the face. The glob of spittle ran down the forehead.

They both stood looking at the gory mess for a moment. François felt nothing. It was as if he had killed a goose or a deer. It was a meaningless act and in the spur of that moment, there was no time to consider the act itself, only the immediate consequences.

She said, 'You were right about it all. Barbie wants all the captured partisans transferred to Lyon and they are transporting them by road.'

'Rachelle?'

'He said there was a girl among them. It might not be her.'

'But it might. When?'

'I don't know. If I'd asked too many questions, he would have become suspicious. As it is, he only told me because he was gloating. He expected promotion from keeping Barbie sweet.'

'We need to go. You know what to do.'

She looked at him then placed a gentle hand on his arm.

'François. I…'

'I know. This isn't the time. We must hurry.'

They left the room and François tried to lock it. The lock must have burst when he forced his way in. The door stood ajar as if it was insistent on revealing their activities to anyone who passed.

He shrugged.

'So what? Everyone in Bergerac will know soon anyway,' he said.

They descended the stairs and stood in the passageway, hidden from the restaurant by the thin cotton drape. François drew his Luger and flicked the safety catch with his thumb.

2

He took a deep breath. Limping fast, he pushed the drape aside. He walked up to the two Germans. One was forking a piece of duck into his mouth. The other held his glass of wine to his lips. He was smiling. Neither German understood what was happening. No words were spoken. François levelled the pistol at the drinking man's forehead. He pulled the trigger. The bullet exited. It took a spray of blood mixed with fragments of bone and brain with it onto a tablecloth behind.

The second man tried to stand up. François' bullet struck him in the chest. It must have lodged in his spine. It did not exit at the back. The German crumpled, his hands scrabbling at the table edge as he fell. François leaned forward, across the red and white chequered tablecloth, knocking the empty wine bottle and its candle to the floor with a crash. He fired again twice. Satisfied, he looked around the room. Jules and Josephine were standing and Amos appeared from around the bar. Bernard sat on a barstool with his head in his hands.

Three men at a corner table sat with their napkins tucked

into their collars and with their hands in the air. They looked ridiculous.

A single shot sounded outside.

François said to the horrified diners, 'Get out. Tell no one, or the Germans will come for you too.'

The men, judging by their clothes, were local businessmen and they scrambled towards the door. François lost sight of them.

Josephine said, 'Let's hope Seppo has done his job. Hurry.'

François stepped across the boards and grabbed Bernard by the arm. The man looked up at François. He was shaking. His face was pale.

'You didn't tell me you were going to kill them. You never told me.'

'You would have agreed?'

'But you never said. I had no chance to say no.'

'You have now. Come with us if you want to live. Your restaurant is now full of dead Germans. You think they won't arrest you? Come, living in the forest isn't so bad.'

'What about my business? Who will run the restaurant?'

'Bernard, there isn't time to argue. Lock up the front, put up the shutters and then come out of the side door. We will wait for you. If you stay, they'll kill you.'

Bernard stared at François. His mouth was open and seeing a tear forming in his eye, François almost felt sorry for him.

'Well? Come on.'

Bernard stood up with shoulders slumped; he walked to the door where he picked up the hook for the shutters. Seppo entered.

'François, I have moved the car and disposed of the driver. We don't have long.'

'Where's the car?'

'In the alleyway.'

'Good. Let Bernard lock up and we can all go. It will be cramped in the car.'

'François my darling, I can sit on your knee. Don't worry.'

For the first time for many months François smiled.

It was almost painful.

Chapter 24

He says no with his head
But he says yes with his heart,
He says yes, to what he loves,
He says no to the teacher,
He stands,
He is questioned,
And all the problems are posed.
– from *Paroles* by Jacque Prevert

1

There was no pursuit. The town remained quiet and no pass-ersby even looked up as the Mercedes drove past, its swastika flags fluttering and the engine purring. Seppo drove and François sat next to him with Shirley on his knee. The close-ness of her body aroused him, but whether she noticed or not he could not tell. Despite his embarrassment, she said nothing and nor did he. They seemed lucky because there was no checkpoint on the bridge and although a military vehicle passed in the opposite direction, no one hindered them. Per-haps Bergerac was becoming used to German cars full of revel-lers.

Ditching the car in the river posed no problems either and François began to wonder how such luck could have come to them. When they arrived at the camp, and sat around the burgeoning blaze, Josephine was the first to speak.

'François, you did a good job back there. What have we learned?'

Shirley said, 'There is a girl among the prisoners in the Mairie. Schultz hinted she was the one who told him about me. It has to be Rachelle. He did't say when the prisoners will be shipped to Lyon.'

'He accepted you would spy for him?' Amos said.

'I don't know. I think he wanted me and was deciding what to do with me afterwards.'

'We will have to watch the Mairie round the clock until we know. There is a shoe shop, closed now, but it is a good place from which to observe the Mairie,' François said.

'You know this? How?' Josephine said.

'I used it myself once. A long time back.'

'So it was you then?'

'Me what?'

'You shot Meyer.'

'What makes you say that?'

'It makes sense now. When he was shot all hell broke loose. The Germans took hostages and shot them north of the town. They searched houses too, they killed people, but no one knew who shot Meyer. Brunner put up a huge reward.'

'Why would I want to do that? I hate the Germans but at that time I was not part of any group.'

'Well if it was you, then I congratulate you. You were the one who showed us the way. You know they shot seventeen men and boys in Saint-Julian for that killing of yours.'

'I didn't say it was me. Could have been anyone.'

'How can we watch the Mairie and still warn the others when they transfer the prisoners? It will be too dangerous to use the radio.'

'I have a cousin,' Jules said, 'who may be able to find out. She cleans the floors and hears a lot.'

'I need to be certain. Maybe kidnap one of the guards?' François suggested.

'I don't see us doing anything inside the town for months now, after tonight. The place will be crawling with patrols. They'll take more hostages, more reprisals.'

Seppo poked the fire with a stick. 'Maybe I can find out. I could drink some beer with one of the soldiers. It will be common knowledge about the transport of prisoners and I don't think the Germans care who knows.'

'They care,' Josephine said, 'they will be expecting an attack on the prisoners' transport if the news is leaked. There may be a way, without us taking too much risk. There is another partisan group in the north of here. We haven't worked with them because they are Communists and they are quarrelsome. They want France to be a communist country like Russia and they have their own political agenda. Even so, they have good intelligence. They know almost every low-paid worker in the area. Someone must know something.'

'You know them?' Shirley said.

'Jules does.'

'Well I wouldn't say I know them well, not any more. One of them was at school with me when we were children.'

François said, 'Name?'

'Fabien, Pierre-Georges.'

'If you are going to ask them for help with intelligence, you had better go now. They may ask for something in return.'

'We have nothing for them.'

'No support once the war is over? They are clever these

Communists.'

Jules looked at Josephine. She smiled that beautiful smile and nodded. Jules picked up his bag and without speaking again set off in a northerly direction. They remained sitting. No one spoke. Time was running out for Rachelle and they all knew it. No one could stand to be in the cells of the Mairie for long.

2

Northeast of Lembras where the Route de Périgueux branches, François knew the German convoy would either take the northern route towards Campsegret or continue east towards Lamonzie-Montastruc. The partisans could not cover both routes so the crossroad became critical to their plan. If they arranged the attack on the wrong branch the Germans might escape, and he did not intend to allow it. They decided to waylay the transport before the crossroad and they laid their plans with care. François satisfied himself the attack would go well and now they waited.

The Communists provided the information as if they knew the date of the prisoners' transport already, and François wondered what resources they had access to within the Mairie, and who communicated with them. They refused to say. He did not care either way; if he could only save Rachelle he would have communed with the Devil himself.

The Communist partisan group had agreed to join them for this assault because the German transport included twenty armed soldiers. Some were in cars and some on motorcycles. The partisans' aim was to stop the truck carrying the prisoners and kill the accompanying troops.

The weather changed the day before, and it became colder than in the previous weeks. The last spring frost on the ground made François' leg ache in the cold. The late-morning sun was invisible behind dull, grey clouds, but there was no rain and the ground was dry enough. He lay on his front on a low embankment overlooking the road. On the opposite side dense woodland marched as far as he could see. A smell of petrol hung in the air but he didn't know where it came from and he didn't puzzle over it. He began listening for the sound of the coming Germans and realised he was sweating despite the cold. His heart thumped against his ribs and he took a bottle out of his overcoat pocket. The rough taste of the Calvados made him purse his lips as he swallowed and passed the bottle to Seppo who lay next to him. Jules and Amos wore two of the captured uniforms, laundered and repaired by fellow partisans in the town. Josephine and the rest of her group lay hidden well out of sight on the other side of the road, while the other partisans hid in the surrounding woods.

'You know, François,' Seppo said, 'there is always a chance they won't stop.'

'True but I think they will. We only have one chance. I'm not a praying man but don't let me stop you.'

'Hah. I don't pray now either. I'm a Lutheran anyway, so we don't even have that in common.'

'Hear that?'

'Yes, I'll get the vehicle organised.'

Faint and far-off François could hear the hum of a large engine and he thought he could hear motorcycles too. He gripped his Mauser. He carried plenty of ammunition and his knife was strapped at his waist, the stolen Luger pistol tucked in with it. He was taking no chances now.

He looked up to his right and waved. He could see Seppo

and Jules, Amos behind them, pushing the now rusting Schwimmwagen into the road. They left it at an angle, half-way across, blocking the road and he watched as the two uniformed partisans laid their weapons out of sight in the vehicle. Seppo joined him.

'I hope you are all clear what to do,' François said.

'You've been over it six times with everyone. If anyone is unclear, then they need to go back to school.'

François grunted and wished his heart would slow. He was breathing fast now. He thought of Rachelle and realised he could not fight if he did not calm down. He whistled a tune.

'Shhh. We don't need the music,' Seppo said.

'You have the grenades?'

'Yes François. The men across the other side have four and I have four. Do you want one?'

'No. I can't throw far since I was shot. Can't run too fast either. It's only been a week. I'm better hanging back and sniping.'

With his heart beating an even faster tattoo, he saw the convoy appear at the far end of the visible road. He made out four motorcyclists at the front, an open military vehicle with six soldiers and a large green truck, metal-topped and with bars above the sides. There was another vehicle behind and more motorcyclists.

He watched as Jules waved an outstretched arm in the air above his head. He looked casual, relaxed and François couldn't help but admire his coolness. The leading motorcyclists speeded up and halted in front of the Schwimmwagen.

'Shizer,' Jules said and kicked the front tyre.

He threw both his hands in the air and walked back towards the other side.

One of the motorcyclists dismounted and leaned his ride

on its kickstand. He approached.

The man saluted, clicking his heels. He said, 'Oberst, was ist los?'

'Fick deine Mutter,' Jules said, reaching into the vehicle.

François almost laughed. He had no idea Jules could swear so convincingly in German.

Then all hell broke loose.

3

Jules began with a sten-gun. He was ten yards from the nearest motorcyclist. The man collapsed, with blood and brains gushing from a head wound as his helmet rolled away. Jules continued, spraying bullets towards where the others stood astride their motorcycles, immobile, ossified. Bullets ricocheted off the motorcycles; one must have struck a fuel tank. The explosion spread flames in every direction. A burning soldier staggered towards François before falling, writhing in smoke and flames.

Seppo threw a grenade. It landed under the open troop carrier at the rear. François watched as the explosion lifted the vehicle a foot into the air and the six men inside disappeared in a column of smoke. The staccato crack of rifle fire, the boom of more grenades and the rat-a-tat-tat of sten-guns filled the air. François saw one motorcyclist heading away down the road, his engine screaming. He fired three shots but the rider slalomed his ride and escaped around the bend at the end of the road. Troops would come. There was no time now.

The Germans were firing from the rear vehicle, but surrounded on all sides, the fire-fight was short. Three men lay under the prisoner's lorry where no one dared throw a grenade. The Germans shot at anything moving around them. François could see the driver slumped across the steering wheel beneath a smashed windscreen. The truck was going nowhere.

François wondered how long reinforcements would take. He estimated half an hour at most. They had to remove the remaining soldiers. Dense smoke covered everything and the irritant stink of it made him grimace as tears ran down his cheeks. He crawled forwards. From his vantage point, he saw a booted foot under the truck. He aimed and fired. The victim screamed and tried to roll further under the truck but succeeded only in exposing more of himself. François put the next bullet in the man's back. He lay still.

Sidling along the bank, he popped his head up ten yards away and this time had a clear view of one of the men under the truck. It was an easy shot and he saw the bullet take the man in the face. The last man held a grenade. François had no way of knowing whether the German had pulled the pin already or whether it was safe to shoot. One last man and it could still go wrong. If the grenade exploded, the prisoners might all die.

He thought of Rachelle then. Was she there? Could all this have been for nothing? There was silence now. The smoke remained, obscuring his view from time to time.

'You there,' François called in German.

No answer.

'You under the truck.'

Silence.

'Look, all your comrades are dead. You are surrounded. Come out with your hands above your head and I promise you, we will let you go.'

'No. I am waiting for more troops. You won't take them so easily.'

'They won't be here soon. Not soon enough for you.'

'Come near me and the truck goes up with me. I have a grenade.'

'It's a big truck. One grenade won't make much difference to it. Come out.'

'Forget it, Wichser.'

He could see the man. He could see the grenade. Maybe the pin was there, maybe not. He weighed the alternatives. Never before a gambling man, he wondered whether shooting the grenade out of the man's hand would distance the explosion and save the truck.

Seppo, now by François' side again, said, 'If you shoot him it will all be a waste of time.'

'If I don't, the Germans will be here any minute. I'll try to hit the grenade handle. It may be enough to send it away from the truck.'

'You're mad. It will go off.'

'We have a choice?'

'Maybe I can get behind him and use a knife.'

'He'll blow the truck as soon as he knows you are near. Anyway, the moment he dies, he'll let go of the grenade.'

'The risk, François. Think what you are doing. It's an impossible gamble, you know that.'

'Huh. I'm a good enough shot.'

'You'd better be. Rachelle is in there.'

François swallowed. The taste was bitter, smoke and fumes were in his mouth. He checked the rifle. He placed the stock against his shoulder and looked down the sight. It was no sniper rifle, the short barrel made it inaccurate compared to the one he used in the last war. Wisps of black smoke intervened from moment to moment, but he needed only one second and he knew he could do it. No choices left, he took a deep breath, held it, and began to squeeze the trigger.

It was a strange moment for a man who always professed to be uncaring. For the man who only months ago, wanted the world to leave him alone, who kept out of the fight, it was enlightening. Now he knew who he was. He was once lost, loveless, angry and bitter. The child in the truck was his lifeline. He had to succeed. It was more than Rachelle's life at stake, it was his very soul.

The kick of the rifle took all thoughts away for an instant; then, when the puff of smoke from the barrel dissipated, an explosion greeted his ears. In the haze and mist of the burning vehicles, he stared, hoping, wishing, desperate.

Then it was relief; it was joy. His bullet must have ejected the grenade from the soldier's hand and the force of the missile must have thrown the explosive far enough away. The truck stood, battered and shaken, but intact.

He waited, and then saw the limp and lifeless body of the soldier under the truck. Something, shrapnel or even stones must have travelled under the truck. There was a bloody mess, unrecognisable to François, where the soldier's head once perched.

François stood. He waved through the thinning smoke to the others and they came, slowly at first, then at a run. They shot the lock from the truck's door and began to help the battered scarecrows who once were their friends, out of the truck. François stood at the periphery staring hard at every face as the prisoners descended from the doorway.

One, two he counted. Here was a man he recognised, here a woman, her face bruised and battered. Some could not stand, others seemed strong. Arms reached up towards them and they descended, light as gossamer it seemed to François, each man held up lest he stumble.

Then his heart leapt. It was Rachelle. Beaten, almost unrecognisable, skinny and weak, the welcoming arms helped her down. He limped towards her as fast as he could. He took a deep breath, a thirst for air born of relief. She was safe.

Amos pushed past him. He ran to the girl. He enveloped her in his strong arms and François stopped, watching. His heart beat fast as he witnessed Amos touch her bruised lips with his, in the gentlest kiss he could imagine. François could see what was in that kiss and even feel it. It was love, relief, tenderness, all expressed in a way he never thought could be so clear. Standing there, it felt as if he was on the outside, looking in, displaced and superfluous. They had each other and each of them had been uppermost in the other's thoughts, all through the week, when he had been drinking with the pathologist and moving with such sloth.

He felt like an interloper in their love. Although he knew he had no right to interrupt, he too, like Amos, wanted to hold her, to make her safe. He hobbled towards them, jostled by the other partisans as they helped their comrades away.

'Rachelle, Ma Petite,' he said.

Holding on to Amos, as if unable to stand alone, she turned to him.

'Uncle? Uncle?'

She held out her free arm towards him and he found himself in a strange embrace, for it included Amos, but he did not care. He even hugged them both.

'You're safe now, my little one. Safe. If they had shot you I don't know what I would have done.'

'Uncle. I knew you would come for me. I knew it. In the dark, terrible, painful nights, I knew. I knew you would come.'

He patted her shoulder, the only part of her he could

reach.

'Amos too. He fought with us and he did his job to free you.'

'Yes, but I knew you would be here as soon as the shooting started. I never doubted.'

Between them they supported her as the entire group melted into the forest. It was not the familiar forest south of Bergerac: they were further north than usual, where the Communists hid. They would, after this, have to lie low a long time. The Germans would tear their world apart with myriads of searching soldiers, and they knew it.

'Uncle,' she said when they stopped to rest on a forest track, 'where is Cognac?'

'I could do with a drink too.'

Her bruised and misshapen mouth twitched in a painful smile.

'Please. Where is she?'

'I left her with a doctor who is not a doctor. A partisan and a collaborator. She will be fine with him.'

'What will happen now?'

'Now? You will rest and eat and we will travel north, you, me and Amos. Bergerac is too hot for us this time of year. I have a cousin who lives in Dun-les-Places in the north. We can stay with him a while until the Germans are defeated.'

Amos, who had spoken little since the rescue, said, 'We should stay. There is more fighting to do here. I don't want to run away.'

François said, 'Rachelle can't go back. Look at her. It will take a long time for her to heal. The damage is not all on the outside.'

'Uncle, I told them everything. About you, about Josephine, even about Amos.'

She looked at the ground and François noticed a bloody tear descend in a grimy journey down her face. He reached out at gentle hand and touched her cheek.

'My little one. We all know everyone talks under torture. It is nothing to be ashamed of.'

'They know about Shirley. She has to escape.'

'I know this. She knows it too. No one blames you.'

'They will hate me for my weakness.'

Amos said, 'I will come with you, Rachelle. I understand, just as François says. No one can blame you for talking.'

She sobbed on the lad's shoulder. François stood up and walked away, leaving them alone. There was a sinking feeling in his heart.

He wanted to speak to Shirley. During the previous two days, they had hardly communicated and he felt, now the tension was resolving, there might be time to talk. He needed to make plans. It was the first time since the outbreak of war that he considered moving to another part of the country. The prospect filled him with fear, but he knew Bergerac was too dangerous for him. He came there, running from his past and from the bitterness in his heart over everything he had lost. He was leaving now, because he had found some part of what he had lost and also in one sense, a love he was losing. Age and time took away that hope.

He could not help but think of Shirley as someone he loved. She never showed such feelings for him yet he often wondered whether he was reading her right. There had to be some chance, some semblance of hope. He wished he could turn back the clock and become the man he used to be. He wondered if clean and brave was still accessible to him after years of living alone, away from people, untroubled by the real world.

The real world.

It was a state coming to everyone at some time in their lives, whether they dreamed and pondered for most of their lives or not. He knew he would have to face it and the thought perturbed him. He knew however, he would risk anything for this English rose, this danger-loving young woman whose very presence lit up his otherwise dark and dreary world.

Chapter 25

I learned very late to love birds,
I regret it a little,
But now it's all arranged,
We understand each other,
They don't occupy themselves with me,
I don't occupy myself with them.
– from *Paroles* by Jacque Prevert

1

François found Shirley talking to the leader of the Communist group. There was an argument in progress and as he drew near, he heard the words "interference", "foreign powers", "workers' rights".

Shirley wagged her finger at the man. To François, she looked like a schoolteacher admonishing a pupil and it made him smile. It was, after all, too familiar for him.

'Why won't you understand, we have no interest in interfering with your politics? SOE don't care about that. We are there to support the freedom fighters of France. To do what we can to liberate your country. What you do with it is up to you, but we have to get the Germans out first.'

'I won't work with them. They are unprincipled and they obstruct the progress of the country. The Communists in Russia now fight on our side and this will be a communist country, whatever you Rosbifs say.'

'There won't be a country left if you don't all work together. Jews, Catholics and Communists. Can't you see? When the real fighting starts, partisan groups like yours will be of enormous value in hindering any German response.'

'May I interrupt?' François said reaching out a greeting hand towards Fabien, a tall man in a dark coat, long enough to cover his knees. The man's clear brown eyes had a piercing quality.

'You are the poacher? We've heard about you.'

'Nothing nice, I hope?'

Ignoring François, Fabien turned back to Shirley.

'You don't come here telling us what to do.'

Fabien made a mistake then. He poked Shirley in his rage with his index finger. His face was a picture of ebullient anger.

François reached forward so fast neither Fabien nor Shirley realised what was happening. He grabbed the poking finger in his hand. It was a grip of steel, bending the digit back until the Communist fell to his knees. François experienced difficulty speaking through his anger.

'Never treat a woman this way. You are a disgrace. Even if you disagree with the English politics, you don't behave this way to any woman. You have no manners and even less sense.'

He let go and Fabien scowled at him, his hand on a knife at his waist.

'Use your anger against the Germans. I'm on your side,' François said.

He placed an arm around Shirley's shoulders and turned her away, keeping a cautious eye on the Communist just in case.

'Damned Communists.'

Shirley looked sideways at him, 'You didn't need to do that. He was just irritated.'

'It's a disgrace. If only he understood what you have done here in Bergerac.'

'Me? I've done so little I expect them to sack me when I get home.'

'I wanted to talk to you about that. You can't go back to Bergerac now, you know this.'

'No, I know. The entire SD department will be looking for me, once they discover that bastard's body.'

'Come, let us walk,' François said.

They went north through the forest, away from the others, the camp and the noise. François still kept his arm around her and she showed no signs of rejecting him.

They walked in silence, perhaps half-a-mile from the camp, and stopped at a field filled with yellow spring flowers. Peace surrounded them as they looked out on the gold flowing before them in the breeze. They stood for a few moments, then turned almost at the same time, facing each other. François touched her cheek. He dared not hope. He could not analyse his feelings, but something was happening to him and he felt he knew where he was going and what was required of him now.

Shirley for her part looked him in the eyes and smiled. She turned her head and kissed his hand. To François, it felt like the caress of an angel. His heart beat faster and he drew in a sharp breath.

'Don't,' he said.

'Don't?'

'You tease me.'

'Tease? No François, I'm just showing you how I feel. You cannot deny you feel the same, surely?'

'The... the same?'

'When you killed Schultz my heart skipped. I looked at you and saw someone whom I could believe in. My protector if you like. I have wanted you for a long time. I told you so, but you did nothing.'

'I... I never understood anything like that. I only know I am too old for you. I will soon be fifty. What could a beautiful young woman want with me?'

'You know a lot, you are strong and yet your ignorance at times is bewildering. You never saw how I looked at you?'

He took her in his arms and their lips met. François remained uncertain, as if this was something stolen, to which he was neither entitled nor able to accede. They lay in a yellow world, in which they stole time to escape from the realities of their lives. He touched her breast, his hand gentle, trembling. He began unbuttoning her shirt. She caressed his face and drew him to her. François gave no more thought to the act. It seemed more natural to him than breathing. They made love, a slow but increasingly intense act, one of giving and taking, with neither of them holding back. It was as if François became a young man again, with everything in life ahead of him, and this was his young bride. She aroused him, she held him and she moaned when they came together. When she climaxed it was intense and short, a shuddering and quivering reaching into his very soul, as if this was someone with whom he could share the depths of his feelings at last.

Spent, they lay in the meadow staring up at the blue and grey cloudy sky. François turned and stroked her hair, and his eyes, softened by love, roved over her slim and beautiful body.

'You know François, I am almost tempted to stay here, with you and Rachelle. I could take a chance and fight the Germans and be one of you.'

'You are going home?'

'London wants me to return. The last time I radioed, they told me it was too risky to stay. I just don't want to leave.'

She turned her face towards him. 'I don't want to leave you.'

'I love you, you know that,' he said.

'You never told me. I have thought about you all the time. I have never met someone like you. I have a past you know and it is not something I want to talk about yet.'

'The past is gone. What we have now is all that matters. I am angry that I love you. I find it hard to believe you could ever want a man like me and I have denied my feelings because I never really believed it could be possible.'

'Yes, I know, but there are far worse things in this life than to be truly loved by another. Believe me I know.'

'Maybe one of them is to be loved by an old man.'

'No, my dear François. You are not an old man. You are everything I ever wanted in a man.'

'It would be a short relationship. I will be fifty soon. Jean-Paul would accuse me of being a dirty old man.'

'Don't say that, François. I do love you. Even if we don't have a long time together, it could be worth a lifetime.'

'It would not be a good thing for you. I am old enough to be your father. We should not have…'

'Have what? Made love? I want you. I needed you just now. There is nothing wrong in that.'

He fell silent, wondering about what he had done; he was twenty years older than she was. This girl was too young for him and he was too old for her. He had to let her go back. He had to release her to her normal life. In a few short years, he might be dead. And what would she be left with then, aged fifty? A grave to visit? Regret she ever came to France? No. He loved her and he wanted her but it could not be enough. If he loved her, he would let her go and allow her to live her life with someone who could give her all the things he could not.

Unable to analyse his thoughts further, he said, 'You know how we say everyone talks?'

'You mean Rachelle?'

'No, Arnaud.'

'Arnaud?' she said.

'Yes. He never talked. Dr. Dubois told me how they tortured him. He did the post-mortem. The old fellow never talked. He told them nothing to the point of death. That was why they did not come looking for me. I owe him my life.'

'Strange, isn't it? We all try to make rules about life, yet sometimes strength and bravery destroy them.'

'Yes. Like us now. Truth shows us both we cannot be together. What am I, but a rigid, vicious old man? I kill Germans and I grieve for my dead family. You should stay away from me. I have nothing to offer, but this moment you have given me is more than I deserve and something to keep until the end.'

'What is wrong with you? I want to stay because of you. I know I love you. You are honest and braver than any man I have ever met.'

There was silence then. They dressed and walked back to the camp. François felt a heaviness in his chest. He wondered what he was giving up. He could not permit her to stay. It was nothing to do with the risk, it was her future he wanted to protect, and he resigned himself to it.

2

François thought to himself how Steinbeck would have described Dun-les-Places "a one horse town" as they dismounted their bicycles and placed them in the stands outside the church. The village was one any traveller would have passed through and never thought about again. He looked up at the church, its thirty-foot spire, a thick stone tower, old and angry, framed against the grey sky. The shape of the building was that of a cross, the knave running forwards from the rather plain architrave above the double doors and the spire situated at the near end.

He thought about how he had left God behind. He knew too, he was right. Looking back, he wondered why abandoning the habit of a lifetime occupied so little of his thinking process, though it once pervaded everything in his life. Those habits were strong in him when he was a young man. Now, older but not much wiser, he reflected, it was his faith he had lost. How could it be otherwise? There were so many layers of blood on his hands; however God looked at it, that forgiveness would have been a struggle even for the Supreme Being.

Then, as they walked north to the end of the street, he looked at Shirley. She smiled and clasped his hand in hers. He thought she had faith. Not religious faith, but faith in François Dufy. How could she not have? She slept with him and said she loved him. He could not understand why she felt this way. It was illogical, but logic was never a way forward in François' life. If it had been, he would never have trusted Colonel Arnaud; he would never have engineered the ambush saving Rachelle and the others.

Turning left at a crossroad, Amos, Shirley, François, Bernard and Rachelle walked down the street searching for number 43. There was a strange silence as if there was no one in the village. François saw a curtain flutter as some watcher hid from his view. The house they sought was at the far end of the street, detached and neat, the last summer flowers drooping in the beds; the end of their season, the end of their lives. François felt like one of them. Shirley could only stay long enough to get in touch with the local partisans who had an escape route into Switzerland. She was going home and François was staying.

It was a simple choice for them both. If she stayed, she risked censure by SOE, but she said she came into the war to defeat Germany and she had much to do yet. She said she would return. As François knocked on the green door, he knew she would never come back. They waited.

The door opened a crack, as if the tiny chink would admit some disease poised to infect the house or its occupants.

'Yes?' a cracked voice said.

'Albert. It's François, your cousin. Is there no greeting for your long-lost cousin?'

The door opened and a small man of middle years came out. His face looked weatherworn and wrinkled and he seemed to François to have aged badly. He held a shotgun under his arm and his once-white shirt had seen better days, a rip in the fabric hanging in tatters near the armpit, barely held in place by his braces.

'François? Is it you? We thought you were dead.'

Albert unloaded and closed the shotgun then set it down, leaning it against the doorjamb. He opened his arms and François hugged his cousin.

'When I heard about Jean-Paul, I went to find you. The house in Saint Cyprien was empty and the next time I came, they said you had moved away. I thought…'

'No. Still alive. I went on holiday.'

'Holiday? Where?'

'Hah. It's a long story and we have cycled far. My friends are hungry. You have food?'

'Not much but what I have is yours. I have some wine. Welcome,' Albert said, gesturing the entrance to his home.

3

The sun was setting, throwing long shadows across the floor and a chill descended on the house. Albert lit a fire and cooked a lamb stew. He warmed bread in the black range and provided a sharp but not unpleasant red wine. He had pâté and they ate the bread with it as Albert explained how the village survived, day to day, with military patrols and German troops inspecting often. They sat in the kitchen; all six of them, and François told the story of how they came to be there. Albert listened, mouth open, eyes wide.

'Your cousin is a hero,' Bernard said.

'Don't be foolish,' François said.

Albert looked from face to face and said, 'Like in the last war. He was decorated you know.'

Shirley said, 'I didn't know that.'

'Oh yes. He was a military sniper. He killed many German generals and was given a decoration.'

'Shut your mouth. It was a long time ago. Those days don't matter now. All that matters is resistance against the Sauerkrauts. We need to join up with the partisans here and work to expel these vermin from our country.'

Shirley took his hand. 'So, twice the hero.'

'No, I'm not a hero. I have done what anyone would do. It is Shirley and all her compatriots who come here to help, who are the real heroes and heroines. Certain death faces them every minute, and for what? For our country.'

He raised his glass. He said, 'To SOE, "Silly Old English", and for France.'

They all stood and drained their glasses.

'You know, I thought those young partisans would be dead within a month,' François said.

Shirley said, 'You were quite wrong there. I have never met a harder woman than Josephine. She loves Jules, you know, and he always said he was in charge, though we all knew it was Josephine who made the real decisions.'

'I thought Seppo was a traitor at first,' Amos said.

'Seppo?' François said, 'Yes I wondered too, but he wasn't. We were just unlucky. There were no traitors in our group.'

With a violence surprising everyone in the room, Rachelle stood up, her chair clattering to the stone floor behind her.

'No. Only me.'

She ran from the room and Amos made to follow her. François raised a restraining hand. 'Let me. Please.'

She sat in the salon on a low chaise-longue by the window, her face covered by her hands. François approached and sat down next to her. His arm encircled her.

'Ma Petite. Nothing you might have told them was a betrayal. We all knew how you must have suffered. No one could blame you for anything you might have said. Why else do we all fear capture? It isn't the pain. It is because we know no one will come. No rescue will liberate us and we are alone with the pain. It becomes futile in the end to be silent. There is not one Maquis in the country who does not know that. Why hold out anyway after the first day? Your brothers and sisters will have moved away and there remain no secrets worth suffering for any longer.'

She looked up at him. Her face shimmered in the candlelight from the smearing tears and the moisture in her eyes.

'I told them about you, about Arnaud and about Shirley. They…They hurt me so many times. I…'

He rocked her in his arms and patted her shoulder.

'Dear Rachelle. It made no difference. We all knew it could happen and we all escaped.'

'But I betrayed myself.'

'No. You must stop this foolishness. You gave in to pain, which no human being should ever have to endure. It was not betrayal, nor weakness. It was human. It is basic in us all that we have a point where hopelessness comes into our heads and then we give way. I was hopeless too once. You gave me a reason to live. I love you like my own and if forgiveness is needed, you have that, but I don't think it is. You are braver than I ever was. I folded without the physical pain. I gave in to grief and self-pity, until you came into my life and you needed me. Who is the strong one? You. You survived the Germans taking your family. You became a fighter and you suffered. There is more heroism in your little finger than there is in my entire soul. I love you my little one.'

'Arnaud never talked.'

'No?'

'Schultz told me that. He said Arnaud was the only one he ever heard of who remained silent. They laughed then. They said he took days to die. Then they started on me. They kept using his name. They said I could never be like him. They taunted me with it, and in the end, they convinced me. I was all alone.'

Her shoulders shook with crying. The sound stabbed him like a knife and he felt moisture in his own eyes. He wanted to kill them all. However much he tried to placate this young woman, he knew deep inside how his hatred still burned like a flare in the night sky.

A sound at the doorway made him look up. It was Shirley.

'Can I come in?'

He motioned her to a chair.

'Rachelle,' she said. 'we all knew you could not resist for long. We know that about all of us who fight this battle. My Control has your name. He is putting you on a list. It is not a list of traitors. It is a list of heroes. He said, he thought you are among the bravest of all, to survive and still fight. I admire you, as we all do.'

Rachelle looked up from François' shoulder.

'It is not what the world thinks in its kindness and sympathy. It is what I have in my heart. Don't you understand?'

Shirley said, 'Look. You have suffered. Does it mean you give up? You are here with Amos and your country still needs you to fight. You didn't die. You live to fight again.'

'No,' François said, 'I don't want her fighting anymore. She needs to get away with you when you go.'

'Never, Uncle. I stay. I take my chance and every German I kill, I will think of Schultz and his red-hot iron and the rape. I'm glad he died like a dog, and no one can make me leave.'

There was silence then, each of them deep in thought. François wondered if Rachelle's hatred could be turned to good use. It might allow her to feel she was avenging herself and it could, he hoped, draw her from the depths of the grief and anger she felt. He smiled to Shirley. He loved them both.

Chapter 26

And despite the teacher's threats,
To the jeers of infant prodigies,
With chalk of every colour,
On the blackboard of misfortune,
He draws the face of happiness.
– from *Paroles* by Jacque Prevert

1

It was raining when they reached the steep slope of the mountain track where Shirley was to meet the two partisans taking her on the escape route to Switzerland. She wore a wool-lined raincoat over her long floral dress and a black beret, perched at an angle over her blonde hair. She carried her small canvas bag over one shoulder, and gripped François' hand, her knuckles white, as they ascended. They both carried stolen Mausers slung over their shoulders, as if such adornments were now part of life and of no consequence.

Her eyes were moist; François could not decide whether from emotion or the cool wind in their faces.

'I wish I could stay, François'

'I know. It's tearing me apart. I want you to stay so much,

but part of me knows you will have a better life in England than I can offer you here.'

'But you know I would stay if I could. My Control insists I return. They are planning something big and they need me. I gave my word.'

'I understand. I will miss you more than anyone. For this short time, you've replaced everyone I lost before. I'll never forget you.'

'I'll come back you know. It's only a temporary parting. You'll see.'

'I wish it were true but part of me says you must be free. I have so little to offer. I'm too old for you, I keep telling you. '

'Oh, don't start that bleating on about my age and yours. I'm grown up. I can make my own decisions. When this war is over, I'll come and look for you. You know what there is between us.'

François was breathless when they reached the top. He faced her and their lips met. Pulling away, he watched a solitary teardrop escape down her cheek and he realised his own eyes felt moist. They embraced.

'We can sit here and wait. I think we are early,' he said.

'This stupid war. Why can't we be together?'

'You will forget me, you'll see.'

'No. I will come back. I'll write to you when I'm free to return.'

A falling rock behind them made François look over his shoulder. 'It's them,' he said.

Two men appeared on the brow of the hill above them. They looked like his people, partisans, peaked caps and carrying guns. Neither of the men spoke.

Shirley stood and hailed them and they came down to where François and she stood.

'You are the English girl?' the taller of the two said.

'Yes. We're going now?'

'Yes. Three days and we get to the border. We used to have a boat but some fellow took it. Left a dead policeman behind and took our boat. We will have to find another so we'll have a day or so to wait.'

'You will be careful?' François said.

The smaller of the men said, 'That's why we're still alive. Come, let's go.'

Shirley turned to François. With pallid knuckles, she gripped his arms. They looked long into each other's eyes and he leaned forward and kissed her one last time. Shirley turned away and walked in silence up the few yards of the hill followed by the two partisans. She did not look back. Rainwater dripped down François' face and he knew there were tears there too. He wiped his face on his sleeve and trudged down the hill.

He felt numb. He had lost again. Without Shirley, the whole war and his part in it seemed pointless. He knew Amos was there for Rachelle and what did he have left? Not even Cognac. He wondered whether he had been searching for something to fill the void left by his bereavements. Perhaps, he thought, it was love he was looking for. Then Shirley came into his life. A bright ray of sunshine and an illumination of his world. The sun had now set for him and his search it seemed to him, had ended. It was perhaps all in vain. What can a man do though, but continue?

François felt certain he would never see her again and his whole existence seemed to have become a darker place. It seemed to him that all he had left was fighting and fulfilling his wish for revenge. In some way, he held the Germans responsible for his loss of Shirley, as if her departure was a direct consequence of their invasion. He hated them all and he knew he would fight and continue fighting until they were driven back.

2

In the year following Shirley's departure, François found his grief attenuating like a fading scar. He thought of her less and when he did, it no longer made him melancholy, as if the short time they had together was a treasure to store in his mind and examine from time to time when he needed a lift. Bernard, Amos, Rachelle and he, joined one of several Maquis groups in the area. They hid in forests; they shot German officers and blew trains from time to time. By the time July came, they had caused as much damage as a regiment and they celebrated, drinking wine around their campfire.

For François it had been a strange year. He killed, he hid and he reminisced. He thought of Jean-Paul, he missed Shirley and he tried to protect Rachelle whenever it was needed. But his hatred never departed. There was loneliness in the anger and disgust when he witnessed what the Germans did to his country. He knew it was not the German people he hated: it was the military machine with all its party affiliations and dogma he detested. They took reprisals, they terrorised townsfolk and they were the epitome of evil in his eyes. Yet he never saw the evil they did with religious eyes. It was a pragmatic way of seeing wickedness. He knew inside they believed in their politics, their party and their Fürer.

To François, those beliefs were enough for him to kill without mercy and he did not see his role as if he were some religious avenger. It was justice he sought. Justice for the death of his son, justice for the reprisals against innocent people inflicted by a cruel and to his mind, evil regime.

He sat on the hillside in front of a blazing fire. They all sat there, Rachelle, Amos and the rest. Bernard cooked a stew of rabbits, flavoured with herbs he found growing on hillsides and forests around them. After eating, they sang a song of partisan resistance and even François joined in. He knew he had become one of them and there was a warmth in his belonging. It was no substitute for what he wanted in life but it was kinship. It kindled fear for him too. It was a dread of the war finishing. When peace came, however it worked out for him, he would be alone again. There would perhaps be nothing left. No family to return to, no lover with open arms to comfort him and induce forgetfulness. No. For François the end of the war meant an end to a meaningful life. He had nowhere to go, no one to belong to, or with whom he could share the meaning of what he had been through.

Père Jean, the priest from Dun-les-Place visited often and François was pleased to talk with him. He was an intelligent man who believed in God's justice. François often debated with him how God could allow the viciousness of war.

'My son, it is not God who is at fault but humanity.'

'Then there are no penalties for human behaviour.'

'Yes. No penalties for simple mistakes. It is not the taking of life in this terrible conflict, which is unforgiveable. It is the men who commit atrocities and don't care, whom He will wreak his vengeance upon.'

'Do you think,' François said, 'He means for us to suffer?'

'It is through suffering that we can reach a clear path to Heaven.'

'Sorry father, I don't agree. If He exists, He took away everything in my life that matters to me. I am not Job. I am not his modern equivalent, yet my wife, my son and all the people I love, He takes away from me. And what am I left with? I'm left with Bernard and his lousy cooking.'

François laughed but the sound of it meant nothing to him. There was no real humour in the remark either. His disappointment with life seeped into every conversation, every action. He had lost hope and Père Jean knew it.

'François, why don't you take confession like the others?'

'Père Jean,' he said, 'I lost my faith a long time ago. My son, my beautiful, clever, heroic son was taken away from me. Your God took him away. If you don't agree then you don't believe in God. He is omnipresent and all-powerful, yet He allows evil things to happen. Surely, He cannot expect anyone to trust him or believe in him, for that matter?'

'All things are as God makes them. He has tested you. Will you give in to that trial? Let me take your confession.'

'No. it is too late for me to believe in these things. Don't misunderstand. I value the power of religion I just don't need it myself. There are too may contradictions.'

'François,' the priest said, 'you are running out of time. You could die tomorrow, a stray bullet may find you or you could be captured by the Germans. Would you die turning your back on God?

'Afraid so. It means nothing to me anymore.'

'Then I will pray for you my son.'

'You do that. I hope it brings you more than prayer has ever brought me.'

Neither of them spoke again that night. François never saw the priest again, but in following years, he often considered their conversation. It never brought him back to the church and he never harboured regrets. He sometimes reflected how faith brought that priest no luck either.

Chapter 27

Real and surreal,
Terrifying and funny,
Nocturnal and diurnal,
Usual and unusual,
Handsome as hell
– from *Paroles* by Jacque Prevert

1

François was sitting in the same moth-eaten chair as when he read Charles' letter all those years before, the one containing the news of Jean-Paul's death. Little had changed in the time when the house had been in different ownership. Outside, it was raining and he listened to the patter of it on the window-pane. The clock ticked and he began to feel sleepy. He grimaced as he sipped a glass of Corbières, thinking the taste too tannic for him. It felt as if it gripped the back of his teeth. He put down the glass and thought about Shirley, wondering where she was and whether she was happy. He wanted nothing more than that for her. He had never heard from her throughout the rest of the war.

Picking up his tobacco pouch, he pulled a leaf of the flake out and rubbed it between his fingers. Placing the brown trea-cle-smelling leaf into the bowl, he struck a match and coughed

290

as he lit his pipe. He waved the smoke away with his left hand and blew a smoke ring. Habit. Much of life, he pondered, was habit, even love. When the passion is gone what remains had to be habit. He felt he had lost all the pleasant habits and returned to his drinking and his dubious hygiene. No more clean and brave for François Dufy.

There was a knock on the front door. Finishing his glass of wine, he went into the hallway.

'There you are my old man.'

'Doctor Dubois. It's you.'

'Yes François, I'm here. A short visit.'

Cognac dragged on the lead in the pathologist's hand. She wagged her tail and almost wagged her body. She licked his hand and he squatted scratching her head behind the ears, muttering endearments. François looked up. The doctor looked different. He had a walking stick; there was a scar on his face, puckering his right cheek. In his left hand, he carried a bottle wrapped in brown paper.

'What happened to your face?'

'Nothing worth talking about. Look, can I come in?'

'Naturally.'

Dubois handed his bottle to François muttering something about being pickled in spirit was better than being pickled in vinegar. François opened another bottle of wine and poured a generous glass for his visitor. They sat in his drawing room. A truck thundered past and a child laughed outside the window.

'What made you to return to St Cyprien? I thought you hated the place.'

'I did, but Bergerac held too many memories of those days. When I was there, I was not a man. I was a shadow of one.'

'And what do you do now?'

'I am teaching again. A man has to earn a living. The head teacher, Mme. Lusard died in the war. They took me back. You know, I was rude to her once. I regret it now. SS soldiers shot her out of hand when she tried to obstruct them taking one of her Jewish children away. I always thought she was a stuck-up bitch but she was braver than most.'

'We all suffered in some way in the war.'

'And you?'

'I have no real tales to tell. I did a little work for the partisans during the year after you left. I'm going to England to live. My family wants to stay there and I have the means. That's why I'm here.'

'Oh?'

'I have to give you back your companion. Cognac cannot go with me. They have very strict quarantine laws, the Rosbifs. You will take her back? For company perhaps?'

'She was a working dog, nothing more than that, until Rachelle came into my life.'

'Rachelle?'

'Yes, the Jewish girl who lived with me.'

'Ah yes, I remember now. What happened to her?'

'She's married. Married a Jewish partisan. They moved away seeking a new country where everyone is Jewish. She writes sometimes.'

'You will take the dog?'

'Of course. Someone must look after her. You went to a lot of trouble to find me then?'

'No. Many remember you and how De Gaulle mentioned the twice-decorated sergeant who killed so many Germans. It makes you quite the celebrity in Bergerac. You were easy to find.'

'Ah.'

Silence descended. There seemed to both of them little left to say. François thought they had nothing in common in the end. He was indebted and the doctor was leaving. They viewed each other through an empty bottle, as empty as François' life.

2

François looked across his desk into the St Cyprien street. Snowflakes were falling outside, settling on his windowsill, like a soft, frosty tablecloth spread there by some icy hand. He questioned why, after all he had been through, he moved back into the same house in which he once grieved for Arlette; in which he had waved goodbye to Jean-Paul. He felt safe here, cosseted with his grief and his memories. No one disturbed him and he disturbed no one, not even at Christmas-time. Another Christmas Eve. The birth of Christ. He wondered what it meant to him now and he concluded it meant nothing.

In front of him on the desk were a half-empty bottle of Calvados, a Luger pistol, a pen and a blank sheet of paper. There was a faint smell of damp but it did not bother him now. He was leaving. He was not ready yet. He poured another glass of the sharp liquor and braced himself as he drank. He refused to go without letting them know why. He stared at the empty page.

He cast his mind back to a vision of the first war. He could see the man's face. A man of middle years, he was stepping from an armoured car. He was proud. It was apparent from his face, solid, strong and smiling. François could see it now. He relived the moment. Did the man have children? A wife?

Who was he, apart from being a target to which they had pointed François? He recalled the feel of the trigger as he squeezed it, the smoke from the barrel-tip. He envied the man. After the bullet entered his face, he would feel no pain. He would never ache as François did now. No grief, only blackness. It was the same blackness François sought now, peace and rest. He was finished with it all and he felt so tired.

He recalled General de Gaulle. His serious face, his small moustache as he kissed François on both cheeks after pinning the medal to his chest. De Gaulle muttered something about bravery and valour but François could not recall the exact words. He remembered his feelings; he felt nothing. He was there because they told him to be and none of it meant anything to him.

The endless killing, the wickedness he witnessed when he fought alongside Bernard among the Partisans still gripped him, and he could not shake the memories away.

His mind wandered as if in a fog. Every now and again, the fog cleared and he saw sights, scenes from the wartime struggle. Those memories made him cry when he was drunk, but when he was sober, which was seldom, they made him angry. He felt as if he had nothing left now, no peace. For everyone else, the end of war meant freedom and justice. For François it seemed to mean shackles of pain and memories of hatred. He missed Jean-Paul, he longed for Alma, Arlette, but above all, he wished he could have turned back the clock and kept Shirley with him. It was ridiculous this feeling for a girl almost twenty years younger than he was. He knew as soon as she set foot on British soil he would have been forgotten.

Of all his memories, the one haunting him the most was Dun-Les-Places. They were returning there, cycling through the forest when Amos halted on a rise ahead. He held up his hand and François could still picture the young man's raised hand as he looked down the hill towards the village. When they all came level with him, they saw smoke. A house was burning. They looked with scrupulous care for any sign of German military activity in the early morning sunshine below. They cycled on and came to the church. The scene greeting them was one François would never forget. It would haunt him from that day on.

In the small churchyard at the front of the church, were bodies. They lay sprawled and piled in the uncomfortable postures of the dead. Blood-stained, torn, and immobile, lay the corpses of twenty men. Their ages varied, some were adolescent others adult. There was blood too, but that was not what François' mind focussed upon. It was the way necks were turned, arms were twisted and faces were contorted in death, carrying a caricature of expression. They cycled nearer and Amos pointed upwards. Hanging from the spire was Père Jean; hung there, a rope around his neck and a white card sign with the word "partisan" scrawled in red. Amos cut him down and the body tumbled to the church steps below. It lay there on the stone flags, themselves damaged and chipped by bullets. There was silence all around them, no birdsong, not even the sound of a car. The church was as quiet as a grave.

They found the women and children locked in a barn and for the rest of the morning François endured the cries and the weeping of the women as they recognised the faces of their loved ones, husbands and sons. The four partisans helped dig the graves and each one was marked with a wooden cross.

'Why have they done this?' Rachelle said, tears in her eyes.

François said, 'The carpenter's wife said it was a reprisal for four German officers who were shot twenty miles away. They came yesterday evening. There was nothing anyone could have done.'

'I want to kill them all.'

'They will get what they deserve these murdering swine,' François said, but in his heart he knew it was not so. He also knew once the war was over, there would be almost as much bloodshed in revenge, visited upon collaborators and German spies. He was sick of the killing now. Tired of the constant layers of blood on their hands and yet it was not remorse for the deaths he caused. It was a feeling that enough people had died; it was as if the poor earth must be saturated with blood from all the death and carnage he had witnessed. And where did it all go this blood? This river of hatred? François felt at times, as if he needed to know but there was no one to answer him and he had no answers himself.

3

François was searching for a reason, a glimmer of an explanation as to why he still lived. He fought, German soldiers shot him, yet he lived. Was his body sacred, he wondered?

He wished he could believe in God. All his formative years he believed. Jean-Paul too was a good Catholic. François wondered whether, when his son died in Charles' arms, he sought God or adopted a more pragmatic approach to the end of his life. For François, Jean-Paul's departure from the mortal coil ended every aspect of life, which possessed any meaning. He thought Rachelle and Shirley were distractions from what really gnawed at him. He was intestate, bereft of any offspring and yet he had lived through a dangerous, life-threatening war. In the end, he thought he had nothing to show for it. He wanted so much to love. He looked back at his last few years and realised it had all been a search. For revenge? No, all he wanted was love, and what happened? Shirley returned home and Rachelle departed to fight for a Jewish state and pursue Nazi criminals. Better to go now, rather than wait and die alone, incontinent, grumpy and useless; a retired teacher, whom no one would miss. Yes, they would say, he was a brave man in the war. A partisan. He killed Germans, lots of them, but look at him now: pickled in Calvados, wetting his pants and swearing at everyone. Is this how our heroes turn out? Is this what happens to old soldiers, bereft of love?

It was all too much this mental flagellation. François checked the magazine. Two bullets. It was enough. One for Cognac and one for himself.

'Cognac, ici,' he said, pointing to a place beside his chair.

Her eyes lit up, as if obeying him was all that mattered in her life. He took hold of her collar. The Luger felt heavy in his hand. She looked up at him. Her dark eyes showed no trace of fear, no mistrust. Trust was the deepest instinct in them both and for François, the most painful.

'Au revoir, Ma Petite Amie,' he said and pulled the trigger.

There was a loud click. No explosion, only a click.

He swore. He ejected the bullet. He examined it. The cap was scored. A faint indentation, a pathway to death leading nowhere. Not today, not for Cognac. He had one bullet left. François knew he could not waste it on his canine companion. There was work to do.

Reconsidering the moment, he did not want her shut up with his body, so he pulled on her collar and ejected her through the back door, into the yard behind. She scratched at the door, she whined, and then began to bark.

It was no use, he decided. He let her back in, leaving the door wide-open. At least she would not be wandering alone in his house, with a corpse in the front room. He sat down again. He wrote:

To whom it may concern.

He started this way and the foolishness of what he had written came home to him. He was a man of letters after all. He knew no one was "concerned" and the absurdity of this statement made him reject it. He screwed up the note.

He began again.

I am François Dufy.

Yes, that's better.

I have served my country, but it is enough. I have no family. I have no dependants. It is better to end it all than to endure. Please look after my dog. Her name is Cognac.

Yes, it had a certain ring to it. It was enough. True it was not Balzac or Gogol, but who cared anyway? François felt he had no friends. Bernard had returned to Bergerac to re-start his restaurant. Amos and Rachelle left too. Nothing remaining.

And Shirley? God, he missed her.

The Luger weighed heavy in his trembling hand. François placed the tip of the barrel in his mouth. The metallic taste felt repulsive. He changed the angle of the barrel so the shot would pass through the base of his skull. With any luck, he would be dead within a second. He began to squeeze the trigger with his thumbs. Somewhere in his head, he wondered what damage it might do if the recoil spoiled his aim. He decided he did not care much, so he gripped it with both hands.

Life was a gamble and so was death. If you fail to get it right this time, then try again.

Two things happened then. They were not simultaneous but the effects were similar.

Cognac whined. She grabbed his jacket with her teeth. She pulled and François had no choice but to look down. He put down the pistol.

'Damned creature. You spoil my aim.'

He pointed to her bed in the kitchen.

'Allez,' he said.

The dog ignored him. She tugged. He pulled. With his free hand, he raised his open palm and she let go. The dog continued to whine.

'What do you know?'

She wagged her tail.

'Damn it. What do you know? She's gone forever so has Rachelle. You will be all right. Allez.'

For anyone, he thought, there comes a breaking point, a place where tolerance of pain becomes unendurable. For François then, that point had come. He wanted death. He wanted to be free of the endless visions of death and the cruelty he knew men were capable of inflicting upon each other. He needed a finishing line and he felt like a man who runs a race but there is no tape across the track.

Damned dog, he thought. Damned distractions. Dante Gabriel Rossetti never has such nonsense to stop him.

And then he stopped. He thought he had not created anything in his life. Rossetti did. When he was gone, from the lake of Choral and his drink in which he lived, he left behind a legacy. François realised he left nothing. No poems, no books. His despondency increased. Not even that, he thought.

He ignored the dog. He placed the pistol in his mouth. He

aimed low.

Then the doorbell rang.

'Christ and all his fucking Saints! Now what?' he said aloud.

He wondered whether, if he ignored it, the caller would leave. He placed the gun on the blotter in front of him and stood. The sooner he got rid of them the better. He needed peace, he needed concentration. Whoever it was at the door, they should leave him alone with his grief and his misery.

François ambled to the door. He felt dizzy. It was as if he had drunk too much, but what was a half-bottle of Calvados to him? Since he bought the house back, he was drinking two bottles of wine every evening. He knew he could not be drunk. If he was sober, then why did he feel this way?

How any man responds to a sudden change in their existence may vary. In the case of François Dufy, the change and the termination of his suicide plans came in an instant as soon as he opened the door. He said nothing, spellbound.

'I told you I would come back.'

Stock-still for a moment, he remained silent.

Then, 'Shirley?'

He stepped back to let her in, into his home, and into his life.

A Note From the Author

This book, a work of total fiction like my first book *The Cyclist*, is dedicated to the heroes of the French Resistance, men and women who gave their lives to protect and preserve their culture and their heritage during the Second World War.

Although all the characters and some of the places are fictitious, I have tried to draw a picture of a terrible time and the measures needed for those involved to get through those times, with their grief, their anger and most of all, their love. None of my characters are based upon real people.

The events and much of the geography of the town of Bergerac are fictitious, there is no point letting me know that for example, the Mairie is northwest of the main market square. I know this and have changed locations in the book to dovetail with the story. The interdigitation with *The Cyclist* may seem imperfect but this is another story although it overlaps.

My interpretation of the geography of northern Spain may seem inaccurate to some. This is not a history book, it is a character-based fiction and as such I needed to create atmosphere not truth. If my juggling of reality offends, I humbly apologise.

The premise is that one should never give up hope; love will find you in the end if only you are open to it.

ALSO BY FREDRIK NATH FROM FINGERPRESS:

THE CYCLIST

A World War II Drama
by Fredrik Nath

"The story is brilliantly executed... Nath's biggest success is
the sustained atmospheric tension that he creates somewhat
effortlessly."
-LittleInterpretations.com

"A haunting and bittersweet novel that stays with you long
after the final chapter – always the sign of a really well-
written and praiseworthy story. It would also make an excellent screenplay."
-Historical Novels Review – Editor's Choice, Feb 2011

http://novels.fingerpress.co.uk/the-cyclist.html

GALDIR: A SLAVE'S TALE

Barbarian Warlord Saga, Volume I
by Fredrik Nath

"Highly commended"
-Yeovil Literary Prize

A tale of love, brutal battles and conflict, in which a mystical prophecy winds its way through an epic saga of struggle against Rome.

MAGIC AND GRACE

*A Novel of Florida, Love, Zen, and the Ghost of John
Keats*
by Chad Hautmann

"Quirky and funny and heartfelt and rich"
-Ft. Myers News-Press

"A compulsively readable mixture of fast-paced plot, likable
protagonist, and subtly deep theme"
-Magdalena Ball, CompulsiveReader.com

"Highly entertaining, often thoughtful, and strategically
humorous"
-Ft. Myers & Southwest Florida Magazine

**http://novels.fingerpress.co.uk/magic-and-
grace.html**

Interested in visiting France?

Find crowdsourced travel guides on all your favourite destinations at Fingerpress Travel:

www.fingerpresstravel.com

While you're there, check out our unique travel writing contest: the most voted-for articles will be published in Fingerpress travel books.

FIND MORE GREAT BOOKS AND DETAILS OF AUTHOR EVENTS AT:

www.fingerpress.co.uk

Lightning Source UK Ltd.
Milton Keynes UK
UKOW03f1402040614

232821UK00003B/65/P